Up and coming romance novelist sensation, McKayla never could have imagined that the medieval Scottish Highlands she wrote about were anything more than pure historical fiction. But little did she know that her Broun ancestry would prove an irresistible pull for one very remarkable highlander.

Colin MacLomain, skilled assassin and fierce warrior, is ready to make right his jaded past. Newly seated as chieftain, he's determined to win over his clan and one true love. But when she's pulled back in time will McKayla, his unknowing best friend, be able to see past his shaded history to the man he's determined to become?

Find out in Mark of the Highlander.

Mark of the Highlander
By Sky Purington
COPYRIGHT © 2014

Edited by *Cathy McElhaney*
Cover Art by *Tamra Westberry*

Published in the United States of America

Mark of the Highlander
The MacLomain Series- Next Generation
Book One

By

Sky Purington

Dedication

For my Broun cousins, Rebecca, Michelle, Debbie and Lee
Ann.

Acknowledgements

Andrea Snider, you went above and beyond to help make this
novel shine. Many thanks, lass!

Prologue

"'Tis simple really, take the dagger and slice her throat."

"Just like that, run the blade and be done with it?" he said.

A sharpened dagger was pressed into his hand. "Precisely like that."

With a heavy sigh he shook his head. "A lad is one thing, a lass another."

"And that, my boy, is where you will go wrong every time."

Frustrated, he clenched the weapon tighter and tried to see her more clearly. At least if he saw her face he would have something to hold on to. It was important to remember who one murdered. It was crucial to never forget. But did he have it in him this time?

"What a shame. You have not the gumption to do what is necessary."

"And why again is this necessary? What did she do?"

"'Twas not what she did but what she *will* do."

A heavy rumble started in his ear. A pressing urge started behind his temple. The calling came as it always did. This was necessary. She must die.

"I see you know the right of it. Dinnae doubt the gods."

"The gods," he murmured and nodded.

"Aye, the gods. They urge you to continue."

He closed his eyes and took a deep breath. Never before had he hesitated. Never before had he questioned.

"I just wish I knew more," he whispered.

"Nay, 'tis the verra reason you were chosen. Because you dinnae ask. You dinnae question."

Should he though? When the lass stirred he clasped the blade tighter.

It was time.

The air thinned. A chill raced over his skin.

It was past time.

He would do this. He *could* do this.

He put his lips against her ear and said, "'Tis for the best."

Clenching his jaw, blade to her neck, he inhaled the sweet scent of her hair. He knew that smell, *her* smell.

Her eyes opened slowly.

Familiar eyes.

"Nay," he whispered, shocked. "This cannae be."

Before his palms grew slick, before he could further doubt, he swiped the blade.

Chapter One

North Salem, New Hampshire
2014

"Just slice the blade and be done with it already."

"Oh, I don't know." Trevor shook his head. "What fun is there in cutting the cake if I can't smear it in your face when you try to eat it?"

McKayla grinned. "I suppose that's the beauty of Skype. We chat, pretend, all that good stuff."

"Look at this." He pouted and held the cake up to the screen. "I bought it especially for today."

She licked her lips. "No doubt it's delicious. You know you didn't have to."

"Hey, it's not every day my best friend lands a book deal."

"Good timing is all," she said. "Scottish highlanders are a hot topic. Women eat them up."

Trevor chuckled. "In your books they certainly do."

"Hey, it sells." McKayla stretched and yawned. "So when are you coming home?"

"Soon I hope." He frowned. "I just need time off."

"You always do."

McKayla kept her voice light but she was worried. Trevor was determined to rule the world of technology. Though gainfully employed, he had several top companies beating at his door. He was purely half computer geek, half Einstein with a mind most would pay billions for. Clean cut and handsome with dark brown hair and magnetic green eyes, he had an ambitious hunger few possessed. Even now, as vice-president of one of the top tech companies in the United States, he remained unsatisfied. She'd never met anyone who craved greatness like he did.

But she was concerned it would take its toll.

"Stop that," he muttered.

"Stop what?"

"You're worrying about me again and I wish you wouldn't." He set aside the cake, determined. "I'll book a flight in the near future and visit. It's been far too long."

"Please do." She glanced at the clock. "I have to go soon."

"I know." He pulled on a suit jacket. "Me too."

"I love you."

He leaned in close to the video camera. "I love you too, sweetheart. Good luck with your meeting. Remember, *you* wrote this book, not them. Fight any changes you don't agree with."

"Oh sure," she said, and winked. "Talk soon." Offering her best 'I rock' smile, McKayla blew him a kiss and disconnected.

With a heavy sigh, she sat back and stared out the window. There was still time before the meeting but she didn't want to listen to Trevor rave more about her accomplishments. Most people would be over the moon, screaming it from the rooftops. But not her. She didn't want to talk about it. The truth was the publishing world terrified her. It was a hungry beast that craved money. But she supposed that was the whole point.

Or was it?

She eyed the manuscript on her desk. They were going to try to make adjustments to ensure its popularity.

"Hey there."

McKayla smiled at her cousin, Sheila, who stood in the doorway. "Hey."

Breezing in, Sheila plunked down on the bed. "Was that Trevor I heard?"

"The one and only," she confirmed.

"And how is he?" Sheila answered her own question before McKayla could respond. "Missing you more than ever I'm sure."

Her cousin thought more existed between her and Trevor than actually did. "Yeah, the distance is hard." She switched topics. "I need to borrow your car today."

"Of course." Sheila waved away the request as if it shouldn't have been made to begin with and cast a dubious eye at McKayla's closet. "So what are you going to wear?"

"What they expect," she assured. "A well-tailored black pant suit."

Sheila grinned and her powder blue eyes rounded. "What they expect from *you* are comfy sweats and a worn out sweatshirt."

McKayla shrugged. "Maybe Leslie does, but not the rest of them."

"How is your *agent* nowadays?" Sheila asked dryly.

As if she knew they were talking about her, Skype buzzed with an incoming conference call. McKayla bit the corner of her lip and considered ignoring it.

"Go on. Take it," Sheila said. "But I'm staying. Just don't tell her I'm here."

"You're bad."

"Yep. Go on."

Even though Leslie and Sheila were related they'd been battling one another since childhood. Now they would be living together. McKayla couldn't imagine it going well. But they all needed a place to live. And as it turned out, their cousin Caitlin MacLomain had a house to rent. Sheila and McKayla had moved in several months ago, and Leslie would be joining them in a few more days.

"Go on, Kay," Sheila said again.

She hated being stuck between her warring cousins. After a deep, calming breath, McKayla clicked and received the call. Sheila kept out of sight.

"I see you're not dressed yet," Leslie said in greeting.

"Nearly." McKayla nodded toward the closet. "Clothes are ready to go."

"This meeting is far too important to take for granted. The publishing house has a cover for your book. Have you seen it?"

"Aye, I mean yes." Oftentimes McKayla slipped into medieval Scots tongue. It was no wonder considering it was all she wrote lately. "It's definitely something." *That* was an understatement. She'd been up all night staring at it. "Who's the cover model?"

"That's a good question. I have no idea. But does it really matter? Even without a full face it makes a stunning impact." Leslie with her olive-skinned good looks and French-manicured nails leaned in close to the screen. "Do you want that tattoo removed? I mean really, it doesn't fit the story."

Sheila rolled her eyes at the computer then held up a sample of the cover, fanning herself with one hand as she gazed at it. She winked at McKayla then stuck her tongue out at Leslie.

McKayla hid her irritation. Granted, she hadn't tied the tattoo into the story but the small mark on his upper collarbone suited him. Heck, it was downright sexy. Whether or not it suited the story didn't really bother her. Nor did it seem to worry the publishing house.

"It's fine," she assured Leslie and made a 'cease and desist' motion with her hand toward Sheila. Sometimes she wanted to strangle the pair of them.

"Maybe so," Leslie muttered. "But it might be worth bringing up in the meeting."

"Maybe," McKayla replied, not intending to do so in the least.

"Either way, I wanted to touch base and let you know that I'll be thinking of you today."

That's all Sheila had to hear. Her face screwed into an angry little ball and she bounced up, acting as though she'd just entered the room. "And why won't you be there?"

Leslie's eyes narrowed and met Sheila's as she became visible in the camera. "*This* is a private meeting, Sheila."

"Answer my question," Sheila said. "You're her agent. Why won't you be there?"

"Oh no," McKayla said, shaking her head. "This isn't happening. Today is too bloody important." She swung her gaze to Sheila. "Go. Now."

Sheila looked from her to Leslie then back. "Me? Why? *She* should go. Shut off Skype."

"I'm her agent," Leslie reminded her. "If anyone should go it's you."

Already, a headache blossomed. But business was business. Again she said, "Sheila, please hon."

"What was that you said?" Leslie asked.

But McKayla was focused on Sheila who seemed undecided. "I need this day to go smoothly. I can't stand the business end of book deals. You know all I really want to do is write. *Please*."

Leslie narrowed her eyes and shook her head. "That was strange. Say that again."

Sheila was about to respond but McKayla continued. "Please don't make me ask again."

Her cousin frowned and looked from her to the computer before she shook her head. "All right then."

After Sheila left, McKayla sunk into her chair and turned her attention back to Leslie. "Her intentions are good."

"No worries. Sheila's, Sheila. We all know that." Leslie's expression was nothing less than confused. "But I'm curious about what you said."

"You heard what I said."

"I did. But what did you mean?"

"Oh, come on. You heard every word. Sheila's just being protective and as usual, frustrated when it comes to you."

"Yeah, I got that from her. But what language were *you* speaking?"

"Seriously? English. Albeit frustrated English when it comes to the two of you."

Leslie shook her head and looked at her watch. "Whatever. I wrote down the words you spoke. It was definitely a foreign dialect. I guess I'll have to research it later. Meanwhile, get dressed and get going." Her eyes rounded before she ended the call. "Now."

McKayla sat back. Foreign dialect? What was she talking about? Maybe Leslie was feeling the stress of the contract more than she was willing to admit. After all, it was big for them both.

As McKayla began to dress, she tried not to dwell on what life would be like with all three of them living under the same roof. Pure hell, she supposed. Her only hope would be frequent visits from Caitlin and Seth. Otherwise, she'd go nuts.

She smiled thinking about them.

Caitlin owned the house but she'd made it abundantly clear that it belonged to the whole family. And Seth, her paranormal investigator friend, was a light in her oftentimes self-induced seclusion. He wouldn't allow her to get overwhelmed by Sheila and Leslie's drama. Other than Trevor, Seth really was her favorite person. So in her own little writing world she counted on five people, Sheila, Leslie, Caitlin, Trevor and Seth.

She'd bet that was more people than most writers had in their entire social circle.

Pantsuit on, she stared into the mirror. What would the bigwigs think when they looked at her. Oh, here comes another one! Did she look like all the rest? Lord, if she knew. Her pale blond bob hung straight and boring. Her peculiar pale slate gray eyes slanted up a little too far. Trevor had always called them elven eyes. Exasperated, she held a dark red and dark pink shade of lipstick in either hand. *Ick.* Neither suited her. She tossed both aside and smeared a peachy cinnamon shade over her lips.

"McKayla!"

She smiled and sighed with relief. Of course, Seth remembered it was her big day. That's the way he was. He never forgot anything important. Within seconds he bounded up the stairs and leaned against the doorjamb, a wide smile on his striking face. "I see you're halfway ready."

"Yeah, halfway to calling all this off."

He took in her attire. "The outfit is good enough. The hair will do. The face?" He shook his head. "Could be much better."

Seth grabbed her make-up bag and threw a few items on the bed. "Wipe off what you've put on and use these colors. Then you'll be as gorgeous as ever."

"I hate it all," she reported, sullen.

"Of course you do. But today's meeting means everything."

McKayla fingered the items he'd set aside including brown-black mascara, peach blush and a light, tasteful shade of pink lip gloss. "I can't stand this stuff."

"Up," he ordered. "Stop thinking and start doing. Within a few hours this'll all be behind you."

Though reluctant, she wiped away the old stuff and started reapplying her make-up. "You've planned a party for me, haven't you?"

"Me?" Seth sat on her bed and leaned back casually. "Never."

"You." She arched a brow at him in the mirror. "Definitely. With Alana away, you're restless. A party would suit your mood."

"It would," he agreed. "Not because my wife's away but because you've accomplished something phenomenal." Though he seemed relaxed he radiated unspent energy. "Don't you realize that?"

She sighed and finished applying her make-up. "Maybe I will once the meeting's over."

"I know you're not happy unless you're typing away on that computer but consider this, if you don't revel in all this in-between stuff now you might not be so content when you write the next bestseller."

McKayla tossed the lipstick aside. "Don't jinx me. Nothing says *this* will be a bestseller."

"Nope. Nothing does. But I'd put money on it." Seth stood and smiled. "You're gonna do great today. You know that right?"

"Sure," she said absently.

"Seriously, you are," he said, helping McKayla with her jacket.

And he was right. The meeting didn't go too bad.

Nine hours and one very long commute later; it was Seth's warm eyes that greeted her first. He helped her take off her jacket as a foyer full of people yelled, "Congratulations!"

Blushing, she managed a smile. "Thanks everyone."

"No need to thank us. You deserve it, girl!" Sheila said.

"Yes you do," Leslie agreed.

"How could you not?" Caitlin added.

McKayla pulled her cousins into a group hug and mumbled, "Thanks," once more. One way or another, they kept her whole. They, as diverse as they were, made real life a little more bearable. Because if she had her way every last inch of her existence would be part of a medieval Scottish novel. And that just wasn't good. Or healthy.

When she broke away from her well-meaning family she came face to face with a portrait size portrayal of her book cover propped up on an easel. Again she found herself staring. Yes, her editors loved it. She loved it. But did it really represent what she'd written?

As if on cue, Caitlin's husband Ferchar walked up beside her. It was a hard thing not to find him incredibly attractive. Tall, muscled, hot as heck with a deep Scottish brogue, he was impossible to ignore.

"Bloody odd, that mark," he said.

She touched her collarbone absently. "You mean the one here."

"Aye. Scots dinnae have marks like that. At least not then."

McKayla rolled his dialect over in her mind. Though she wrote it, did her words sound as good as they did when they came from his mouth? If in fact he sounded like they did in medieval times. After all, Ferchar was from modern day Scotland.

"The cover artist, or should I say cover model, is responsible for that," she explained.

Ferchar's pale blue eyes narrowed but he didn't grow too serious. "I'm sure." He paused and frowned. "I dinnae much like the title."

McKayla tried not to be offended but her sensitive nature made it tricky. "The title?"

"Aye." He shrugged. "*Plight of the Highlander* doesnae seem quite right."

The writer in her kicked in as she stared at the cover. "But the whole story revolves around his plight. There's no more perfect title."

Caitlin came between them. "Is he telling you it's all wrong, then?"

McKayla frowned. "Yeah, so it seems. What do you think?"

"I think only you should be the judge of what you want to call your book, nobody else." She wrapped arms over McKayla and Ferchar's shoulders. "This is a happy day. Let's step away from serious talk."

"But now he's got me thinking," McKayla murmured.

"Naturally. That's all you do!" Caitlin grinned. "*Think* too much. So let's not, eh? Let's drink, eat and party."

Ferchar offered her a knee-buckling smile and agreed. "Aye, let's be merry."

Yet even as the crowd celebrated, McKayla was eager for the party to be over. She wanted to be back in front of her computer. Another story waited, another highlander. While the meeting had gone smoother than anticipated, she felt edgy. Even though she'd signed the contract, edits were underway and she had her release date, something very important was still missing. But what? Everything was ready to go.

"She's driving me crazy," Sheila said under her breath.

"She always does," McKayla responded and shook her head.

Sheila, of course, referred to Leslie who was now surrounded by three admirers.

"Are we sure she's even our cousin?" Sheila said, scowling. "She looks nothing like us. And who are those guys anyways?"

"She's definitely family," McKayla said. "And not so bad most of the time. As for the guys, I'm not sure. Maybe they're Seth or Caitlin's friends. I don't know who half these people are."

"Hmph." Sheila frowned. "You're too damn forgiving. She's an arrogant tyrant. Not sure what men see in her."

McKayla did. Leslie was a knock-out. But so was Sheila. Both were constantly dating which made her realize she hadn't gone on a date in far too long. In her defense, it took a lot of focus *and* time to write a book. Still. It'd be nice to have a man waiting in the wings. Though that's probably where he'd have to stay while she worked on developing future characters and fleshing out plots.

As if she'd been reading her mind, Sheila said, "It wouldn't hurt you to socialize with a few of the men here tonight. There are a lot of good looking ones."

"True," McKayla said, eyes narrowed on Seth. "Too many I'd say."

He grinned at her from across the room. These guys were his friends for sure. It seemed he was determined to set her up. Push her into getting out and maybe even to date a little. But as she gazed at all the faces and found a few gazing back, McKayla's stomach grew queasy. The idea of mingling and going through the whole 'get to know you' process suddenly seemed like way too much.

15

Seth recognized the telltale signs, and made his way over. "So you figured me out. I only had the best intentions, sweetie. C'mon, let's go outside and get some fresh air."

She followed him out and they sat on a bench beneath the old oak tree. A rope swing hung lazily on the opposite branch. The warm summer night felt welcoming. Without a doubt, the old colonial full of life suited her much better from a distance.

"One of these days you're going to have to return to the real world," Seth said.

"I did the real world today. The T's were crossed, the I's dotted."

Seth shook his head. "So you stuck your head out for a sec then retracted." Before she could respond he cut her off. "Eventually you're going to have to join the rest of us." He nodded at the house. "Outside of here."

Head leaned back, eyes closed, she responded, "It's here that I find them, everyone I need."

When he sighed she opened her eyes and looked at him. "You know what I mean."

"Real life, McKayla." He glanced around at the yard and once more at the house. "Not just this."

While he was one of her best friends, he was just like the rest, clueless. They lived one life, she another. Why couldn't they understand she was fine living life the way she did. Even if it seemed terribly dull, she was content.

"You say you've read my books, Seth. I'm obviously not bored."

He chuckled. "Matter of opinion."

Yet his eyes swung her way with appreciation. Outside of Trevor, she had no greater fan. Only God knew why because neither man was into reading romance. Still, Seth thought her passion for writing outstanding and Trevor, well, he just loved that she didn't give up on her dream.

"When is Alana due home?" McKayla asked. It was the perfect time to change the subject. She was over talking about her life, or lack of one. "You've got to be missing her."

16

"Like you wouldn't believe." He shook his head. "And she's not coming home soon enough for my taste."

"I still think it's great she's traveled to Europe to scoop up authentic pieces for your house," McKayla said.

"Ah yes, nothing but the best for the Tudor Revival." Though he smiled, she saw the strain around his eyes. He adored his wife. Married only a year, McKayla could truly say she'd never seen Seth so smitten. Free-spirited and more alive than most, her friend had once prided himself on independence and extreme adventure. Now, when his other half wasn't around things weren't nearly as fun as they used to be. The truth was Alana had not turned Seth into a boring man but into a far more interesting and dynamic one. And perhaps more mature. But she'd never tell *him* that.

"She'll be home soon. Then you'll be back to redecorating." McKayla smirked before issuing a proper pout. "Then you'll be back in Vermont and I won't see you very much."

"True," he said and slanted a look at her. "Unless, you come up for a few months and work on your next novel at our place."

"Oh, I don't know." The very idea ignited a strange sense of trepidation and her gaze once more settled on the old colonial. This was where she wrote *Plight of the Highlander*. This was the place that marked the beginning of her mental affair with Colin of the MacLeod clan. A man born in the wild, Scottish highlands when times were perilous, and tumultuous. Where men were brave, honorable, loyal and relationships were meaningful. A time before chivalry died. While McKayla always loved elements of medieval history, she still didn't understand why moving into this house had inspired such a sweeping saga.

"I know you're determined to stay here and write," Seth said softly. "I'm sure this house knows as well."

"This house?"

"Yeah, sure. Houses have their own souls. And this one inspires you to write well and often. Why, I've no clue, but it does."

It was hard not to reflect upon how mature Seth had become as of late. The old Seth would never say anything so profound. At least not on purpose.

17

"I suppose you're right," she admitted. "The minute I sit down at my computer a whole new world blossoms...one that never existed before. Sort of strange, don't you think?"

A grin split his face. "I don't think anything's strange, love. After all, I hunt ghosts for enjoyment."

"Right." She smiled and nudged his arm lightheartedly. "Weirdo."

He shrugged and threw his arm around her shoulders. "What fun would life be if not for the afterlife, eh?"

"If you say so." She chuckled. "I suppose it can't be much different than being infatuated with a world that only exists in my imagination."

His eyes widened playfully and he huffed. "Are you saying that ghosts are as made up as the characters in your book?"

"Not to me," she replied, always respectful of his beliefs. "But surely they are to most. Face it; our passions walk a similar but bizarre line."

"Only because you hint at witchcraft in your story," said Caitlin's husband.

McKayla was surprised to find Ferchar sitting on the rope swing. How had she missed him walking out? Never mind sitting so close to them.

"How did you?" she started.

"What?" Ferchar asked.

"I never saw you walk by," she said.

"I did," Seth said. "Perhaps you were too engrossed in your thoughts."

McKayla frowned. This sort of thing had been happening a little too regularly. She'd miss small things like people approaching her. While it wasn't overly alarming she was starting to take note. Granted, she always lost time when she wrote. One reality replaced another. When it did, time seemed to slip away. But it wasn't normal not to hear someone approach. Was it? Shouldn't she hear something? The sound of a footfall, breathing, anything?

"He's right," Seth said, interrupting her thoughts. "You did add a little witchcraft to your story, right?"

"Yeah, a little. Just enough to flavor the time period."

Ferchar smiled. "I thought it was a nice addition, lass. One that will make a difference."

"A difference?" She cocked her head. "How so?"

"Well who doesn't like a bit of fantasy in their romance?" Seth offered.

"Most people," she replied. "Straight historical romance usually prevails. I'm still a little surprised I landed a contract on this one."

"Dinnae be," Ferchar said absently. "It will do the world good to ken a wee bit more about what really went on back then."

"What?" she asked, confused. "Of course everything I wrote is purely fictional. Unless..." She eyed him, a little flutter in her stomach. "You know something I don't."

Seth eyed Ferchar as well. McKayla swore she heard a hint of mock amusement when he asked him, "So what *do* you know of a time long gone in your country?"

Ferchar was about to answer when Leslie walked out the front door. She released one last peel of riotous laughter for her admirers before she slammed shut the door, demeanor once more serious. She stopped short in front of them and eyed her notepad. "Okay, so here's what you said this morning."

McKayla frowned. Had it been Sheila who did this she would have rolled her eyes. But it wasn't. It was Leslie. And Leslie was the most level-headed, logical minded person she knew, oftentimes to the point of frustration.

She almost said 'huh' but Seth beat her to it. "What do you mean?"

"This morning. On Skype. She was talking to me and Sheila, when she started to speak in what turns out to be a very old form of Gaelic."

McKayla's mouth turned dry. "Gaelic?"

"Yes. And a form of Gaelic primarily used in Scotland during the early medieval period." She paused for a moment, her perfectly plucked brows drawing together as her pale green eyes pinned McKayla. "Did you research Gaelic for your book?"

"You know I didn't."

Leslie nodded. "Precisely." Her attention returned to what she'd written. "Though I'm sure the translation isn't exact you said something very close to, "His is the circle that never connects. A means to let me in. If ever it closes, we are forever lost.""

A strange chill shot up her spine. What did that mean? "You must've heard me wrong. I don't speak any language but English and a little Spanish."

"May I see it?" Ferchar asked.

When Leslie handed it to him McKayla got goosebumps. It suddenly felt as though Ferchar and the words written on that paper were interconnected. Why would she think such a thing?

"Do you understand the language?" Leslie asked him.

Ferchar glanced over the words, his expression unchanging when he handed it back to her. "What makes you think I would understand it? They dinnae teach this in Scotland nowadays."

Leslie's shrewd look made it plain she was unconvinced. Strange. Her cousin had a talent for looking straight into a person. When they were kids, Sheila nicknamed her 'soul reader' with good reason. Leslie understood people better than they did themselves. It had always been uncanny, spooky almost. As an adult, the peculiar gift made her a razor-sharp agent amongst many other things.

Instead of answering Ferchar, Leslie handed the sheet of paper to McKayla. "You should keep it. They're your words."

McKayla stared at the sheet and shook her head. "But they're not. You must've heard garbled words from another Skype channel or something. That happens sometimes."

"Garbled words that sounded so clear and actually translated into something halfway coherent? Not to mention ancient." Leslie shook her head. "Doubt it."

"Definitely crazy," Seth said, peering at the sheet.

The front door opened again and this time Caitlin and Sheila stepped out. Laughing about something, they made their way over.

Sheila shook her head at Seth. "How many friends do you have? There have got to be at least twenty single men in the house and believe me, it isn't big enough for all of them."

Seth shrugged. "I didn't think so many would bite when I put out the Facebook invite."

"Oh shoot, really? A Facebook invite?" McKayla looked skyward. "That meant it hit all your Boston friends. Most from the single scene."

"Uh, *yeah*, kind of the whole point," Seth said.

"Not really," she replied. "The whole point was to celebrate my book contract not invite all of Boston's night life to our home."

Sheila snorted and handed her cell phone to McKayla. She'd pulled up the 'event invite' Seth had sent out. There was a picture of her, Sheila and Leslie taken at a party last year. They'd all been feeling pretty good. Their selfie made that apparent. The invite said, "Partying with my girls. Come join the fun!"

"Seth! You made it sound like we're all looking for a good time."

"Well aren't you?" he asked innocently.

Leslie shrugged one shoulder. "I actually *am* having a good time."

"Me too," Sheila said.

McKayla sighed and handed the phone back to her cousin. "You're a sweetie, Seth. Of course I'm having a good time too."

He was about to respond when headlights appeared down the old dirt road leading to their house. In little time, a silver Land Rover pulled into the driveway.

"Another one of your friends?" Sheila asked.

"No idea," Seth said. "Don't think so."

It took all of two seconds for McKayla to realize who was getting out of the car and only another two for her to run and jump into his waiting arms.

Chapter Two

"Trevor, you came!" McKayla said.

"Of course I did." He spun her a few times. "This is a big day!"

She pulled back and looked him over. As always, he was immaculately dressed in dark slacks and a button down white shirt. With wide shoulders and a tall, lanky build she always thought he'd make the perfect cowboy for a western romance. He looked nothing like the techie he really was. So while women were always drawn to him because of his good looks they inevitably found out that the latest gadgets interested him far more than their cloying antics.

McKayla grinned and pulled him over to the others. They all greeted him with big hugs and warm smiles. It appeared nobody knew he was coming. But that didn't surprise her in the least. Trevor, for the most part, was both secretive and spontaneous. She'd bet he hadn't planned this visit. The thought probably popped into his head and he went for it.

Now her perfect day was complete. Everyone who mattered most was here to celebrate with her. After spending a few minutes catching up with everybody Trevor nodded toward the woods. "Mind if I steal McKayla for a few minutes?"

Sheila laughed. "It was only a matter of time."

Leslie gave her a stern look. "Now you know these two don't like each other like *that*."

"Of course not," Caitlin added, a twinkle in her eye.

Her cousins knew feelings like that didn't exist between her and Trevor. At least not anymore. That was the beauty of their friendship. They knew precisely what did and did not work between them. Somehow, eliminating the sexual end of it had only made their friendship strengthen into something impregnable.

As they split from the group and headed toward the dark forest, Trevor grinned. "It's been years since we dated. When are they going to let up?"

"When we're both entrenched in long-term meaningful relationships with other people. I think us remaining so close after all this time has stumped them. They're convinced we'll get back together."

Trevor said nothing to that but leaned into his SUV and grabbed a device. "Check this out. A little something I whipped up."

Only about fist size and square, he placed it on the ground. McKayla squealed with delight when it emitted a faint buzzing sound. Then, long, thin, electronic legs snaked out and lifted the box. The next thing she knew they were following a spider-like, self-controlled flashlight into the forest.

"You're too much." She continued to smile as they followed it. "I imagine it's already pre-programmed to lead us to Stonehenge."

He took her hand and smiled. "Where else?"

When he'd helped her move in six months ago, it'd been one of the first places she'd visited. Salem's Stonehenge was supposedly built thousands of years ago by an ancient people. Now a tourist attraction, it drew in all of those fascinated with a culture long gone. As a history buff, it'd been the main perk to moving into the old colonial. A short walk through the forest and she could enter a slice of time long gone.

"So how are you getting on here, Kay? I know how much you loved the Cape."

She'd grown up in Cape Cod and never thought she'd leave. Very few loved the ocean like she did. But when Caitlin's grandmother Mildred passed away, Caitlin, Ferchar and their son had moved into Mildred's old house at the end of the drive and the colonial became available.

"We Skype nearly every day. You know how much I like it. Especially the inspiration I'm getting from being here."

"I'm still surprised that Caitlin and Ferchar moved so soon after her grandmother died," he remarked as they walked. "But it makes sense. Renting out this place to you and your cousins is a financially sound idea and pulls the family closer together."

23

She nodded. "I think that was some of it. But she was so close to her grandmother and Ferchar was very close to his grandfather, Adlin. They feel like they've kept a little piece of them alive by living in Mildred's house. The move didn't surprise me in the least."

Trevor remained silent for several long moments before he softly said, "It's unusual how they died together like they did."

McKayla only met Mildred a few times and had never met her new boyfriend, Adlin. But she couldn't help agree. As a romance writer she didn't know which aspect of their relationship to focus on first. The fact that they'd fallen in love so late in life or when they died it had been together, hand in hand, sitting on the front porch.

Then again, their whole situation had been peculiar. Caitlin's grandmother fell in love with her husband's grandfather. If that wasn't odd enough, Ferchar's appearance in Caitlin's life caught everyone off guard. He was a man raised in Scotland that no one had heard of a month before. Not even Caitlin! It was like he materialized out of nowhere. And then, poof, his grandfather also from Scotland showed up, and was suddenly living with Mildred. On top of all that Shane, Caitlin's brother, vanished after writing a Scottish war novel. One that still sat securely on every bestseller list. What she wouldn't give to talk to Shane right now.

McKayla and her cousins had been estranged from Caitlin and Shane for far too long. So long, in fact, it was a shock when Caitlin reached out to them. Though she supposed she shouldn't be that amazed. Caitlin was great. She had to be in order to forgive like she did. Not that McKayla, Sheila and Leslie had done anything wrong, but their parents, that was another story.

Sibling rivalry had created a dam between Caitlin's parents and theirs. Nobody spoke for years. Everyone drifted apart. So no one was there for Caitlin and Shane when their parents died. Good thing Mildred stepped in to help or the two would have had to fend for themselves. When Caitlin got in touch with Leslie over a year ago it breathed new life into their family.

The Broun cousins had reconnected.

That's how Caitlin liked to phrase it because they were all descendants of Mildred and her siblings. Hence they were all a part of the great Scottish Broun clan.

"Plotting out your next book?"

She was about to respond but Trevor shook his head. "No, of course not. This time you're deep in thought about loved ones lost then found."

It was hard not to smile. "You know me too well. Yeah, I was busy thinking how lucky I am. It's great to have us all together again."

"Even in the maelstrom of Leslie and Sheila?" he asked.

"Aye, even."

"I like how you've started talking like you write. It's cute."

"What? Oh. Right. Sorry. It's becoming a habit. I've gotta stop."

"Naw, it suits you somehow. Don't stop." They trailed after his little spider flashlight, its glow cutting through the woodland with amazing precision. "It means you're truly becoming part of what you write. Like you always say, 'Show, don't tell.'"

"Rule of thumb in writing," she agreed. "But not really the case here. Love your vote of confidence, though. The truth is I think I'm becoming a little too immersed in the worlds I create. In fact, I think I'm going a little insane."

"How so?"

"For starters people are creeping up on me. Well, I shouldn't say it like that. What I mean is people are suddenly next to me when I don't see or hear them coming. If that isn't enough, I guess I spoke gibberish this morning when Skyping with Leslie. Ancient Scottish Gaelic or something."

A warm summer wind blew through the woods, cooling off her enflamed skin. She'd be lying if she said what Leslie showed her wasn't alarming.

Trevor squeezed her hand in reassurance. "You're just under a lot of pressure, honey. That's why I'm here. I knew things were getting intense for you."

"Intense? That's an understatement," she muttered. But she felt better just by having him here. Seth might keep her upbeat but

Trevor grounded her. The world could go upside down crazy, but with Trevor here it all made sense. Everything that'd been crooked stood upright. "I guess I spoke about unbroken circles and a guy. It sounded almost intimate."

"And Leslie caught this?" he asked, astounded.

"Yep, can you imagine? The most down-to-earth person I know. Which sort of freaked me out even more. Had it been Sheila I might not have taken it too seriously. No offense, but we all know how much she loves fantasy fiction. That type of thing would be right up her alley."

"You're not completely free of the bug yourself, you know," he remarked.

"What bug?"

"The fantasy fiction one. Didn't you imply that Iosbail had a special gift? One that allowed even the most calloused of Highlanders to see women a wee bit differently than they had before."

They'd nearly reached Stonehenge and still it seemed his little spider flashlight had a specific destination so they dutifully followed. "Iosbail was only ever a figment of the heroine's imagination. It was never really meant to be a fantasy element just a voice in my character's head. One of many might I add."

"I thought her pretty special. In fact, I always figured she was sort of your alter ego."

She pressed her teeth together. Only Trevor would think as much. "Which would mean you think I compare myself to my heroine who at first came off as a shy, unobtrusive creature with little or no backbone."

"Well..." He laughed when she scowled. "What?" he asked. "Should I have responded differently? Okay." His face grew serious then his eyes rounded. "McKayla, I would *never* think that of you! You should know better. I've never met a more forthright, my-way-or-the-highway woman."

"Oh please." McKayla rolled her eyes and followed the little tech spider to a spear shaped rock at the heart of Stonehenge. She leaned against the rock and stared out at the forest. This stone fell in line with Summer Solstice. "I really love it here."

Trevor smiled, placed his hand against the rock and peered out over the swath of land. "Me too. It's peaceful."

She picked up the spider flashlight and put it on the rock. As if understanding it could relax, it whirred and preened, its little legs retracting before it settled down. The light vanished and the faint sound of bagpipes emitted from an unseen speaker.

McKayla put a hand over her heart and stared at the little piece of technology programmed specifically to celebrate the release of her Highlander novel. "You are completely insane." She looked at him. "And entirely too sweet. Thank you."

He winked. "If we weren't trespassing I would've had it in a kilt, programmed it to speak with a brogue, and trained it to play a miniature bagpipe, but I knew you'd want to be here. Or at least I'd hoped."

"Why?" she asked.

"Because while you think it's the colonial that inspired your novel, I know it's really this place. Every day you talk about your walks out here. Then you come back, sit down and write like a mad woman. Never forget, I was there with you nearly every step of *Plight of the Highlander*. I think I understand Colin MacLeod better than you do."

"Do you?" She grinned and shook her head. "Actually, you probably do. Good thing I wrote the book in the off season so I wasn't breaking the law too awfully bad."

"Oh, you were a regular outlaw," he promised with a devilish glint in his eyes. "But it was a great thing."

"Was it?" She gazed up at the sky. "The story is so unlike anything that I wrote at the Cape." McKayla couldn't help but look at him and ask, "Do you think my other stuff was totally boring?"

"No," he responded instantly. "While it may have been safer it was still interesting." His eyes covered her face, suddenly reminding her of how he'd once looked at her. "Everything you've ever written is profound, McKayla. *Plight of the Highlander* will draw eyes and eventually your old work will be recognized. I don't doubt it for a second."

In that moment it was hard to remember why they ever broke up. Trevor knew her better than anyone and supported her always.

If only that'd been enough. But with him nothing was ever enough and she'd been smart enough to recognize it. He could never be tied down by any one woman or any one obligation. For that matter by anything that made him feel trapped. In a weird way, he was sick. Sick with fear of something she'd never understand. McKayla remembered well the day she'd discovered that Trevor would never be hers for too long.

It had been the day he proposed marriage.

"To celebrate I've brought you something very special." He pulled an object from his pocket. "A gift."

Ripped from thought she stared down at what he held out. She took the odd contraption. "What's this?"

"It's my latest creation. Actually, I'm an unseen partner in this project. Partly my idea, mostly their money."

McKayla studied the fabric in the dim moonlight. It appeared to be something one would put over their eyes to keep the light out when they tried to sleep. "What does it do?"

Excitement radiated off him. "You know how you've been having dreams about Scotland. Ones that never quite make sense. You never see anyone, never talk to anyone yet you know they're there?"

He was the only one she'd told about the dreams that had started when she moved into the colonial. "Yes, what of them?"

"This device will help make them clear," he whispered eagerly, touching the fabric and her hand all at once. "This will help you see everything you couldn't before. It allows you to control your lucid dream state."

She blinked and frowned. "I don't understand. They were just dreams, Trevor. Why would I want to control them?"

"Why not?" he asked, impassioned. "This is cutting edge technology. Do you have any idea how much this will impact society when it's released to the public? It'll change everything."

McKayla breathed in sharply through her nose and pushed the object back toward him. *This* was the Trevor that made him impossible to love beyond friendship. This career driven, hungry stranger that wanted to rule the world with the next bright idea.

His warm hands clamped around hers and the device. "No," he said passionately. "This isn't like all the rest, Kay. I swear. This is different. It enables you to control the full Rapid Eye Movement state of sleep which by the way is the healthiest form of rest. So not only do you choose where and what you want to dream about, you get the best sleep possible."

"Trevor!" she cried softly. "This is supposed to be *my* day."

"And it *is*," he responded. "I'm giving this to you. Not for me but for *you*."

She glowered at him. Trevor was a handsome sight. But, Trevor passionate about something nearly took one's breath away. His neatly brushed hair was tussled, errant strands askew across his forehead. His brilliant green eyes took on a tempting wildness.

As she'd trained herself to do, McKayla focused on her calm center and let it flow out through her limbs. If not, she'd go nuts on him. If history had proven one thing it was that Trevor didn't handle crazed women well. He didn't hit back. No, not Trevor. He fled. Vanished.

"I hate that you're making me find my calm center," she grumbled.

He pulled back as though she'd slapped him. "Did I just do that?"

"You know you did."

Luckily their friendship had developed to such a degree that he knew precisely what he'd put her through when they'd been in a relationship. "And it sucks. So, stop it," she said. "You're too intense right now."

Trevor smoothed back his hair and stood up straighter, suddenly the businessman he prided himself to be. "I'm sorry, Kay. I'm just so excited about this…for you. It's been in the works for a while. I've got two of them with me. One's in my pocket." He tucked the other in hers. "And now the other's in yours."

Did he really think her dreams were that important? She certainly hadn't. They'd never made much sense. Had they inspired her to write about Scotland? Yes. Had they somehow made her fall in love with a time and place not her own? Highly unlikely.

One thing was for sure, right now she didn't want to know. "It's time to get back. After all, Seth threw this party for me."

"Right," he said softly. "I'm sorry, McKayla. I never meant…"

"No worries," she replied just as softly. "Your heart's always in the right place. Don't think I don't know that."

His tired eyes met hers. "You've no idea."

For the first time in a very long time she felt that old familiar weakening in her knees. With a hard swallow she looked away from his intense gaze. Yeah, call Leslie a soul reader all day long but she had nothing on Trevor. If McKayla didn't play her cards right and keep her emotions locked up tight he'd eat her soul alive and she'd love every last minute of it.

"Don't forget your new flashlight. It might've found its way here but has no idea how to get home," Trevor said.

"Of course," she said and went to grab the box off the rock. The minute her hand was within inches, little spider legs extended and lifted it up. Arms shot out and a little faceless head extended. A short fabric kilt fell from its waistline, then it lifted a little bagpipe and started playing a happy jig, spider legs bobbing the box up and down.

Overjoyed in an instant, she burst out laughing. "You did it anyways!"

"Of course I did," he said happily.

Before she knew it, Trevor pulled her into his arms and they danced. In the dark woods surrounded by ancient rock and the memories of a long forgotten people, they twirled to the tune of Highland bagpipes compliments of a box in a kilt. It was amazing and so uniquely him. She loved it.

Too soon did the song wind down and the kilted creature retracted back into nothing more than a flashlight.

"Congratulations," Trevor said, pulling her in for a tight hug. "I'm so proud of you. I hope you know that."

She pulled back and looked into his eyes. "You know I do. Always. And I'm proud of you too. I'm sorry about my reaction to your gift. It's big. I know."

He brushed her hair away from her face, something he'd done before they dated and still did. "I love you, sweetheart, more than anyone, anywhere at any time. You know that right?"

McKayla wrapped her arms around his neck and put her cheek against his chest. "Yeah, I know. Me too."

His words warmed her heart. It was a sentiment they used when one or the other needed support. She supposed right now she needed his support more than she wanted to admit. Even though today was the best day of her life, it had also been the scariest.

"Time to go back," he said.

She stepped away. "You sound reluctant."

He grimaced and picked up the dormant box off the rock. "Seth threw this party. That means I'm going back to a house full of single men eager to get to know you better."

McKayla chuckled as they walked. "You should be happy for me."

"Happy for you? Why? Because you have a house full of men that only came because they got a Facebook invite that made you look loose?" He shook his head. "Not so much."

"How do you know that?"

"I got the invite too."

"Oh no."

"Yeah. I think Seth sent that invite to every guy he knew."

"He's worried about me."

"So am I," Trevor admitted. "But you don't see me sending out mass invites to perfect strangers who could end up doing God knows what to you."

"Seth would never allow that."

"No, but he'd enable it without realizing. The guy doesn't think."

"He's changed since marrying Alana. But you wouldn't know that, would you?"

McKayla felt the shift in Trevor's demeanor. "Moving to San Francisco was the right thing for me. My office is blocks away from some of the world's largest tech corporations. I'm right where I need to be."

"Silicon Valley? Really?" She huffed. "You're driven enough to accomplish just as much on the East coast."

"For people like me everything starts in the Bay Area. You know that."

"Then why aren't you a billionaire. Where's your fucking techy website?"

They both stopped short at her words. She didn't swear. Not ever. But the truth was she wanted him home. More than she realized apparently. And the subject had been coming up more and more often lately.

McKayla felt his eyes swing her way like one might feel the oppressive heat of a summer storm. His words were like low rumbling thunder. "I refuse to create a site that could be hacked allowing my products to be stolen. As soon as I find the kind of security the monster companies have, I'll offer the public things they never could've imagined."

Suddenly moody, she opposed him with one statement. "You've got enough money to sink a boat. If you really wanted the security you'd already have it. Again, something you could do from here."

"Come home," she complained and kept walking. "You're a New Englander. You don't belong out there."

Trevor didn't say anything. She didn't think he would. Even though he'd been born in this neck of the woods, he was a runner. His very roots scared the heck out of him. Even after knowing him for so long, she had no clue why.

The house was in full swing when they returned and her cousins were joyous as ever. There were no hard feelings between her and Trevor. There never were. They drank and partied. Only scattered looks from Seth and the girls made it clear that she and Trevor weren't exactly where they were supposed to be.

It seemed if they were off a little, everyone noticed. It was kind of annoying.

McKayla didn't meet a new guy which was no surprise. Not with a towering, brooding Trevor overlooking. The Bostonian crowd was easy, smooth, and handsome. And even though he might be the best looking man in the room, her best friend was the total opposite. Trevor roamed the room like an alpha wolf protecting its pack. Quite simply, he acted as if he were better than the rest.

His eyes remained hooded behind dark lashes and his lips wry. Even when he spoke it was with an air not entirely his own. Though raised in Massachusetts by a lower income family he acted more like a man born of privilege. It was strange…and irritating. But most of all, it was uncharacteristic.

"When exactly did you meet him?" Ferchar asked, as he and McKayla plunked down next to one another in front of the fireless hearth.

"Trevor? Years ago."

"I dinnae understand why you're not together. He seems verra…protective of you."

McKayla took a sip of wine and muttered, "Because I don't like cowboys."

Ferchar didn't seem overly fazed by her response. "Nay. But you like him."

"Aye, I did." She slowly twirled her glass, staring aimlessly. "A long time ago."

"What made you stop?"

"Technology."

The Scotsman chuckled. "So he moved across the country and you could only communicate through technology."

McKayla shook her head. Though only on her second glass, the wine was affecting her. "No, it wasn't the distance, it was *technology* itself. He's addicted to it." She narrowed her eyes at Trevor. "Do you know what he has in his pocket?"

"No, but I'm sure you do," Ferchar said easily, a grin on his face.

McKayla rolled her eyes and shook her head. "No, not that. But yes, that. But no." Ugh, did she sound tipsy? No matter, she had a point to make. "In his pocket is a way to control my dreams. A way to get to the very heart of my book."

Intrigued, Ferchar said, "Oh really, the heart of your book?"

"Did you know I'm a Broun?" she asked, distracted.

"A Broun? Aye, of course. But what does that have to do with Trevor?"

"I'm not sure," she mumbled, losing focus. "But we all are, Caitlin, me, Sheila and Leslie. That means something."

Ferchar's arm came around her shoulder in comfort. "Of course it does, lass. Always has."

"Has it?" she said, looking at him. "Really?"

For a second she felt a little dazed, as if he'd seen something within her mind even she could not see.

"Always has and always will, dinnae ever forget that."

"Are you okay?"

McKayla blinked, surprised to find Caitlin on her other side, and speaking to her.

"I don't know? Am I?" she asked.

"Come on." Caitlin pulled her up off of the couch. "I think you've had enough. It's been a really long day."

The next thing she knew Caitlin was tucking her into bed. McKayla yawned. "Thanks cuz."

"No problem, hon."

"Caitlin," she said. "Can you do me a favor?"

"Of course, anything."

"There's something in my pocket. It's meant to cover my eyes while I sleep. Trevor gave it to me. Can you get it for me?"

"Here it is."

Eyes already closed, she felt something cool and silken slip over her head.

"Anything else?" Caitlin asked.

"No. Thank you."

Her cousin shut the door behind her. Yawning again, McKayla found contentment in Trevor's gift if for no other reason than it felt wonderful on her face. She curled onto her side and pulled a comforter over her shoulders.

"Tsk, tsk, not quite yet, lassie."

Exhausted, she mumbled, "Trevor, let me go to sleep."

"Not quite yet. Wake up."

"Please," she mumbled.

He started to shake her shoulders. "Nay, wake up. Now! Right now!"

Startled, confused, she listened and bolted upright.

Not to Trevor but to Colin of the MacLeod Clan.

The hero from her novel.

Chapter Three

The lass had no sooner sat up before she passed out.

Again Colin wondered how his brotherhood had found out about her. For now, it would remain a mystery. With one last disgusted glance at his fallen mentor he scooped her up into his arms and scanned the forest. He had to remain focused, alert. Or he'd end up dead. Because of one deadly action, he was the most hunted man in Scotland. His bloodline didn't matter in the least. Regardless of who he was or how much power he possessed, he would be searched out and killed.

Or his clan would go to war to protect him.

Yet another God forsaken war.

After waiting ten more seconds he knew the time had come. He covered the lass with his enemy's tartan and leapt into the forest. Jaw clenched, body ready, he ran fast and hard.

There was no other choice.

Sawooooooosh.

They shot at him. He dropped to his knees and covered her head, waited three counts, then bounded up and ran.

Zawiiiiiiing.

A dagger-edged boomerang.

He jumped right, then left three times, before falling to the ground, covering her with his body again.

Zawiiing.

It flew back over.

He bounced up, ran at full speed then plunged to the ground.

Zawiiing.

There it went again. Damn, would they ever stop? He didn't know how long he could evade them. If he were a gambling man, he'd bet he was in trouble. But he wouldn't give up, it wasn't in his blood. He would fight until the end, which would be real soon if he didn't do something, and do it fast.

With his eyes closed, he breathed in through his nose, waited two more seconds until a peaceful calm overcame him. Then he ran again, harder and faster than before. One, two, three, four, he counted, and then crouched. An arrow whizzed overhead. He started to run. Two more arrows whizzed over. He jumped over a ledge. His arse hit the slope hard and they started to fall. Oh hell, he wasn't about to die now. He grasped her tighter. Refused to let go. They'd already come too far.

"Hold on," he whispered.

But obviously she couldn't so he locked his legs around hers and wrapped his arms around her chest to protect her. "Stay with me," he murmured.

Though it was a fairly long slide, it wasn't too bad. Soon enough he ducked into a small rock enclosure. Colin held the lass close for a long time, looking up and around, barely breathing. He knew this was supposed to be a safe spot. But truly, what was safe in this country nowadays?

He reluctantly leaned her unconscious form up against the rock and then sat against the opposite wall. It wasn't that he didn't want to be near her. Did he ever. But what he wanted and what *they* needed were two different things. He couldn't concentrate when she was so near, and right now he had to focus on keeping them alive. From where he sat, he had a better vantage point of incoming trouble. At least that's what he *told* himself.

Now all he could do was wait. And pray.

Time went by and still nobody came. It seemed, at least for now, that they were safe. She was safe. That was all that mattered. It was hard to believe that she was really here because in truth she shouldn't be. She should be safely tucked away in the twenty-first century and as far away from Scotland as possible.

Yet look at her.

Here not there.

And as always, so bloody beautiful.

Since the moment he'd laid eyes on her, Colin had been obsessed. Aye, he knew about the draw between the MacLomains and Brouns but assumed he'd be immune. His was a life of danger and no lass deserved such. But since he'd first seen her, without knowing it, she had drawn him ever closer. Colin held his head in his hands. How had he even arrived at the point of killing her?

Dark magic no doubt.

In the end none of it mattered. He'd been tricked.

Now he was in the process of maneuvering through and manipulating time to stay one step ahead. There was nothing he wouldn't do to protect her. *Nothing.*

"Oh heck," she whispered.

He lifted his head. She was awake. Groggy, but awake. Palm against her forehead, she slowly opened her eyes. Their gazes met, held. Pale gray, like moonlight on ice, her eyes searched his. What did they see? Did she recognize him? No, of course not.

"Okay," she whispered. "I get it."

There was no way she understood what just happened. What he had put her through. He never wanted her to know, because then she would hate him. And rightfully so.

"You're Colin. You *must* be."

Aye, but not the Colin she thought he was.

"Aye, lass. I am Colin."

"And you are part of my lucid dream."

Best for now that she think that. "Aye."

"You're not what I expected."

"Speak softer, lass." He really needed her to be quiet. But what did she mean, not what she expected?

She nodded, as if she understood something, then whispered, "Are you not Colin MacLeod?"

A sour taste filled his mouth. He'd allow only so much. He whispered back, "Nay, I am Colin MacLomain."

Her brows furrowed in confusion. "Ah, so in this state I've given you the same last name as Ferchar and Caitlin. Interesting. But I suppose that makes sense in that I'm more familiar with it."

Right. She would think that. He wondered if he should be honest. Either way, things would get far more confusing before they became clearer. After all, she was caught in a time gap that was closing quickly, one that stretched between twenty-first century New Hampshire and medieval Scotland.

Her wide eyes continued to study him, a warm blush spreading over her cheeks. "I can't wait to tell him how well this works.

Amazing," she said. "Though you don't quite look how I envisioned."

"How what works?" he asked innocently though he knew damn well what she was talking about. "And how precisely did you envision me, lass? We've only just met."

Colin knew he should be forthright but these precious few moments of ignorance seemed preferable...especially in light of what lay ahead.

She shook her head, clearly debating how much she should share. "It's just," she began then stopped. "Well, you see you're not." She stopped talking again and frowned. "Okay, here's the thing. You're not...*real*."

He glanced down at himself then back at her. "Are you sure? I feel real enough."

An indiscernible sound escaped as her nervous gaze flickered from him to their surroundings then back. "This is going to sound really strange but you're actually a character from a book I wrote and the only reason you're here is because a friend helped invent something truly remarkable."

"Is that right?" He crossed his arms over his chest and leaned his head against the wall. "So I am but a figment of your imagination?"

Her lips thinned as they always did when she worried about hurting someone's feelings. "Yes, so it seems. I'm really sorry."

"Dinnae be. In light of our current circumstances your imagination would be a preferable place."

"You sound so much like Ferchar," she said, her eyes shooting to his lips.

Colin felt that look as though she'd touched him. A bolt of lust shot through him, unlike anything he'd ever felt before. Having her here in this place was dangerous. He couldn't control the feelings thundering through him. He wanted to touch her for the first time on this land, in this time. But he would not, could not, lest risk frightening her.

"Tell me more about where you think you are," he urged.

"Well, if you're here I'm guessing the setting would have to be thirteenth century Scotland." She glanced around the cave. "But

I never wrote about this place." Her eyes returned to him. "Or you such as you are. It seems my lucid dream has you looking more like the guy on the book cover, at least as much of him as I can see. Your chin is the same but it's hard to say if the rest is."

"The rest?"

"Your...body," she stuttered then snapped her mouth shut.

"My body? What do you mean?" He really shouldn't be putting her though this when truths could be shared. But would she believe him? Doubtful. At least not yet.

Clearly wanting to change the direction of their conversation she said, "My name is McKayla. It seems only fair you should know that even if you're not real."

"'Tis a bonnie name," he replied in kind. One he knew all too well.

"Thank you."

"So I've a question for you, lass," he asked.

"Sure, ask me anything," she replied, obviously still trying to acclimate to her surroundings and to him.

"If I'm but your dream, shouldn't you be able to control my actions? Perhaps even my words?"

She drummed her fingers on the rock by her side. "You'd think so. But perhaps I'm already doing that without even knowing it."

Unable to resist, he stood and walked over to her. McKayla's eyes grew enormous as he approached. Reaching out his hand, he encouraged her to stand. Unsure, she looked from his hand to his face.

"Aren't you curious to see if you can touch me?" he asked softly.

With little hesitation she reached out and took his hand. He pulled her up. The energy fluctuating between them was almost palpable. Their connection here in Scotland was much, much stronger. It took a great deal of strength not to pull her against him, to feel the sweet softness of her curves.

"So tall, so real," she whispered, her eyes roaming his face. "He's going to be a millionaire for creating such a device."

Interesting. He was jealous of someone who was no threat at all. Or was he? Though he knew the answer he asked, "Who?"

"It doesn't matter. A friend," she said absently.

Though it shouldn't, frustration rose sharply to the surface. "A mere friend created something that allowed you to live within a story you wrote?"

Confusion pinched together her brows but her eyes remained locked on his. "Why do you sound upset?" She grimaced. "Though that's possibly something I would've had you say."

His jealousy waned quickly. Was it? A small thrill shot through him. "McKayla, what would you say if I told you that your friend did more than create a device that allowed you to dream of me. A device that also allowed you to do more than dream of medieval Scotland, the setting for your book."

"I don't understand."

Colin squeezed her hand gently. "What if he created a device that actually allowed you to travel back in time?"

A shaky burst of laughter erupted and she twisted her lips. "I'd say scratch him being a millionaire and make that a multi-billionaire."

"Then he must be because you are here. This is Scotland. We are in danger and won't be able to find shelter in this cave for long. 'Tis my hope that you can return to whence you came." He studied her face. "At least for now."

McKayla looked at him as though he were insane but softened her expression almost immediately. "Yes, of course I will. But please know this isn't…" She bit her lower lip and scowled before her brows lifted. "It will all be fine. I'll go and you'll stay here in Scotland."

He knew she didn't believe him in the least. Who would?

"So it seems you are mine until you awake."

He didn't miss the slight quiver in her hand nor her heavy swallow. "So it seems."

Colin felt the air shift. Their surroundings brightened then dulled. He knew she didn't sense it. Before she could be taken from him he cupped her cheek with one hand. "I cannae tell you how glad I am you came, McKayla. Verra soon I will tell you

41

things you never could have imagined. Will you believe me when I do?"

Stunned, she whispered, "You're not only my hero but my muse. I'll listen."

"Aye," he whispered in return. "Then I will see you soon, lass."

She started to fade. Watching her go was more difficult than he'd anticipated. Yet his chest tightened only a moment...for he'd see her again soon.

Inhaling deeply he closed his eyes and focused. Magic stirred. The mark beneath his heart began to burn. Following the path of light within his mind, Colin felt reality shift and warp. Sparks of white hot lightning shot up his spine and his skin turned so cold it felt as though ice water had been poured over him. For a split second he endured such severe pain that he might as well be immersed in acid.

As quickly as the sensations came they vanished. He was whole once more, but different.

Not pausing a moment, he walked into McKayla's bedroom.

****

McKayla shot up in bed.

Though sweat coated her body, shivers raked her from head to toe. Clenching the bed sheets she stared blindly around the room.

"Are you okay, sweetheart?"

It took several long disjointed seconds to realize she still wore the mask. When she tore it off, Trevor was there. The moment he sat on the edge of her bed she curled willingly into his waiting arms and buried her head against his chest. "You'll never believe what happened to me."

His warm hand stroked the back of her head, comforting. "It's okay. Just a bad dream. Was it the mask I gave you?"

Early morning light crept into the room and things began to look more normal. Gathering her composure, she sat back, nodded and looked at him in amazement. "Yeah, the mask definitely works." She shook the cobwebs from her mind, still shocked and in awe about what had just happened. "Boy does it ever work! I still can't believe it. I didn't really have a nightmare but it was intense. I dreamt about my book! About the hero in it. I was in Scotland!"

Concerned but interested, he said, "Wow, really? Nice. Were you able to control the dream?"

She blew a bit of bang away from her face and shrugged. "I have no idea. Maybe. It's hard to tell if I created everything Colin said. It seemed so real. He even went so far as to say I was really there, that I'd traveled back in time to medieval Scotland. But I suppose it makes sense I'd try to rationalize what was happening even though I knew I was in a dream state, right?"

Trevor nodded. "Sure, I guess. What'd he look like? Was he the character you'd created?"

"God no." Her cheeks burned thinking about him. "He was so much hotter!"

Even that was a massive understatement. The man was gorgeous. Trevor didn't have a chance to respond before she rattled on. "He was so tall, even taller than I'd envisioned him. In my book he had dirty blond hair. In my dream it was much darker, almost black with dark brownish highlights. And his eyes were amazing. Not sure what to call the color. Sort of a piercing mix of light green and blue, bright opal maybe? If I were to write it I'd say they were the color of the Atlantic thinned over coral in bright sunlight. Eerie but sexy."

"Eerie but sexy?" Trevor chuckled.

"Yes," she confirmed. "And he wore his hair cinched back. Kind of modern for medieval Scotland I thought, definitely not how I would've written it. Then there was his face."

"Good face?" Trevor asked almost dryly.

"Great face! Again, not how I envisioned him. As you know my Colin was inquisitive so he had those arched brows to match. This Colin's brows were straighter, as if he didn't question much, just sort of already had everything figured out. This Colin also had lips that were used to mocking. I'll bet they often shoot up on one side as if he finds the world a bit ridiculous if not amusing."

"Maybe he does," Trevor muttered, his brows furrowed. "Sounds like you prefer your Lucid Dream Colin over the man you created."

"Actually, I do." She shoved the blanket away and stretched, feeling more and more excited by the moment. "He'll help inspire the hero in my next book."

Trevor fingered the Lucid Dream mask and arched a brow. "So all and all my invention's a success?"

"Oh my goodness, yes! You and your guys totally nailed it. Seriously hit a home run." She grabbed his hand and squeezed. "The only thing you might have to worry about is people getting addicted to it. I mean this thing is crazy surreal."

Trevor smiled and tossed the mask on her bedside table. "So what are your plans for today? Any room for me?"

"You're staying?" she asked, thrilled. "You never stay long."

"I'm yours for the unforeseeable future."

McKayla ignored the odd way he said it, and smiled. "Really?"

After all, the unforeseeable future for Trevor could very likely mean two hours from now. "Good then. We'll grab some breakfast then hop online so you can teach me more about this fabulous new device of yours."

"Or," he said. "We could do normal friend stuff like watch TV, take a walk or go shopping for a new car."

McKayla burst out laughing and looked at him. She stopped laughing when she saw he was serious. "C'mon, hun. Shop for a new car? What, are you going to have it flown home?"

"No, *we're* going to drive it here. Where else would we drive your new car?"

Incredulous, she raised her brows and shook her head. "I appreciate your vote of confidence but despite my book advance, I'd rather wait to see how sales do before I obligate to a new vehicle."

Trevor looked nothing less than determined. "Then don't obligate, let me."

"Let you?"

"Yeah." He shrugged. "Let me buy you a new car. Consider it my congratulations gift."

"Absolutely not. Besides you already gave me a congratulations gift." She stood, pointed at the mask on the bedside table then slid into her slippers. Already in sweatpants and a t-shirt, she padded to the window overlooking the huge oak tree. "I appreciate the offer, I really do. But that takes our friendship to an uncomfy level. Even you know that."

"Does it?" He walked over and joined her. Arms crossed over his broad chest he leaned against the windowsill and looked at her. "You have supported me every inch of the way despite our…break-up. You believed in me when nobody else did. If it wasn't for you I wouldn't be half as successful as I am. What if I said it would ease my conscience if I could do something to help you? You're going to need a car, McKayla. I promise it'll be small and fuel-efficient."

"I love you for offering but it's too much." She touched his arm. "I'm sorry I just can't let you do that, don't be offended. You know I think you're wonderful. And I don't need a new car to prove it. "

Trevor scowled and looked out the window. "Yeah, yeah."

The smell of brewing coffee hit her. "Leslie's up."

"Mmm hmm."

"Oh stop it," she said. "Brooding doesn't become you. Tell you what. When you hit the one million dollar mark from selling your Dream mask, I'll let you buy me a car. Sound good?"

"We'll see," he said. "Let's go get some coffee."

Grabbing a clip off her nightstand, she cinched up her hair and followed him down to the kitchen. This whole 'let me buy you a car' business was Trevor's way of deterring her from talking about his latest technology. Why he didn't want to talk about the mask was beyond her. Maybe he thought it still needed work. Or maybe he just felt like buying a big toy. It was hard to tell with him. If nothing else, he was unpredictable and spontaneous to a fault.

Funny, he should meet Colin MacLomain. They might just get along. She hadn't known her 'dream Scotsman' long but sensed he possessed the same borderline recklessness Trevor did. Both would get bored if they sat still too long. Both would appreciate extreme measures. Why she had that thought, McKayla couldn't be sure.

Colin *MacLomain.*

Why would she call him that? Her mind had been so thoroughly engrossed in Colin MacLeod for the past six months it seemed almost unbelievable that she'd give him any other name. When writing about history it was imperative to learn as much as possible and to be accurate. She'd spent countless hours learning about the MacLeods, there wasn't anything she didn't know about them…but the MacLomains. They were a mystery. Did she bring Ferchar's name into the dream because he was the only Scotsman she knew? Anything was possible. Still, something didn't feel right about it.

"Good, you're awake," Leslie said when they entered. Tablet on, she was busy typing away. "We need to talk."

McKayla groaned and leaned against the counter while Trevor poured them both a cup of coffee. "The sun's just cresting the horizon on a Sunday. Do we really need to talk business this early?"

"Of course," Leslie responded, sipping delicately from her mug while her fingers flew over the keyboard. "Besides, once Seth and Sheila are awake, productive talk gets swept under the carpet. Between paranormal investigating and saving trees, you can't get a word in edgewise."

"It's good that they have passions," McKayla said, grateful when Trevor winked and handed her a steaming cup. It looked like it was going to be a long morning after all.

"They have hobbies." Leslie shook her head. "If they put their efforts toward something worthwhile, that might actually make something of themselves."

Typical Leslie, always a critic.

"If you say so." McKayla yawned as she sat. The coffee tasted delicious. She smiled at Trevor, almost sorry that he was stuck in here too. Almost. Someone had to have her back. When he started to leave the kitchen she shook her head, ushering him back. He didn't need to buy her a new car. Nope. But he did need to hang with her through all 'Leslie' related things because they were downright tedious, bordering on brutal.

"I've been looking over your social networking sites as well as your website. While I like the consistency between them, I can't say I'm completely impressed with the color scheme. Did you approve this shade of yellow with the company we hired?"

"Yes, I think it looks fine," she replied, strongly considering crawling back into bed. Anything to escape.

Leslie's lips curled down. "I keep thinking bumble bee. So much black and yellow."

"They're MacLeod colors. It makes sense to focus on them as I intend to write a series. Besides, I think it looks more gold online."

Trevor nodded, eyeing her website from his cell phone. "I agree. Definitely doesn't scream yellow."

"I can always depend on you to back her up," Leslie said wryly. "For that reason, I can't trust your opinion, Trevor."

"Naturally," he replied.

Leslie ignored his sarcasm and tapped the touchscreen on the tablet, minimizing, maximizing and moving windows around with enviable speed until she finally nodded. "There, I just shot your advertising company my thoughts along with color samples that I think will work better."

Even though she was frustrated that her cousin didn't listen to her, McKayla didn't say anything. What was the point? It would do no good. Leslie always did things the way she thought best. Pushy was her middle name.

McKayla's cell phone buzzed. Grabbing it off the counter she sat back down and read. Trevor had typed, "When are you ever gonna stand up to her?"

After a sip of coffee, she texted back, "You should talk."

"Texting behind your agent's back again?" Sheila said groggily from the doorway. With a nod of approval, she put some water on to boil and plopped a tea bag in her mug.

Though they set their cell phones aside, neither was particularly apologetic.

"They've always thought themselves discreet," Leslie remarked, eyes never leaving the tablet. "And I do have a name you know."

"Do you?" Sheila replied, yawning. Before Leslie could respond she focused on McKayla and said, "So did you enjoy your party? Better yet, I'm dying to know if the Lucid Dream mask worked."

When McKayla looked Trevor's way, he grinned. "I couldn't help but share."

"Caitlin and Ferchar are super curious too." Sheila said. "They want details,"

"What's this about a Lucid Dream mask?" Leslie asked though she couldn't be bothered to look away from the screen.

"Without a shadow of a doubt, it's a multi-billion dollar invention," McKayla said.

This got Leslie's attention. Lowering her reading glasses, she looked over them at Trevor. "Created by you then?"

"So it seems." He glanced at McKayla. "Though it's only in its trial period."

Something about the gleam in his eyes and the way he said it made her breath catch. Why did it seem he referred to them and not the device? Was this some sort of side effect from using the contraption? Because any romance that'd existed between them was long gone. Wasn't it? McKayla almost laughed. Of course it was.

"What's in a trial period? Are you talking about your new invention?" Seth asked, entering the kitchen, eyes half-mast as he poured coffee then sat on the counter.

"Wow, you're up early," McKayla said. "Both of you actually."

Seth nodded. "Tell me about it. I decided to hit Mount Washington today with a few friends. Overdue for some rock climbing."

"Nice." McKayla sulked a little. "I suppose that means you'll be heading home after."

"Afraid so." He nodded at Trevor. "But I'm leaving you in good enough hands."

Trevor seemed a little surprised by Seth's remark but said nothing. Though they'd known one another for years, their friendship was lukewarm at best. McKayla supposed it was because they were so different. Seth was the dare-devil, Trevor the techie.

"Let's hear more about this device," Leslie said, removing her glasses. "I'd like to see it."

"It's on her bedside table," Trevor said.

McKayla stood, intending to go get it. The men frowned and Sheila nixed her actions when she said, "Sit, sweetie. I'll go get it." But not before she shot Leslie a look that said 'why don't you get off your ass and get it?'

McKayla refilled their coffee mugs then sat down again. She abandoned her cell to fiddle with Trevor's. Naturally, it was the latest and most expensive phone on the market. One way or another he'd always been good at making money.

Sheila dangled the contraption from her finger as she entered the room. "I assume this is it?"

Trevor nodded and Leslie held out her hand to take it.

"Yeah right," Sheila responded and studied it rather than handing it over. "It looks fairly simple. Weighs next to nothing. If I didn't know better, I'd think it was a normal sleeping mask." She peered closer. "If there's wiring in here it's undetectable."

"It contains something similar to fiber optics," Trevor said. "It's woven into the fabric so it won't affect the comfort."

"What does it do exactly?" Seth asked.

McKayla couldn't help but gush, "It literally turns your dream into another reality. One I think you can control. At least you're supposed to be able to."

"Really?" Sheila said. "That's incredible."

Leslie snatched it out of her hand and studied it closely. "Tell me what happened when you wore it, McKayla."

"Oh, you might want to wait a sec," Sheila said. "Looks like Caitlin and Ferchar are here."

"Did they bring Logan?"

"Yep."

As it turned out, their three year old son was half awake when Ferchar carried him in. He was a miniature version of his father with jet black hair and light blue eyes. Logan always seemed advanced for his age. There was an old wisdom in his young eyes. As if somehow he'd been here before. So it didn't shock her when his gaze went straight to the Lucid Dream mask in Leslie's hand.

He pointed at it and screeched. "Scotland!"

A sharp thrill raced through her. Ferchar's eyes narrowed slightly at the mask. Leslie's fingers clutched it tighter and McKayla knew her soul-reader abilities had kicked in. In fact, it occurred to her that the air crackled with a mixture of tension and curiosity.

Caitlin came in and stopped, her posture changing. Her eyes shot to the mask that she'd put on McKayla the night before. She looked at Ferchar and said, "I'm going to lie Logan down in the living room."

Ferchar kissed his son on the cheek then handed him over. The moment his arms were free he held out his hand to Leslie. "May I see it?"

Leslie handed it to him, a rattled look on her normally composed face.

The instant the Scotsman took the mask; he inhaled sharply. His eyes flew to Trevor. A few seconds went by as the men stared at one another. She couldn't ever remember Ferchar looking quite the way he did now. Refrained rage seemed to pulse around him and something else, something baffling. Love? The room became deadly quiet.

"You hid yourself well, cousin," Ferchar said bitterly.

Caitlin returned, her gaze shooting between Ferchar and Trevor. "What's going on?"

He took her hand and said, "It seems the connection between the Brouns and MacLomains didnae end with the rings or with the death of my grandfather, Adlin."

McKayla had no idea what was happening. Seth's behavior was the oddest. She'd never seen him look so tense and swore his blue eyes turned black. But that couldn't be. Sheila and Leslie were clearly baffled, their gazes flickering between the men.

"He's Iain's boy," Ferchar said through clenched teeth.

"That's impossible!" Caitlin's eyes rounded. "Isn't it?"

Trevor's eyes remained locked on Ferchar's. "I never meant to deceive anyone."

Seth growled.

The ground felt like it dropped from beneath her. What the hell were they talking about? She looked at Trevor with confusion. "I don't understand. What's happening here?"

The desperation in her voice tore his gaze away from Ferchar and he took her hand. "It's okay, Kay. Just take a deep breath and I'll tell you everything."

"I don't need to take a deep breath. Just tell me why Ferchar said you're his cousin. That makes no sense. You didn't even know him until you met me."

"Didn't he?" Seth said, voice low and dangerous.

She swung impatient eyes his way. "Why are you acting like this? What the hell is going on?"

"You had a dream when you wore that mask, didn't you McKayla?" Ferchar asked, never taking his eyes off Trevor.

"Well, yeah, but what's that got to do with any of this?"

"Why dinnae you share your dream with your cousins," Ferchar said. "Then I have a story to share as well."

It was impossible not to look at each and every person in the room as she spoke. It felt like every word was somehow, in some way, changing the very course of their lives. But she shared regardless. "I dreamt about my book, about medieval Scotland. Though all I saw was a cave I did meet the hero from my story, Colin MacLeod, I mean Colin…MacLomain."

She frowned and looked at Ferchar. "He sounded like you. At the time I assumed my mind picked out your voice because you're the only Scotsman I know. But that's beside the point. I wasn't there long. We didn't have a chance to talk too much. He told me he'd saved my life and that I wasn't dreaming, but that I'd traveled back in time. It was all a little wacky but still an intense, unforgettable experience. What does that have to do with any of this? Speaking of…what exactly is this between you and Trevor?"

Caitlin's eyes hadn't left Trevor. "*Holy shit*," she said, eyes wide with amazement.

Ferchar didn't take the same obtrusive approach. "McKayla is one of many that you owe an explanation to, lad. If I didnae love your Da so well, I'd probably have a blade to your throat."

McKayla was surprised when she saw Trevor's expression shift to anger. "Everything I did was for the good of the clan."

Chill after chill ran down her spine. "What are you talking about? What clan?"

Trevor's eyes met hers, determined. "The MacLomains." He closed his eyes then met hers again. "McKayla, I'm not who you think I am."

"Yeah, got that," she said, shaking her head.

"Who are you exactly?" Leslie said, blatantly curious.

Sheila sat next to McKayla and held her hand. Seth had become nothing less than a pent up beast. There was no doubt he used a great deal of restraint to remain silent.

"The mask," Trevor said softly. "Though it can invoke control of lucid dreaming it didn't do so in your case." His green eyes locked with hers. "You truly traveled back in time, McKayla. Where you met me…the real me, Colin MacLomain."

Chapter Four

McKayla blinked a few times and narrowed her eyes. What was he up to? This had to be some sort of joke. Unable to help herself, she chuckled. Then she laughed when it occurred to her what they were doing. Looking around the room she shook her head and said, "All right, I've found you all out. Is this a 'step into the book' sort of party? Because if it is, you've outdone yourselves."

Nobody smiled. Trevor's disposition turned more and more troubled. "I never wanted you to find out this way." He frowned at Ferchar. "This should've been handled differently."

Ferchar's eyes darkened. "I couldn't agree more."

"She'll never believe him unless he shows her." Caitlin put a hand on her husband's arm. "Unless he shows all of us."

Trevor shook his head. "Nay, 'tis not a good idea, lass."

It felt like someone had sucker punched her. "Did you just speak with a brogue?" McKayla asked.

"Aye," Trevor muttered. "I'm sorry. It takes a lot of effort to speak as you do."

What? She kept shaking her head. "I've known you for years. You've always spoken with a New England accent. Never once did you…why didn't you tell me you were from Scotland? I wouldn't have cared."

"None of us would have," Sheila assured, her tea bag long over-steeped in now cold water.

"It might have proved helpful when she was writing this book," Leslie said. "You could have given her great feedback."

"*What* are you," Seth growled at Trevor.

They all looked at Seth, astounded by the sheer fury on his face.

"Enough," Ferchar said and stepped forward.

Seth seemed to pull back into himself and everything quieted.

Caitlin made Trevor get up so she could sit on the other side of McKayla. Taking her hand, she scowled at all three men. "Make

53

this clear for McKayla or so help me I'll take you all out. And don't think I won't."

Seth looked genuinely upset. "I'm so sorry. Trust me, McKayla this is going to be one helluva day. I experienced something similar three years ago."

Inhaling deeply, she nodded. He was obviously hurting right now. "Okay, tell me then."

"Me, Andrea, Leathan and Devin had gone on an investigation unlike any other."

"And?"

He started to take a swig of coffee but stopped and lowered his mug, clearly upset by what he was about to tell her. "It was at this Victorian house where I learned that a lot more exists in this world than we think."

"Like what?" Leslie asked, completely intrigued.

Seth's brows arched in resignation. "Like magic, vampires, bad things." He cleared his throat, uncomfortable as he looked at McKayla. "Even warlocks."

She held Caitlin's hand tighter. "You've got to be kidding me. Why are you saying this?"

"Because he's trying to come clean with you," Caitlin said. "About all that's out there that normal people don't know about."

It was impossible to swallow as she looked at her cousin and whispered, "How would you know?"

Caitlin twirled the sapphire centered Claddagh ring on her finger. "Because I'm a witch, sweetie."

McKayla instinctively pulled her hand away. "I'm not sure what you're all up to but I'm ready for the game to be over, okay?"

"This isn't a game," Trevor said, voice both sad and resolute. "There's so much out there beyond what you all know. Always has been and always will be."

"Trevor," she whispered, pleading with her eyes for him to stop, to start laughing, to send her a text saying, 'Got ya!'

But his phone was still in her hand and he wasn't laughing.

Sheila seemed to be handling this with as much stride as Leslie. But perhaps they thought this was a joke, too.

"I think the easiest place to start is at the beginning," Ferchar said, compassionate as he looked at her. "And that was in Scotland a verra long time ago. You are familiar with my grandfather, Adlin MacLomain, are you not?"

"Yes, of course, he was in love with Mildred, Caitlin's grandmother. They lived in the house you now live in."

"That's right, lass," he said gently. "Yet they didnae meet here in New Hampshire but in early eleventh century Scotland."

"She traveled through time to meet him," Caitlin said, nostalgia in her eyes. "Theirs was a great love, one that went through many trials and tribulations. In the end they were together as it was always meant to be."

McKayla looked from Caitlin to Ferchar. They were speaking truthfully.

"But Adlin was born long before he found Mildred," Ferchar said. "It was he who birthed the great MacLomain clan. He was able to do this because he was an immortal wizard."

Slack-jawed, Sheila shook her head and whispered, "I always speculated this stuff could exist." She looked at McKayla. "Didn't I tell you it wouldn't hurt to slip some of it into your book!"

"When he was younger Adlin created something called a Highland Defiance. A way to travel through time. As he got older he no longer needed it. Between his power and the rings, time travel became much easier," Ferchar said.

"What rings?" Leslie asked.

Caitlin held out her hand. "Gem centered Claddagh rings. They're meant to bring true love together. They transport members of the Broun and MacLomain clans through time so their souls can be joined. The gem in the ring matched the wizard's eye color and brought forth a powerful bond that could never be broken."

McKayla stared between Caitlin and Ferchar, not looking in Trevor's direction. "Is that one of them?"

Caitlin nodded, a warm smile on her face. "It brought Ferchar and me together."

"Across time," Ferchar said. "McKayla, I am not from modern day Scotland but medieval Scotland...early thirteenth century to be more precise. I was not only chieftain to the MacLomain Clan but one of four wizards."

She pinched the bridge of her nose and tried to make sense of what they were telling her. Though their story was extremely far-fetched she couldn't help think about the inspiration this property had lent her. Never once had she contemplated writing about medieval Scotland before moving here. Yet that could be just coincidence...couldn't it?

But she was not so blind that she didn't see and feel what was happening around her.

Especially between Seth and Trevor.

They had put as much distance between one another as possible which wasn't much in the small kitchen. Seth looked ready to drive a stake through Trevor's heart and Trevor had become the uncharacteristic brooding beast from the night before. Their arms were crossed over their chests in defensive, unyielding postures.

Caitlin looked at the three women. "You are all Brouns and like me, witches."

McKayla's throat went bone dry.

Sheila sat up a little straighter but said nothing.

"You are all completely out of your mind," Leslie said with assurance and once more focused on her tablet before she looked at McKayla. "But what a great inspiration for your future work." Then she rethought that because she shook her head and said, "Paranormal and fantasy doesn't sell nearly as well as straight historical or even contemporary. So, keep that in mind."

Unable to help herself, Sheila shrugged. "I don't know. There are several paranormal and fantasy authors who have made it huge." She cast a flippant look at Leslie then focused on McKayla. "You just have to set aside the influence of tight-assed, close-minded advisors and be willing to take chances."

"Or," Leslie said smoothly to McKayla though her eyes narrowed on Sheila. "You can take the advice of an agent who has already locked in a five-figure book deal before your novel has even hit the shelves."

Being surrounded by witches and time-travelers seemed less daunting by the minute when faced with being pulled into a Leslie/Sheila blow-out. However, for the first time ever, she could admit she preferred the ever-annoying distraction they provided. Without them she'd have to look at Trevor...then Seth.

And both were scaring the heck out of her right now.

"Are you okay, McKayla? Because there is more you need to know. Much more," Ferchar said.

Caitlin again squeezed her hand, eyes reassuring.

Whether she truly believed it or not, McKayla could think of only one response. "Do I have a choice?"

"Nay," Ferchar said without hesitation. Though his concerned eyes still flickered with a hint of compassion it was soon replaced with a driven, somewhat hard gaze. "Do you remember what we talked about last night? About the connection between the Brouns and MacLomains?"

She nodded.

"The connections continue it seems." He glanced at Trevor. "While I dinnae ken the reasons yet, he's here for you and rest assured, he is a MacLomain. Born to be a chieftain, I cannae speak about the details of his life save he's important and should never have approached you as he has." This time Ferchar's eyes grew turbulent. "He has been here without me suspecting it in the least for far too long, which means either he is more powerful than I or he has others protecting him who are."

"You make me sound like a monster when I'm nothing more than a shifter. I love Kay. I'd never do anything to hurt her," Trevor said.

"I'm not sure you should call me Kay anymore," she said.

Wounded, his eyes pleaded with her briefly before he looked away.

"Shifter," Sheila said, looking at him. "Like a shape-shifter?"

"Aye," Trevor said softly.

"And you're also a wizard," Seth ground out. "Don't think I don't know."

"Which, naturally, is so much worse than you being a warlock," Trevor said sarcastically.

They were *what*? Her heart pounded. "Both of you shut up!" McKayla barked then snapped her mouth shut. Had she just said that?

Everyone looked at her. Nobody said a word. She wasn't a confrontational person so although she'd lashed out, McKayla didn't have much to follow it. Time to think this all over would be her first choice. Alone. With no fighting, accusing or distractions, but evidently that wasn't an option. Overwhelmed, she looked at Leslie. If anyone could make sense of this, it was her.

Not needing further prompting her cousin looked at Trevor and Seth. "You two mean the most to her. If we're to move forward with this tall tale there needs to be proof." When she continued speaking McKayla realized Leslie didn't believe them in the least. "Seth, do something *warlocky*. Trevor, leave the room and return as this Colin person. I only say to leave the room because the very idea of someone transforming in front of me is nauseating. So out of the room for five seconds then back in. Sound good?"

Seth's brows drew down. "Something *warlocky*? Are you serious?"

"Verra," Ferchar said, arms crossed. "And make it good."

"Aren't you worried about your son in the other room?" Seth said caustically.

"If it wasnae for my bairn nobody would be the wiser. Seems he's brighter than the lot of us. But no worries, he's watching cartoons."

Seth shook his head. "Fine." He looked at McKayla. "Can I sit next to you?"

The idea sort of irritated her but she said, "Yeah."

If looks could kill the one Trevor shot Seth would've put him in an early grave.

Seth sighed when he sat down. "Do you know how much this blows?"

"Which part," she replied, "That you lied to me or...wait, there's nothing worse than that if this proves to be true." McKayla frowned. "So it better not be."

"Damn, Kay," he started but she interrupted.

"I don't think I'm Kay to you either right now."

Seth ground his jaw and nodded. "Understandable." He took her hand and said, "Though my craft is dark magic, I can do good things with it. So tell me, what do you want me to do right now. What will prove to you that I am a warlock?"

"Make it rain."

"Inside or out?"

"Inside."

"That'll ruin your appliances."

"Then make it snow."

"You don't think that'll do the same?"

"Really, guys?" Sheila broke in.

McKayla couldn't help but feel a bit lighter. This *was* Seth after all.

A brilliant idea occurred to her. One she knew would put them all to the test. Maybe. And Seth would surely back out when he heard. "Okay, summon me a Claddagh ring with a gem the exact shade of Trevor's eyes."

"Nay, dinnae do it," Trevor said, angered.

"Nay, dinnae," Ferchar agreed.

"Why not?" Leslie asked, obviously impressed.

Hurt, McKayla looked at Trevor. "If Seth can summon it then he should be able to unsummon it. Worse case, you or Ferchar will. No worries, I don't want to be with you, anyway."

"You dinnae ken," Trevor shot back.

Too late.

Seth must've somehow seen an opportunity to lash out at Trevor. Clasping her hands he began to murmur. "Irish ring of gold, green at center, her one true love. *Irish et inaurem auream unam. viridem ad centrum. illi qui in amore veri.*"

Trevor roared in rage but it was too late. A ring similar to Caitlin's appeared on her finger with a bright emerald at its center. McKayla felt nothing but a cool breeze wrap around her finger before the ring appeared. Dumbfounded she stared. This couldn't be!

"You bloody bastard, I dinnae have green eyes in my true form!" Trevor said.

"Sucks to be you!" Seth roared back. "If you hadn't been deceiving her all these years you might not be in this position."

Before Trevor could get to him, Ferchar was between them.

It took more magic than any of them were ready to witness for Ferchar to keep them apart. Black sparks spit around the room. The microwave crackled then lit on fire. Dishware exploded. Even the overhead light popped and broke.

The girls screeched.

Caitlin waved a loose hand and put out the fires.

Only little Logan's declaration seemed to halt them all. "No more Scotland!"

"Och, nay laddie," Ferchar said and lashed out one last time. Whatever he unleashed had both men falling back, motionless. He scooped up his son and walked away, whispering, "Always Scotland for ye me wee bairn, just not for the likes of them, aye?"

Caitlin stood, hands on her hips, and looked between the paralyzed men. "Never a good idea to piss off a Scotsman's bairn. It tends to piss off the Scotsman himself." She looked at Trevor, disappointed. "You especially should know that."

Shaking her head, Caitlin pursued her husband and son out of the room.

McKayla, Leslie and Sheila all remained motionless, looking back and forth between the unmoving slack-jawed men. Never in her wildest imagination could she have dreamed up what she'd just witnessed. Not only did she wear the very ring she'd requested of Seth but Ferchar with one quick motion of his hand turned both of these big men senseless.

Leslie waved her hand in front of Trevor's face but he only stared back unseeing. Sheila did the same with Seth but his expression remained frozen. The women looked at each other before they sat down at the table. McKayla, for the life of her, could summon no fear for either man. Shouldn't she be afraid? What if they remained this way? Lifeless.

"Do you think…" Sheila started but stopped.

"Perhaps they're just…" McKayla started but stopped.

Leslie stared blankly for several long seconds before she stood and grabbed the coffee pot, careful not to nudge Trevor's lifeless form. After she filled hers and McKayla's mugs she sat down again, not touching what she'd just poured. She folded her hands neatly on the table.

"Do you suppose we're all wearing a Lucid Dream mask and don't realize it?"

For the first time in a very long time Sheila smiled in Leslie's direction. "I'm not sure if I hope so or not."

McKayla placed her hand on the table and they all stared at the ring. "Do you think I should take it off?"

Leslie touched it then glanced between the two men before her eyes returned to McKayla's. "It couldn't hurt, right?"

"Who knows. Maybe it could," Sheila said.

"Well she won't know unless she tries."

"Look at everything we just witnessed. God knows what might happen," Sheila argued.

And just like that, the two of them were at it again. So she took matters into her own hands and tried to pull it off. No luck. The elegantly carved ring didn't budge an inch. Instead of panicking she asked logically, "What do we know about Claddagh rings?"

Sheila and Leslie shook their heads and said simultaneously, "Nothing."

It took everything she had not to look at the men. They were her best friends! Any normal person would call 911 but not her or her cousins apparently. Why was that? She laid her head in her hands on the table. She knew why. Ferchar wouldn't hurt them. The Claddagh ring Seth put on her finger proved magic was real. Ferchar had simply sealed the deal when he punished Seth and Trevor.

But what did all of this mean exactly?

"Magic," Sheila said. "Unbelievable."

"And I believe it still is," Leslie replied.

"How, after all of this, could you think that?" Sheila asked.

"Everything has a practical explanation. Somehow, we'll make sense of this."

"You're unbelievable, Leslie," Sheila said. "But at least you're still predictable."

"And you, as always, take everything at face value. Had you listened to my advice when trying to save your forest last year you might've...I don't know...saved a forest!"

Sheila frowned. "You don't understand my endeavors."

"Nobody understands your endeavors. Not even you."

"Shh. Wait. He's moving," Sheila said.

McKayla lifted her head. It was Trevor. His eyes were alert and his arms were moving. She might be frustrated but he was her friend. Scooping up his cell phone she stood.

Sheila grabbed her arm. "You sure you want to do that?"

No, but she would mainly because she'd expect the same from him if their positions were reversed. So she brought the phone over. Fingers moving fast, he texted, "I'm so sorry."

"You should be," she said.

"I will show you me," he texted. "Soon."

Eying him, McKayla breathed deeply and sat back on her haunches. What was a shape-shifter exactly? What if Trevor wasn't Trevor at all? Which he obviously wasn't. She nodded and turned to check on Seth. He remained completely motionless.

"Oh sweetie." She cupped his cheek. "You'll be back. Make me a promise? When you come back don't kill Trevor, all right? I'll owe you one...maybe a thousand. But you know how much I care about him."

Seth stared aimlessly. Please, God, let him hear me.

Thump.

Trevor fell forward onto his hands, gasping for air. "Bloody hell, lad's got some kick-arse magic," he croaked.

Putting her arm around his shoulder she helped support him as he stood.

"McKayla," he gasped and pulled her close. "Forgive me."

Before she could respond he set her aside and stumbled from the room. She was about to go after him when Seth gasped.

She once more crouched and cupped his cheeks. "Seth, are you okay? Talk to me."

His hand shot up and clasped her arm the moment his eyes shot open. "So sorry, hon."

Before she could respond he started coughing. Eventually, he fell back, his body moving more and more. He whispered, "Never met a vamp, werewolf or reaper with more power than Ferchar. Scary shit this." After another deep breath he asked, "Are we sure he's not a demon?"

She tried not to think about the creatures he implied existed. "Logan got involved. He's always been an overprotective Dad."

Seth wiped a hand across his mouth and winced. "Was I drooling?"

"Yes," Leslie said.

"No," McKayla assured. "Stop stressing."

"Or maybe he shouldn't stop stressing quite yet," Sheila said in awe.

Huh? Looking up, McKayla nearly toppled over backward.

As though she were right back in her dream, Colin MacLomain, tall and kilted, held out his hand to help her up. She cocked her head as though looking at someone who wasn't there. Broad shouldered with muscles rippling down his arms, Colin wore a dark tunic with a blue and green checkered plaid wrapped around his waist and over his shoulder. Licking her lips, McKayla tried to focus on his black boots, on the hand he still held out, on anything but his face.

But in the end she couldn't focus at all.

The world tilted, swayed and then went away.

A loud buzz filled her ears. All vanished. Within seconds reality surfaced and she was in his arms. Trevor? No, it couldn't be. Colin? Had to be.

"I always meant to just look once and then leave you to your life," he murmured as he carried her. "But it turns out I was too selfish."

He smelled of outdoors, fresh cut grass, warmed cedar, and fresh air. Trevor had always spelled of soap and woodsy cologne. But it couldn't touch this new smell, the very scent of this man's skin. "Who are you?"

Then she was lying in her bed with a warm comforter pulled over her. Sunlight tried to stream through drawn crème-colored curtains. "I'm not tired," she whispered.

"You were tired the moment Leslie started on you this morn. Take a nap, love. Then you'll see me again. The way you were always meant to."

McKayla tried to respond but couldn't. Instead her heavy lids slid shut. Though it seemed only a few minutes had passed, when she next opened her eyes the sun's cast on the curtains was low. Wind blew the oak tree and spikes of sunlight danced across the room. Somehow, it was tremendously peaceful.

Could it be she'd simply dreamt it all? No. It had happened. Of that she was sure.

"This was Arianna's room even before it was mine."

Startled, McKayla sat up to find Caitlin sitting in the corner.

Settling back some she said, "Sorry, I didn't know you were here."

"I should be the one apologizing. Not you." Caitlin smiled. "How are you feeling?"

"A little off honestly." She took a deep breath and said, "It all happened, didn't it?"

"It did." Caitlin pulled the chair closer, her golden eyes compassionate. "You and your cousins are handling this really well. I suppose it's in our genes to adjust to all of this quicker than most. Are you all right? How can I help make this easier?"

Passing out like she had was handling it well? But she supposed it was better than going into hysterics like any normal person would.

"Are Seth and Trevor okay?" McKayla asked.

"Yes, they're fine, just worried about you."

"Okay. Good. I mean that they're okay, not that they're worried about me."

"It's good they're worried about you," Caitlin said. "They're just as guilty as Ferchar and I in this terrible deception. We all deserve your anger."

McKayla fingered the ring Seth had put on her finger. "Why was Trevor so upset about this?"

Caitlin schooled a frown. "I think mostly because Seth was showing you magic before he was."

Never. Trevor wouldn't act that way over something so trivial.

64

"You're lying," she replied quietly. "Tell me the truth."

Caitlin took her hand and rubbed her finger over the ring. "You're right. I just don't want to overwhelm you though it's likely far too late." She grimaced. "While I think Seth did this with your best interests in mind it might prove to make things difficult."

"For who?"

"Trevor of course. He's in love with you." Caitlin frowned. "This ring bars that love. There's no way around it."

"Though I'm not buying into the whole Trevor loving me part, how would this ring bar it if it did exist?"

"Well, as far as I know the wizard's eyes must match the stone. When Seth did this he ensured that Trevor could never be your one true love." Caitlin shook her head. "What is it between them to make him act so harshly?"

McKayla sighed. "Who knows? Seth and I have long been best friends in the most unromantic sense. I've never quite understood it because we're polar opposites. He loves a mountain cliff with no rope. I love a quiet, safe room where I can write. The only thing Seth and I shared were a few years of Youths Care Club boating when we were children. He was an inner city kid from Boston. I was privileged from the Cape."

"There's got to be more than that."

"Does there?" McKayla responded.

Caitlin looked at her then away, nodding.

"We've always been there for each other. Simple as that."

"All right," Caitlin said gently. "Lord knows I don't want to pry, Kay. For now I won't but know this, I wish somebody had been there to lay all the facts on the line for me when I hooked up with Ferchar. My gram, Mildred, helped some, but there were a lot of semi-truths and I was thrust into a lot of scary stuff without knowing much."

Before McKayla could respond, Caitlin said, "I would've given anything to have the sort of knowledge at my disposal that you do. And this was only four years ago."

Caitlin looked concerned, almost frightened for her. It was hard to know what to make of that. "Thanks, Caitlin. I appreciate you being here for me. I'm just taking baby steps right now. If only I were strong enough to take leaps."

Her cousin smiled. "Maybe you are taking leaps and don't even know it."

"I'm hiding under a blanket in the middle of the day. Pretty sure I'm regressing."

"But you're doing so in an important room."

"Right, Arianna's room. Now who is she again?"

"Well, I'm not sure how I should say this." Caitlin scuffed her foot on the floor. "I suppose direct is best. Arianna Broun is Trevor's mom...or should I say, Colin's."

McKayla bit her lip. "Oh." A terrible feeling rolled through her. "So we're actually related."

Caitlin shook her head. "No even though it seems like it. She was from the eighteenth century and still a few generations removed. His Dad was from medieval Scotland and is Ferchar's uncle."

"I don't know. Are you sure?"

"Completely. The blood lines are many, many generations thinned between you and Trevor. I assume you're more comfortable with me saying that name. Rest assured, the clans in medieval Scotland and England, alongside many cultures in the world, were guilty of much, much closer blood relations."

McKayla swallowed hard. She supposed her cousin had a point.

"The hands are holding the heart facing you," Caitlin commented.

Once more swirling the Claddagh ring on her finger she asked, "What does that mean?"

Caitlin's cunning eyes met hers. "That your heart is already taken. If a potential suitor kisses your hand he'll know it immediately."

Pressure tightened in her chest as she looked at the ring. Her heart wasn't taken. Or at least it hadn't been for some time. Swirling the heart so she wouldn't have to look at it, McKayla asked, "Are you really a witch?"

"Kinda sorta," Caitlin said. "I can manage parlor house tricks but nothing nearly as profound as Ferchar." She sighed. "Again, I'm so sorry for not telling you. I guess I'd hoped none of this would affect you."

"But you don't seem all that shocked that it did."

"No," Caitlin said. "I guess I'm not. I mean it hit me out of nowhere and though the rings were supposed to tie together the last great Broun/MacLomain loves I couldn't help but think in the midst of all that magic...really? If something as simple as the flu can mutate and survive why can't something as simple as love mutate and survive as well? Because love, like all determined things, will find a way. We just tend to complicate it. Wish we'd stop doing that."

McKayla couldn't help but smile. "Only you could compare the flu with love and come out ahead."

Her cousin grinned and shrugged. "I've learned to see things in the best light possible. Everything serves a purpose. Everything happens for a reason."

"It better," McKayla said on a yawn. "If not, I've no idea what to tell Fate about how I lost both a warlock and a shape-shifter in one lifetime."

"Oh, you do bounce back well!"

Not really. But she wasn't about to let Caitlin worry about her much longer. With a small smile she said, "'Tis what we Brouns do, aye?"

"Give or take," Caitlin said. "But I still worry about how much you're really ready for."

She was about to respond when another voice overrode hers from the bedroom door.

"Dinnae worry, lass. She's now in verra good hands."

Chapter Five

There was never a stranger moment than when a medieval Scottish Highlander walked into her twenty-first century bedroom.

Trevor...no, Colin, sat slowly in the chair Caitlin had abandoned after she was sure McKayla would be all right alone with him. A long, uncomfortable silence stretched as they eyed one another. He appeared much as he had in her dream. Except now his eyes were even more startling, clearer to her vision somehow. Nowhere near green, as he had assured earlier, they were a sharp almost disconcerting shade of pale bluish green. She supposed they were turquoise. With the same black brows and lashes she remembered from before, his eyes certainly had a way of pinning a person.

The pure strength radiating off him struck her almost as acutely as his piercing gaze. It was something that he'd never seemed to possess when in the form of Trevor. Or maybe that wasn't entirely true. Trevor had a strong presence around others. Perhaps he just seemed softer with her because they were so close.

Trevor...Colin.

It would take a very long time to wrap her mind around this one.

When he finally spoke his deep voice and brogue again caught her off guard. "You have a right to hate me, lass. More than I hate myself for how much I've deceived you."

He was right. She did. Pulling her knees up against her chest, she said, "I don't think I could ever hate you." McKayla cast her eyes down, discomforted by looking at a stranger while speaking to her best friend. "But right now I'm feeling a lot of anger...and confusion, even fear. If my cousins hadn't seen the same things I saw and Ferchar and Caitlin hadn't confirmed all of this, I'd think I'd gone crazy."

"'Tis a lot to take in all at once," Colin agreed. "And is only bound to become..."

When he trailed off she looked up. "Become what?"

"Far more confusing and mayhap even frightening. But know that I'll never leave you alone. I'll protect you with my life if necessary."

Alarmed, McKayla eyed his tartan, the build that was clearly a warrior's. "It's unlikely I'll need much protecting. If you haven't noticed there are no warring clans here. Only in my book."

"Aye, in your book. About a time and place that I call home, love. A place that I must return to so that I might face all the havoc I've created."

Worried, McKayla pulled her knees tighter against her chest. It would be one thing to watch Colin go. She might relax a great deal. But to watch Trevor? The thought made her panic. "What exactly did you do? What are you facing? And again, what does this have to do with protecting me?"

She pushed back against the headboard when he stood. Upset but determined he said, "McKayla, 'tis me…Trevor, your best friend, once your lover. Allow me to sit next to you, offer comfort."

Sizzling flame erupted beneath her skin when he said lover. It was impossible to imagine she'd lain with…*him*, the overwhelming Scotsman standing over her. When her eyes started to lower to where they shouldn't she immediately brought them back to his face, mortified. *Damn.* There was no doubt that she and Trevor had chemistry. Would the same hold true with Colin? She bit down on her lower lip and did all she could not to envision it. Pretty hard not to considering she'd written love scenes about just such a man.

He cleared his throat. "McKayla, please. At least let me hold your hand."

"You expect too much," she replied swiftly.

"Rest assured that this will be the least of it."

"The least?" she said weakly but quickly regrouped. Colin certainly had more nerve than Trevor. Or she was finally meeting the man he'd always been. "You have a funny way of trying to endear yourself to me right now."

Without her permission, Colin sat on the bed. Though she tried to pull it away he took her hand. Larger and rougher than what she was used to, she closed her eyes and tried to control her thundering heart. So this is what a weapon-calloused hand felt like.

"McKayla," he whispered.

When she opened her eyes it was to a magnificent man staring at her with desire. Was it as Caitlin said...did he truly love her? Though he'd pushed her away, had Trevor remained interested in more than just friendship? It seemed likely based on the look in his eyes now. She started to snatch her hand away but stopped. Despite her anger, she didn't want to wound him further. At least not right now. She cleared her throat. "Please answer my questions."

"Aye, I suppose I better." He shook his head. "Some would say mine is a long story but after spending time in the twenty-first century, I've learned better than most how to simplify." He gave her a careful look. "Are you ready then?"

McKayla doubted she'd ever be ready but nodded regardless.

"I was born in the Christian year twelve hundred and twenty-six. Born too early, some said the gods were in a rush to get me here and that I'd serve a greater purpose than most. The way I see it, my early arrival just put my Ma through more worry than needed. But there I was, bairn of Iain and Arianna MacLomain. Bairn to the former chieftain and in line to become laird after Ferchar's nephew William."

The author in her couldn't help but ask, "Wouldn't William's son become laird next?"

"Typically, but Adlin MacLomain made it clear that Iain's son was to rule for a time. Aye, William's son would get his chance in due time."

"And Adlin, of course, was obeyed as he'd all but birthed your clan."

"Aye, lass. If Adlin had stipulations before he left, they were heeded."

"So did you become chieftain or is William...still alive?"

"William lives," Colin responded with a deep frown. "And none too pleased with me, I'm sure."

Intrigued despite the remarkable circumstances she'd been thrust into, McKayla said, "Clearly, so is Ferchar. What did you do to upset him besides the obvious?"

Colin scowled, obviously recalling the paralyzed state Ferchar had inflicted on him. "That's a loaded question, lassie. But my guess is I upset him by fleeing on the day William declared he wished me to take over." He shrugged, a flicker of guilt crossing his face. "Then there were the verra *reasons* I left."

"Reasons? Plural?"

"Aye." Colin slowly entwined their fingers, the action so subliminal she barely noticed...until she did. The motion kicked her heart into high gear again. He seemed to notice the affect he was having on her because his next words were huskier than before. "I didnae want to lead the MacLomains quite yet. Only twenty-five winters, I craved excitement beyond the everyday life of overseeing a castle and leading men into battle. I wanted more." His words grew almost too soft to hear. "Then there were the lasses."

The romance writer in her could only imagine the amount of lasses Colin would attract. Too many for her taste. She experienced a distressing mix of curiosity and jealousy. "I'm sure you handled the lasses just fine."

He rubbed the back of his neck and again shook his head. "Nay, I left one at the altar and the other—" His eyes met hers. "In Cape Cod."

Her heart nearly skidded to a halt. It was an easy thing to forget she still spoke to the man she'd always known as Trevor, that they'd spent so much time together. Here. Not there. He'd been here with her while simultaneously being there? "How?" she started but answered her own question. "Time travel. All this time you've lived two lives."

Before he could speak she asked, "Did you really move to California? Or is that a lie too?"

"Nay! I did. But I dinnae spend much time there."

McKayla got irritated with herself when tears welled. She hated being sensitive. For this reason she always wrote about strong heroines. Women who could handle themselves no matter what life dished out. Seems reality was a bit different because the idea that Trevor could have remained in a relationship with her but didn't, hurt like heck. All the while, his shape-shifting self was traveling back and forth having one hell of a time.

"You dinnae ken," he murmured.

Before she knew it he pulled her onto his lap. A surprisingly solid lap. Not giving her a chance to speak he cupped the back of her head so that she wouldn't turn away. "I only left you because I knew I'd have to go back to Scotland. It was not only dangerous but unfair to keep you in my life, McKayla. Gods know I love you, lass. Since the moment I laid eyes on you and every moment since."

Senses overwhelmed by both his nearness and words, she only shook her head.

"Do you remember when we first met?" He didn't give her a chance to respond. "You were sitting on the beach writing." His thumb sifted through her hair. "Your hair glistened in the sun as though covered in diamonds. I never expected you to glow like you did. Or look like you did."

McKayla wiped away a stray tear, grateful no more followed. "You introduced yourself by saying, "I could make you a laptop that sand won't damage." Mckayla chuckled. "I remember thinking that was the worst pick up line I'd ever heard."

He grinned. "But effective, aye?"

Wow, was he extra hot when he smiled. Her eyes went to his sumptuous lips. Though overly aware of their closeness she was feeling more and more comfortable with *Colin*. "You were good looking enough to get away with it."

"Was I?" he asked, flirting. "If you're not careful I might get jealous of…well, myself."

It was hard not to smile. "You would have every reason to be."

Colin seemed sobered in an instant. "I am still the lad you fell in love with, McKayla. What we had…*have*… means everything to me. More than I ever thought I'd find in this life. More than I ever wanted until I realized how powerful it could be, how *important*."

"Then why not stay here in New England with me?" She didn't care if she sounded petty or selfish. "Why not leave Scotland behind altogether? You wanted to leave behind your obligations to your clan anyways, right?"

Colin's free hand clenched slightly. "Nay, I would never abandon Scotland. She's my lifeblood." His eyes roamed her face. "But neither would I abandon you. Or willingly put you in harm's way. 'Tis why I fled. I should have ended our friendship. But I couldn't. And now I've brought more harm than good."

"You say you need to protect me." McKayla wasn't sure she wanted the answer, but she needed to know, so she pressed on. "Why, Colin?"

Darkness settled over his features and for a moment his gaze grew distant. "When I left my clan three years ago, it was with fierceness in my heart. Restless, reckless, I craved excitement. While the battling gave me some, it was never enough. Something else lived inside me. A craving I didnae ken."

A shiver of warning rippled through her but the desire to know more prevailed. "And?"

"I did something verra foolish." His clouded gaze turned her way. "Not long after I left the clan I joined the ranks of a rather clandestine brotherhood. One that did unspeakable things for what they considered a greater good. Being a wizard and shape-shifter with a taste for violence I was a favored addition to their ranks."

McKayla could feel his muscles tighten beneath her. Her question when it finally came was barely audible. "What did you do?"

His distant gaze seemed to clear when he looked her straight in the eyes, obviously wanting her to understand. "I became an assassin. I killed not for money but to alter the paths of destiny, of fate itself. Through the limitless magic provided by my brotherhood, I changed the course of people's lives."

Her mouth dropped open. Unable to move, she only stared at him. Was he serious? Deadly, it seemed, based on the unabashed way he looked right back. Uncomfortable but determined to understand more she asked, "So you murdered not for money but to…help people?" She pulled back. "Do you know how insane that sounds?"

"Insane," he breathed. "Something I've been called way too many times." For a second he sounded so contrite she thought he'd set her aside. Instead, he pulled her closer. "I willnae pretend to look back on all I've done with a sense of rightness and conviction but willnae look back on it as insanity either. I thought I was doing good. I thought I was helping people. 'Twas only recently that I began to realize that the path I'd chosen wasn't exactly what I thought." His determined eyes met hers. "I willnae say I'm sorry."

Brows furrowed, she searched for the Trevor she knew. "So while we were together, first as *lovers* then as friends, you were traveling back to medieval Scotland to murder innocent people?"

Colin's brows shot up. "Innocent? Not one of them was that. These were men who molested their bairns, who killed for the sake of bettering their stations, who manipulated and stole from the poor. Nay, not one was undeserving of my blade."

Child molesters? Shoot. Now killing them sounded pretty darn good. Still. How to make sense of all this? She decided to focus on the obvious. "So what made you realize you were on the wrong path with this brotherhood?"

"Which brings us to why I said I'll always protect you," he murmured, his arm locking tighter around her, barring all escape. "There's something I need to tell you, lass."

"Obviously," she said, trying to ignore the feeling of dread welling inside.

"Do you remember the cave in which you awoke during your lucid dream?"

She nodded slowly.

"I'd carried you there, McKayla. We'd been running from my brotherhood, from my newborn enemies…. enemies because I killed my mentor instead of you."

"*Instead* of me?" Eyes wide, she tried to pull away but his grip was unyielding.

Pain apparent, he said, "They'd used dark magic on me. I didnae know it was you until nearly too late. But even then my blade would not have cut."

Her heart beat so loudly she could barely hear herself speak, "I don't understand. Why? How? I wasn't even there yet."

Colin ground his jaw. "Nay, you weren't. At least not at first. You see I was tricked. While I thought 'twas you it was but an illusion. *You* had been an illusion. Which meant they had discovered who you were...what you meant to me. That in itself is dangerous. As soon as I realized such it was imperative to have you with me." He frowned. "So I purposefully fed into their trap and gave you the Lucid Mask to bring you back in time. It was the only way to keep you safe."

"How did you know the illusion wasn't me?" she whispered.

"A lad knows such about his lass." He appeared sheepish for a moment. "And my magic helped."

A lad knows such about his lass? Her pulse skittered through her veins. "But why bring me back? Why not come forward in time and protect me here like you eventually did?"

"Two reasons." His eyes grew darker. "The first being that they knew *where* I'd killed my mentor. It was a set of circumstances that was going to happen just as it did. They also knew that it was only a matter of time before I'd realize you were an illusion alerting me to their knowledge of you. Hence the trick...I brought you back as they'd planned. Had I traveled to the future from there or whisked you back, I strongly suspect they would have been able to follow. So I laid out a plan by manipulating time-travel and moved you as quickly as I could."

McKayla shook her head, only a little less confused. "So the mask was designed to bring me to the very spot in which you'd killed your mentor."

"Aye, and designed to bring you back to the future when it did."

"What of the second reason for not protecting me here?"

"I am at my strongest when in my true form, and in Scotland. I would not risk having to battle here in New Hampshire. 'Twould be far more perilous for all."

"I won't pretend to understand half of what you just said." Trying to keep her frayed emotions in check she clenched her hands on her lap. "I get the part about you wanting to protect me there. But how can you be so sure they won't come *here*?" She wouldn't be surprised if he could hear her pounding heart.

"I dinnae know with certainty, Kay."

She ignored that he'd called her by her nickname. "But wasn't I still technically here dreaming?"

Colin shook his head once. "I'm good at what I do. You didnae dream at all but truly traveled back in time."

McKayla curled into his protective arms without realizing. Strangely enough, fear seemed just out of reach. Was she in shock? Most likely. The very idea that she'd already stepped foot in thirteenth century Scotland was mind-boggling. Then again, it was only slightly harder to believe than the fact she now sat on a medieval Scotsman's lap discussing it. If all that wasn't enough, there was the part about her being on some sort of supernatural brotherhood's hit list.

That sort of sucked.

A lot.

"Are you well, lass? I'm so verra sorry for all this, for my part in it. If not for me, your life would be far less ..." He stopped and seemed to consider his next words carefully. "Bloody complicated right now. You dinnae deserve this."

McKayla frowned. Maybe not. But she suspected all of this was meant to be. Yes, she'd written a book and landed a great book deal but she had to wonder, would she have done so without the influence of this house and its history? Better yet, would she have written as passionately had she not known Trevor? After all, though he didn't know it, he'd been the love of her life. None could compare. At least not yet. She was about to respond when Colin ground his jaw and leaned forward slightly in what appeared to be pain.

"What's wrong?" she asked.

"The mark," he said through clenched teeth, hand over his tunic. "Burns on occasion."

Concerned, she lifted the material. There was a three-quarter circular tattoo on the side of his abdomen. A second before the tattoo had been black, now the circle was an angry, blazing red.

Worried for him, she instantly put her hand against the mark, cringing but not pulling away when his skin burned her hand.

Colin closed his eyes, covered her hand with his and groaned in relief. She closed her eyes as well and she sighed as the burning sensation slowly faded from her hand. Nothing was left but the feel of his warm, hard skin beneath hers. A small wave of exhaustion washed over her and she mumbled to herself in contentment.

"McKayla," he said, alarm in his voice. "Open your eyes."

Doing so, she was surprised to find his regard uneasy. Curling her fingers against his skin she said, "What, it's okay now, right?"

"Aye," he said, bringing her even closer. "The coolness of your hand drove away the pain."

"You must've let me in," she said then blinked several times as a strange understanding dawned. Leaning back slightly, she pulled up his shirt and eyed the mark. As she ran her finger around the circle she whispered, "His is the circle that never connects. A means to let me in. If ever it closes, we are forever lost."

His body trembled and McKayla quickly realized it was not because of her words but because of her touch, because of the lazy trail she made with her finger.

"I dinnae ken your words," he managed to push past suddenly strained lips.

"I spoke them to Leslie yesterday over Skype," she said breathlessly, still tracing the circle.

"Did ye then?" he said, his brogue turning thicker and thicker, as did other things. Amazing what one little finger was doing to him. Doubly amazing what sitting on a sexually aroused medieval Scotsman's lap was doing to her.

"Remember, I mentioned something about it. An old Scots Gaelic," she murmured, unable to keep her lone finger from wandering up his broad chest.

"Hmm," he murmured in return, one arm drawing her ever closer while his free hand once more buried into her hair.

It seemed the most natural thing in the world to tilt her lips to his, to feel not a kiss from an old flame but the searing new fire of lips that'd never touched hers. Yet neither reaction was tentative. Instead, the moment his lips closed over hers, McKayla swore the room dropped away. The air thinned to nothing. Sound, whatever it might have been before, ceased to exist. A heady rush of desire washed over her. Feelings of lust were so strong she dug her nails into his chest and wrapped her other hand around the back of his neck.

Desperate, their tongues wrapped and twisted, searched and explored. The hungry motion of their lips moved in perfect unison, as though they'd been made specifically with the sole purpose of kissing one another. She reveled in the heavy thud of his heartbeat beneath her hand; by the way his strong heart seemed to throb within the deepening unending kiss. Groaning, she met the thrust of his tongue with hers, met the pure, sexual desperation of his need with more of her own.

The thick evidence of his arousal pressed up eagerly against her bottom. When moisture flooded between her thighs, McKayla kissed him with renewed eagerness. Breathing heavily, she clutched him tighter while rocking her bottom back and forth slowly, purposefully. Even through her sweatpants she could feel the abrasive wool of his plaid. Rock hard muscles rippled beneath as he too moved to assuage his own needs.

While she might have felt some of Trevor in his touches, most were foreign, different, and almost painful in their pleasuring newness. Colin introduced a stinging, sharp awareness of not only what he had to offer but what she did as well. Somehow this man made her feel like a sensual, underused siren with one, long astounding kiss.

"You never did that before," he growled against the tender skin of her neck as he trailed down using both his lips and teeth creatively.

His cock pulsed against her and she all but reveled in his tightly wound self-constraint. He was so energized, almost powerful in his lust, that she didn't know whether to be flattered or petrified. Gasping for breath, she didn't stop him when his touch came between her legs, when his large hand cupped over her center and kneaded. Further aroused by her obvious wetness his eager lips searched out her pebbled nipple through a too-tight sweatshirt.

"So this is your way of respecting her, eh?"

Both froze. Colin pulled away far slower than most men would when confronted with an irritated warlock. Embarrassed, McKayla looked at the doorway and said, "Really, Seth? *Really?*"

Arms crossed over his chest, Seth leaned against the threshold, casual but clearly tense. "Yeah, McKayla, *really*. He was supposed to come up here to tell you he was leaving instead he's about ready to screw you."

Adjusting her clothing, McKayla carefully unraveled from Colin's arms and stood. His hand, however, remained entwined with hers. "He's told me everything."

Seth cocked a brow.

"Well, he's told me a lot," she said defensively. "As I'm sure you can imagine there's bound to be more."

"More than you being on 'Scotland's Most Wanted' list by a bunch of medieval fucked up mercenaries? I hope not."

So she was the last to know. Though irritated, she supposed it was for the best. Trying to maintain some sort of an upper hand she walked to the window and stared out onto the remnants of a brooding sunset. A summer storm simmered in the distance. "He's not a mercenary. Mercenaries take money."

Seth snorted. "Well then, that makes all of this bullshit so much easier to swallow."

"Enough with the swearing, okay?"

"You sound like Andrea," he muttered. "Fine. Whatever."

"We've got more to be concerned about," Colin said. "Where are the others?"

"More to be concerned about? Say it isn't so."

"Seth, come on!"

"Things got crazy when I found out I was a warlock. I'm worried your story is going be as bad if not worse, especially with this guy leading the way."

McKayla crossed her arms over her chest and turned around. Colin lounged on her bed, making it very clear he belonged there. Seth leaned against the threshold, eyes narrowed on the Scotsman. The highlander obviously thought himself above a rebuttal because he only continued to stare at her as though he belonged not only on her bed but covering every inch of her willing body. She tightened her thighs, refusing to give into her immediate response.

"So I see you two are getting along better than ever. As if Leslie and Sheila's bantering wasn't enough," she remarked with a frown.

Tongue-in-cheek, Seth commented, "Trevor, or is it Colin, slept with you for how long, a year or so? Then dumped you to remain long distance friends. Sure, that was sleazy enough but doable. You still cared about the guy. Then it turns out he'd been lying all along. He's from another time, knows magic and has been messing with you all this time while simultaneously being part of something really sinister that could end up killing you."

McKayla ran a hand through her hair in frustration and bit back, "You have no room to talk, Seth. Your lie was just as harmful."

Seth almost defended himself but stopped short, pain crossing his face. "Awe, hell, McKayla, I can't tell you how sorry I am."

"I know how sorry you are. Enough said." McKayla opened her closet door and eyed her clothes. She seriously needed some space so she could sort out her thoughts. "Both of you out. I need to change."

Thankfully, neither gave issue and left. She and Colin locked eyes one more time before he shut the door. How could they not? They'd nearly had what she suspected would have been outrageously awesome sex. Which left her to wonder, had she really almost done such a thing with a man she'd only just met? Though she'd technically known him for years. None-the-less, Seth might've been on to something.

The minute they left she closed the door and sank down against the closet. While she wanted to cry her heart out she wouldn't. While she wanted to revel in the phenomenal feelings Colin had just pulled from her she wouldn't. No, now was the time to think clearly and get her thoughts in order.

"McKayla, can we come in?"

She exhaled through her nose and hung her head. Sheila and Leslie, of course. "No, I'm changing, be out soon!" she called.

The door burst open and both entered. Leslie closed the door, her clipped voice ringing through the room. "Then we'll help you change."

McKayla bent her knees, rested her elbows on them and held her forehead. "Seriously, I'm good, just needed a few minutes alone."

"Yeah, you're as good as I would be if I had that hot-as-hell highlander in my bedroom alone with me for twenty minutes," Sheila remarked, sitting down on the floor opposite her. "How'd that go, anyways? Let me guess, he almost had you, huh?"

"You're as bad as Seth with your speculations," Leslie said sternly, though a hint of curiosity marked her ever-focused tone as she sat on the bed. "I'm sure he told her what she needed to know and they talked it out."

Sheila smirked.

McKayla couldn't help but grin.

"I'm quite sure that with Kay's logical, albeit creative writer's mind she kept things focused. After all, that would be the most prudent thing to do in light of all we've learned," Leslie said.

"Ah," Sheila said. "So I suppose you would've turned your attention from the kilt and the killer body and of course, the smoking hot chiseled face. After all, a business arrangement must be made when one's being targeted by thirteenth century Scottish wizard assassins."

"Are you listening to yourself? A business arrangement?" Leslie paused. "Then again, maybe assassins can be reasoned with. I mean really, who says they might not be interested in letting all this go in light of living a very wealthy life here in the twenty-first century. With McKayla's book sales we could pay them off. Living here with modern day medicine has to be better than with what they're dealing with there."

On the edge of cracking up, McKayla lifted her head and looked at Leslie in amazement. Sheila was doing the same. She wasn't actually being serious, was she?

"What?" Leslie asked. "Don't look so shocked. I'm sure even barbarians can be bartered with."

Sheila put a hand to her chest. "Who, us? Shocked by something coming out of your mouth? Never."

"Sheila, enough," McKayla admonished but couldn't stop grinning. Leslie had truly lost her mind. "Leslie only has the best intentions."

"Will you ever get tired of saying that?" Sheila asked.

"Excuse me," Leslie kicked in. "At least I've got her smiling."

"So it appears." Sheila shook her head and turned a very concerned eye McKayla's way. "How are you? Really? Tell us the truth. We've been super stressed waiting for Trev, I mean Colin, to talk with you."

McKayla wanted to say she was doing fine but faced with her two closest cousins she couldn't lie. "So scared I can't tell you."

"Oh honey." Sheila sidled over and put her arm around McKayla's shoulders.

Leslie started to pace, her stern eyes narrowed. "I've got money saved. We'll get you protection. Nothing will touch you, not even that stranger you called Trevor. Or the other one you call Seth."

Both watched Leslie in renewed amazement. They'd never seen her act this way. She was trying her best to form a protective shell around McKayla the only way she knew how. And McKayla loved her for it.

"They're not strangers, Les," McKayla assured her, mostly because it felt good to calm down the one cousin that never, ever needed to be calmed down. "It's okay, we'll figure this out."

Leslie continued to pace. "Of course I'll figure this out." Then she stopped short, her shrewd eyes locked on McKayla. "But I need to know one thing."

McKayla nodded. "Sure."

"Are you in love with him? And I'm not talking about Trevor but Colin. You were in here with him for approximately eighteen minutes and thirty-seven seconds. That, as far as I'm concerned, is more than enough time to figure out love."

"Was it really that long? Could have sworn..." But the rest of her words were buried in a chuckle which turned to full out laughter that had her holding her stomach.

Exasperated, Sheila wiped a hand over her face and looked at Leslie, repressing her own chuckle. "So in your world, love is figured out that fast, is it?"

Perplexed, Leslie looked at them as though they'd lost it. "Yes, love is figured out that fast. Either you know it or you don't. Simple as that."

McKayla's chuckles subsided as she thought about the first time she met Trevor. How tousled and handsome he'd appeared when he'd stopped to tell her that he could build her a sand-proof laptop. If she didn't know better she'd have thought the planet stopped spinning the moment he spoke, the very second he'd looked down at her. She could still smell the salty Cape Cod wind. And see every detail of his self-assured, cocky grin.

That singular moment had been the most profound in her life.

"I kissed him," she said softly. "And it was better than amazing."

"Trevor? Of course you did. Old news," Leslie said.

"No. She's talking about Colin." Sheila cast a dubious eye Leslie's way. "And you're supposed to be the savvy one."

Leslie sank down on the bed, expression a little too judgmental for McKayla's taste. "Really, you kissed a man who not only lied to you but put you in danger?"

"Did you see him?" Sheila asked, incredulous. "Besides, we all make mistakes."

Whether or not they were right, McKayla was growing more and more exasperated. "Granted, this whole situation is way out of control, but kissing him wasn't a mistake. Yeah, I'm still super mad at him but it's not the first time and certainly won't be the last."

"He ensured that, didn't he," Leslie said curtly, "When he wrapped you up in a dangerous situation that only he seems capable of saving you from. I've had issues with Trevor since he broke your heart years ago and don't say he didn't. I remember sharing ice-cream and cheesy late night movies with you while you tried to hide the tears." Jaw grinding she said, "Now this. A whole new round of fresh pain."

Sheila looked sad but said nothing. Obviously she agreed with Leslie.

Angry, McKayla stood. "I need to change. Give me some privacy please."

"No," Sheila said, standing as well. "Not this time." She shook her head. "No avoidance this go around, Kay. Because something tells me your life's about to become all about confrontation and I'm genuinely worried that it's going to be in a time and place completely different than this. But what worries me even more is that it seems less and less likely that Leslie and I are going to be there to help you."

"She's right." Leslie took a deep, measured breath. "And though I might not show it I'm frightened. For you, for all of us. What we learned today is…difficult."

"Difficult," McKayla whispered. Why then, despite how true their words were, did she feel so calm? Yes, there was fear and confusion. Even blatant rage. Yet somehow despite all that, she wasn't flying off the handle. She wasn't trying to hide in a corner. All she really wanted were a few moments alone. Moments, she realized, her cousins wouldn't give her.

"Okay," she said firmly as she opened her closet door and pulled out a pair of white shorts and a spaghetti-strapped blue tank top. "I'm changing and we're going downstairs because we need to have this conversation with everyone."

"You feel safer talking about it if he's there," Leslie stated blandly. "Coward."

Suddenly furious she whipped around and met her cousin's eyes. "No actually, the opposite. I'm ready to face this head on and yes, with him there. Not because he makes me feel safer, which he does, but because he's the only one who can keep things in perspective. This thing that has happened to me might be because of him but rest assured, somehow all of this is meant to be. The house, the book, what we've discovered we are…all of it."

A hint of a smile appeared on Sheila's lips and she nodded slowly. "You know, Leslie. Maybe she's right. At least about some of it. This is meant to be. *Has* to be." She looked at them both. "And at least we were together when we found out."

"Why aren't you more upset with him?" Leslie asked Sheila. Then her attention swung McKayla's way. "And for that matter, you!"

"Oh, I am," Sheila said. "But what difference will it make right now?"

"Precisely," McKayla said. After she slid on her shorts and tank, she donned what she hoped was a determined look then tucked her feet into heelless white sporty sneakers. "Yes, me and Trevor…or Colin, whoever he is, have some things to work out but I'm thinking our relationship woes pale in comparison to the bigger plot changes that just literally re-wrote our lives."

"Plot changes?" Leslie shook her head, grabbed a brush off the dresser and took to styling McKayla's hair. "Even so, this story's heroine is acting totally out of character."

"Any good writer will tell you that the worst thing the heroine can do is not stay consistent with her character," Sheila agreed, rummaging through McKayla's make-up until she opted on a light pink glossy lipstick.

McKayla rolled her eyes but allowed Leslie to style. "Actually, the story would be no good without character growth. Which means changes in the heroine's personality might be a good thing."

"Would it? I don't know. I think a good, solid, consistent character is important. There," Leslie said and pulled away the brush.

McKayla smiled. Her simple hair cut made styling an all but obsolete notion. Leslie had only brushed it out. "Thanks."

Sheila tugged briefly on McKayla's shorts. "Based on the clothes you chose, I'm thinking plot changes are taking a backseat to the heroine's baser desires."

McKayla eyed herself in the mirror. So, maybe the shorts were a little too short and the tank a little more fitted than what she normally wore. But the day was already proving to be warm and she expected it to get a whole lot hotter. And wasn't she allowed to take a break from being the conservative one in the family? Though she doubted anyone would call her mousy, she knew she wasn't far off. So, yes, consider this a little 'character growth' or even 'out of character' but today she wanted to be different, just didn't want to be who she always was.

Then again, as it turned out, she wasn't who she'd always been after all!

So the outfit and her attitude made enough sense to suit her.

McKayla was about to say as much when a loud crash came from downstairs. The house shook as though it'd been hit by a semi. She ran for the door only to fall back when it swung open and a searing blast of frigid air rushed through the room. In a single moment it became impossible to see or hear anything.

Colin roared.

She cried out, a pain deep and burning gripped her body. There was no making sense of what was happening. Impossible. Too much, too fast. Colors blazed by. The smell of burning sugar filled her nostrils. The ground fell out from beneath her. Petrified, she clenched her body into a ball, squeezed her eyes shut and screamed. As quickly as it started it ended but she couldn't stop screaming.

"McKayla, 'tis all right lass. Please, love, you're okay," Colin said

"She might be, but you bloody hell are not, lad."

Opening her eyes, McKayla cringed against the bright sunlight. Confused, she shielded her eyes to find Colin nearby and a tall highlander standing over them. Colin locked eyes with her long enough to know she was okay before he hung his head then looked over his shoulder. "Aye, Da. I'm home."

Chapter Six

Cowal, Scotland
1254

McKayla sat up and slid away from Colin. Though clearly in his later years the other Scotsman was surprisingly fit and while his emerald eyes stared down at Colin with condemnation there was also blatant relief. His sharp gaze shot to her and softened.

He held out his hand. "Come. Stand, lass. I know how jarring this is for you but all will be well. You are on MacLomain land." When she hesitated he said, "I am Iain MacLomain, Colin's Da. I mean you no harm."

Barely able to breathe, she looked from Colin to Iain.

Colin nodded. "'Tis all right, lass. He is who he says."

She took Iain's hand and allowed him to pull her up. Though her legs were wobbly they held. Iain's hair was white and his frame frailer, but McKayla could see the resemblance between him and Colin. She couldn't help but stare.

"I am so verra sorry we had to meet like this." He smiled warmly. "But I cannae tell you how happy I am that you're here."

It was impossible not to smile in return. He seemed genuine. And he already knew her. She supposed she should wonder *how* he knew her, but with everything else going on it hardly seemed important. Odds were she'd find out eventually. "Thank you …nice to meet you as well."

Iain's smile widened as he studied her. "Aye, indeed."

His attention turned to Colin when several horsemen broke from the tree line. All wore plaids. All had longer hair. Wide-eyed, she watched them approach. Though she knew she'd traveled back in time, why did she feel like she was dreaming? Maybe she was?

Colin's posture grew stiff and his hand slipped into hers.

Yank it away? Hold it? It didn't much matter. She was motionless. Scared and curious, all she could do was gawk.

Most of the horses held back. But four moved forward and surrounded them. Hard eyes assessed them. McKayla counted three men and one woman. Colin pulled her closer as the horsemen bore down. Iain, it seemed, had no intention of calling them off.

Colin eyed them all and nodded but spoke only to his father. "You brought us here now let us go. No harm need come."

McKayla remained quiet though the others didn't. Some sniggered, others downright laughed. Colin stiffened, but said nothing, his indifference almost frightening.

"Not the best of greeting's for your clan, lad." Iain said. "But I imagine none of us are surprised."

"I know I'm not," a red-headed woman scoffed, and then veered her horse closer.

"Even with his life on the line he shuns us. I say let him leave. May no MacLomain protect him," another said. With almost blue black hair, his features were nearly as striking as Colin's.

Colin looked up at the man. His gaze narrowed, making him look even more dangerous. "I'm speaking with my Da. If you've a need to say your piece, Malcolm, do so like a man, face to face."

McKayla tried to step back, but Colin wouldn't let go of her hand even when Malcolm dismounted, and came nose to nose with him. His light brown eyes narrowed. "My Da gave you this clan and you turned it away. You dinnae deserve to step foot here again. You dinnae deserve your Da's forgiveness."

The man spoke with such passion that it was impossible not to gape, almost impossible not to agree. This was obviously William's son. He would rule the MacLomain's after Colin. And he was pissed.

Not backing down an inch from Malcolm's confrontational stance, Colin said, "'Twas never mine to rule, cousin. When I walked away it was with a different heart than I now possess. 'Twas with a confused soul." Colin lowered his head but never lost eye contact. "I can only now beg forgiveness."

Before Malcolm could respond Colin turned his head, looked Iain dead in the eye and continued. "Forgiveness from my Da and Ma." His eyes traveled over Iain's shoulder to the horsemen grouped behind. "And from my laird, William."

McKayla forgot to breathe when all turned deadly silent.

After what seemed far too long a horse cantered forward. This Scotsman seemed sterner than the rest as his silver dusted hair blew in the wind and his unreadable pale gray eyes stared down at Colin. All her senses came alive. Sea salt tainted the air. Sunlight warmed her cheeks despite a cool, crisp wind gusting down from the mountains. Hooves shifted restlessly over dry grass.

Colin stood straighter but never let go of her hand as he looked up. "My laird. I deserve your wrath but hope for mercy, for forgiveness."

William looked down at him for another long minute before he dismounted. Handsome and as tall as Colin he possessed a strong bearing. Older, perhaps in his late fifties, his tartan was wrapped proud and the notch to his chin even prouder. Based on the look on his face, McKayla suspected this homecoming was bound to go poorly.

She was wrong.

Malcolm was just about to speak when William's face broke into a wide grin. "I told them from the beginning you were only on a wee bit o' a journey to find yourself." He clasped Colin's shoulders and locked eyes even more securely. "I told them!"

Colin's hand was yanked from hers when William pulled him in close for a long, heartfelt hug. So strongly did it seem the chieftain felt for him that he clasped the back of his head and didn't let go until he was good and ready. When at last William pulled back he clasped either side of Colin's face and laughed, his eyes merry as he again said, "I told them."

Tension left her shoulders as William released Colin and said to all, "Welcome home Colin MacLomain, our true kin. A man that meant to leave but never really meant to leave at all, aye?"

Iain grinned though strain edged his tired eyes. Malcolm ground his jaw and swung back onto his horse. The others remained silent. No doubt they wouldn't stay that way long. McKayla guessed the minute each had Colin on their own turf they'd have plenty to say.

Though the chieftain said nothing, his interested wise eyes swept over her and she suspected strongly he'd have words for her later. Not for a moment however, did she think they'd be harsh.

William proceeded to shake Iain's hand. "'Twill be a grand celebration this eve, indeed. Your lad is home!"

Iain's eyes skirted between Colin and William. "Aye, my Laird, Arianna will be most pleased."

Arianna! She still lived. While McKayla was happy about the news it made the fear she'd felt up until this point seem trivial. Why, she couldn't be certain.

When William swung back onto his horse and trotted off, most followed. Well, all except for one. She came up alongside McKayla, her savage gaze as harsh as her words. "Let's see how well ye do here, lassie. Let's see."

Even after they all left in a flurry of hooves and dust, Iain remained, his eyes on Colin. She didn't need to be from this time period to see a father's sadness. She'd do just about anything not to be here to witness it. The pure heartache Colin had caused was apparent in this highlander's old gaze. Iain said nothing more, just seemed to soak in the sight of his son before swinging back onto his horse and turning away.

McKayla stood, unable to move, as Iain, like the rest, vanished into the forest. Clenching her teeth, she squeezed her hands and wiggled her toes. Anything she could do to ground herself in this reality. When Colin turned and took her hands, she pulled back. "No."

Brow lowering he didn't allow her to flee but grabbed her hand and shook his head. For some reason, the way he looked at her, his pure self-assurance, made her stop short. "Aye, McKayla. You cannae run. I have unintentionally trapped you in a place that willnae make sense to you for some time."

All of her repressed anxiety released once the threat was gone. There was no way in hell she was going to make this easy for him. So she yanked her hand out of his warm grasp. Good looks and crazy chemistry didn't make up for all that she'd endured. But damn was the chemistry, *crazy*. Making him suffer a wee bit was not going to be easy. But suffer he would.

Colin didn't try to take her hand again but stood, legs slightly spread and arms akimbo. He looked at her, with the mountains behind him, and the wind at his back. Now she saw him as he was always meant to be seen...in the Highlands.

"I never," she whispered then stopped, determined to speak strongly, determined to make sense. With a deep breath she focused on him, not the land around them and certainly not on all she'd just witnessed. She was exhausted and overwhelmed and couldn't tame her tongue.

"My cousins didn't like that I kissed you. In fact, they don't like you at all...Trevor."

She'd never quite know why she called him that in the midst of what was so obviously not her home or time but she did. Maybe she needed an anchor. Maybe she needed to make sure he was still the guy who helped her celebrate a book release with a kilt-wearing flashlight.

Or maybe she just needed to find out if she was dreaming.

Not moving any closer, voice gentle, he said, "And you said if the sand ruined the laptop then the words you'd written really didnae matter."

It was clear he wasn't overly concerned about what her cousins thought of him. No, he was worried about her and understood that she needed time to ease into this reality. If that meant speaking of the past, so be it. If that meant reflecting on a moment she'd spent with Trevor, so be it. Emotion welled up fast but she tempered it. "I spent all of my money on that computer."

"You said you meant to stop writing once the sun crested. That it was impossible to see what you'd written once it was broad daylight."

McKayla closed her eyes. "You said that it was probably best that I didn't see what I wrote. Only the best stories are those that are hidden, even oftentimes from those who write them." She nodded to herself. "That statement helped fuel my novel."

He didn't come to her, didn't overpower her. When McKayla opened her eyes, Colin looked right back, eyes unwavering, sad, caring. But most of all he looked concerned, even determined. When he spoke it was with patience and respect. "The next move will always be yours, love."

She shook her head. He lied. "No, it won't. I'm here when I shouldn't be. What are you going to do now?"

"Find a way to fix my wrongs," he sighed. "Find a way to make all this right."

"How?" she whispered.

When Colin wrapped his arms around her, McKayla didn't pull away. It was just as Leslie had said. She had no choice but to rely on him. She should push him away. But she couldn't. Instead, her body betrayed her. She leaned her head against his chest, and when she shook so hard her teeth chattered he held her even closer.

How had it gone so quickly from her searching for Trevor in him, to needing Colin and the safety he offered? Still shaking, her rage grew. She knew how. When Colin trapped her just as Leslie and Sheila had said. Why hadn't she agreed with them? Was she really as compliant as they thought? None of this was okay and he bloody well knew it.

"No." She vehemently tried to push him away.

But he didn't let go. He didn't budge an inch.

Blood burning beneath her cheeks, McKayla tried to shove away again but he had her locked tight. "No, Trevor. Let me go!"

"Nay," he said softly, his deep voice rumbling against her cheek. "Never."

"Never," she cried and no matter how half-hearted tried to knee him.

He angled away. "Stop, McKayla."

Even as she flailed she felt foolish. But she'd been made to feel such! "Bring me home now."

"Nay."

"Aye!" She didn't care if she sounded crazed. She wanted out. This was too much. Suddenly *way* too much.

With a heavy sigh, he said, "Would it help if I looked like Trevor? Would that ease you, lass?"

Would it? But how bizarre would it be to see Trevor *here*? She shook her head. "If I see Trevor...I mean you, I think I'll probably try to kill him...you. Seriously. I almost think I'm angrier at that version of you."

"Me too," he whispered.

She mumbled 'why' into his unyielding embrace.

"Because he should have been honest with you from the start. He was the verra mask of my deception."

"Creative way of looking at it," she said, calmer by the second. But she felt Trevor inside of him and though they looked nothing alike, the inherent comfort she experienced when with her best friend rose to the surface. As such, she wasn't afraid to tell him what she thought about what he'd said. "But I tend to blame you. Was Trevor not your ultimate escape?"

Sensing that she'd relaxed; he pulled back and looked down into her eyes. "As always, you're perceptive to a fault. Aye, I was a coward going there to begin with, but it took more courage than you can imagine for me to stay once I saw you, Kay. For a man who didnae want much to do with commitment, meeting you was a life-changing moment." His eyes dropped to her lips. "Everything about you made me reevaluate who I thought I was. That says a lot because rest assured, I am…was…amongst the most arrogant and cocky in my clan."

McKayla couldn't help but think of the highlander she'd created for her novel. He too had been arrogant, someone she'd never be overly interested in. Until, that is, she developed his character. Strange how that angle of *Plight of the Highlander* bore a strong parallel to what was happening now. Granted, in the story the heroine didn't travel through time but she *did* have a positive effect on her hero…Colin.

And even though every moment in his arms was having an overwhelming effect on her body, McKayla couldn't help but ask, "What's next for me? My anger may have faded some but I'm still scared. If you got me here, why can't you get me home?"

"Dinnae be scared." He cupped her cheek. "You're safe here on this land. You're safe with me."

It was impossible not to be aware of every *single* inch of him. And it didn't help that she was recalling every tingle, heart palpitation, every bloody emotion he'd made her feel while they were still back home. She had to stop this, or she might go nuts. If she hadn't already. McKayla inhaled deeply and tried to remain focused. But Colin here, in this place, this time, aroused her even more. She was screwed. Her body and mind were both betraying her. She shook her head and closed her eyes briefly before opening them. "Safe," she murmured. "Maybe partly."

She might be safe from would be assassins, but she definitely wasn't safe from *him*. And it seemed his body was responding to hers equally. Colin's voice deepened. "It's been a verra long time since I've had you, lass."

Oh hell, she really was in trouble now. McKayla's eyes rounded and she pulled away. This time he let her go. "You didn't have me. *Trevor* did. And I don't think that's something we should be worrying about right now, do you?"

But she only took one step back, finding it impossible to look away from the hungry desire in his eyes. Had Trevor ever looked at her quite like this? In this predatory fashion? For the life of her she couldn't remember, didn't think so. But he must've. Though they stood a good foot apart they might as well have been entwined with all the attraction crackling between them.

"You may find this form more enjoyable." He arched a brow and though he didn't move toward her, his words certainly yanked her back against him. "More muscles. Far more strength. A tireless perseverance that I promise will make you weep."

"Tireless," she whispered.

"Perseverance," he promised. "Determination."

She licked her lips and tried to look away. Impossible. He looked so bloody good standing there in a plaid with the mountains cheering him on and the highland wind working fully to his advantage. The idea of sleeping with him made fire ignite beneath her skin. She recalled having sex with Trevor and knew Colin would undoubtedly put his shifter self to shame.

But her mind refused to push away images of her and Trevor together. And with those thoughts came old pain. Pain she didn't want to relive. "Let us not forget that *Trevor* chose to end the intimacy." She narrowed her eyes. "You said it was to keep me safe but it's gonna take me time to forgive you for that. I loved you. More than you will ever know." She shook her head and took a deep breath. "You have no idea how hard it was for me to transform those feelings into something platonic. But I did. This.

94

You." She made a loose gesture in his direction. "Reignites old wounds."

Colin nodded and instead of continuing to undress her with his practiced eyes he grabbed her hand and pulled her towards him. However reluctant she followed, mainly because she had nowhere else to go.

"So let's start over, Kay, sorry, McKayla." He cast her a sidelong glance. "I promise not to call you that until I earn back your trust. I don't deserve that level of closeness. Not yet. But I promise you one day I will. I want to earn back not only what I lost when I ended our relationship but what I lost because of all the lies. While I beg for my clan's forgiveness, allow me to ask for yours as well, a thousand times over."

A small shiver rippled through her. Did he really crave her forgiveness as much if not more than those who raised him? His very family? It was hard not to be humbled because she knew he was being truthful. She wasn't being naïve, not this time. He meant it. Regardless, he wasn't getting off that easy. "Let's work at rebuilding the friendship and not worry so much about the relationship, okay?"

Colin nodded and led her into the forest. "Seems like a good start."

That sounded like he intended the friendship to be a mere formality and for them to pick up where they left off. If he thought she was jumping back into a relationship, he was in for a rude awakening. "Friends, Colin. That's all I want right now."

"Aye," he agreed. "Friends. Once earned."

Again, something about the way he said it made her think he was a lot more arrogant than he thought he was. About to say as much, her tongue caught when the pine-ridden woods thickened and sunlight streamed through the trees, dappling the pine-needles beneath. While New Hampshire, even Massachusetts woodlands, possessed a certain beauty, McKayla was instantly caught up in the utter enchantment that was medieval Scotland's forest. "What part of Scotland are we in?"

"Cowal Pennisula, Argyll," Colin replied, nostalgia in his voice. "The year is 1254."

Even though she should be nervous if not downright terrified it was impossible not to think of all her research. She'd landed in the exact year of her book! "William Wallace is yet to be born." Awe infused. "But he will be twenty or so years from now. The guardian of Scotland. How incredible, is that?" McKayla was like a kid in a candy store. She couldn't take it all in fast enough. So many thoughts were crowding her mind.

"So that means his father Malcolm is alive as we speak. Young but alive!" She shook her head. "And Robert the Bruce! I mean *Roibert a Briuis*. According to records, he'll be born exactly twenty years from now. Wow." She looked around, more and more aware of where she *really* was. "I'm standing in Scotland *before* such great men are even born with knowledge of what incredibly important lives they'll lead. It's a little overwhelming."

"Aye," Colin said, hesitating.

"What? Why are you looking at me like that?"

"You remember what they fought for right lass?"

"A number of things, including freedom. I mean the Bruce led this country in the Wars of Scottish Independence against England. Who could forget that?"

"Many. Scottish history is like all history, remembered by those with a passion for remembering. But that's not what I'm getting at."

McKayla looked at him, again astounded by his bearing, by the plaid and boots, the small braids woven into his hair. Yet now his expression was bleak, eyes troubled. Then it occurred to her. Scotland, *his* Scotland, was not his or any other Scotsman's right now. She'd been firmly plunked in the time that led up to the bold actions and fierce fighting of men like Wallace and Bruce. The English were causing havoc in this country, more so now than any time before.

Shame on her for being so self-centered. "I'm so sorry, Colin. It's one thing for me to research this time in your country, another altogether to meet someone, you, who lives or who's lived in such trying times. Forgive my excitement. I was out of line."

"Nay," he said easily. "My time. *This* time-frame, is what you spent months researching. Dinnae think for a second I would fault you for your passion. 'Tis half of what makes me adore you as I do. McKayla, you were brought here against your will. At the verra least, I want you to enjoy what my country has to offer. Few cherish it as you seem to. Your appreciation will be most welcomed by the MacLomain clan. For this country is part of who we are."

Offering a slow nod and a tentative smile she said, "Thanks for that. While I might still be mad as heck at you, it's safe to say being able to see the land I wrote about firsthand is…well, special." She took a deep breath. "So long as I get home safe…which I will, right?"

"If I have to die getting you there, aye, I'll get you home, lass."

Her smile faded. "Well, I'd rather you not die trying."

"Then I willnae," he said, eyes solemn even as they twinkled.

Which brought to mind what should have worried her from the start. "I know the first time I traveled back in time it was because of the Lucid Dream mask. How did it happen this time?" She shivered, recalling the thunder before she was deposited here. "And are my cousin's okay?"

"'Twas my clan," he replied. "And I know not why but suspect we soon will find out. It was more than I deserved that they allowed you this time to acclimate."

"Me?" she said weakly as understanding dawned. They'd brought her here with him on purpose. "Right."

"But dinnae overly worry. That we are permitted to stroll back alone says much about the level of threat against us."

Level of threat? Dear Lord. McKayla again worked on breathing evenly. "What of my cousins?"

"They're safe with Ferchar. Nothing will get near them." He squeezed her hand in reassurance. "The enemy is after me, not them."

McKayla cringed. The idea that there were assassins eager to take out Colin scared the hell out of her. And even though he wasn't saying it she knew she was in as much danger from this *enemy* as him. Words faded away when the forest soon thinned and something she'd only ever imagined existed slowly appeared.

When they reached the edge of the woods, her jaw dropped. Spread out far and wide was a deep green field speckled with purple heather. Children giggled, women worked and warriors trained. But, it was what lay beyond that froze her in her tracks.

A castle.

Not just any castle, certainly not like the worn-down tourist attractions back in her time period, but a thriving, majestic stone castle. With double moats, dozens of wall walks and turrets, it was by far the most impressive thing she'd ever seen.

"Holy hell," she whispered, not caring in the least if she swore.

Colin pulled her closer but said nothing. When she glanced his way she saw a man full of nostalgia. He was a Scotsman who looked upon his home with pride, love and something else, something undefinable. Perhaps remorse? Did he regret leaving it all behind? Would *she* end up being his biggest regret? For wasn't *she* part of the reason he'd left it all behind? McKayla realized that there remained so much she didn't know about him. Yes, she could say that about Colin but she knew he was Trevor too and that her friend repressed great pain.

"'Tis more bonnie than I remember." He shook his head and whispered, "Why didnae I see it before?"

"Sometimes we have a hard time seeing what's right in front of us," McKayla said gently. "Your judgment was clouded by youth. A mistake we've all made."

"'Twas but three winters ago, lass. At least in this time period. And given my position twenty-first century outlooks hold no place in my betrayal."

Though stung by his sharp response, McKayla didn't allow herself to be offended. Not now. The warring expression on his face told her he wasn't fighting her, but old demons, ones that belonged to him, his clan and Scotland.

Several long moments passed before he snapped out of whatever spell he'd inflicted upon himself. He brought her hand to his lips, kissed the back gently and said, "Would you like to come to my castle, see my clan, and a time that's long gone?"

Caught off guard by the old-fashioned gesture, she could only nod. Because it clearly wasn't long gone for him…if anything this time was his in every way possible.

They started to walk but McKayla stopped, suddenly aware they might have a problem. "What about my clothes? Look at me! I'm wearing shorts, a tank and…" She cringed. "Platform sneakers."

"Aye, 'tis sexy." He winked. "Was all this for me?"

Holy hell, he was going to be the death of her. Cheeks burning she shook her head. "It was gonna be hot. I dressed appropriately."

His gaze roamed over her with appreciation. "Then I pray to the gods for hot days."

She felt like an idiot. "Ugh, seriously?" Pointing at the castle she said, "I can't go there and meet your mother dressed like this. What'll she think of me?"

"My Ma?" His grin grew wider. "Is the last person you should be worrying about. Between the lasses casting stones and lads wanting to cast something else altogether, I think ye'll be just fine, lassie. We Scots like a wee bit o' excitement."

"No, Colin." Though it remained hard to wrap her mind around it, she had no other choice but to ask. "You're supposedly a wizard right? Then conjure me up a more appropriate outfit."

Colin looked at her with regret. "Aye, I am a wizard. But, nay I do not possess that particular power."

Hands on her hips, McKayla narrowed her eyes. Really? Colin had to be pulling her leg, because this wasn't happening. Of all the wizards she had to get *this* one. What wizard couldn't cast a spell with the wave of his hand? *This one*! If she clenched her teeth any harder they might just crack. "You mean to tell me, you can shape-shift from Trevor to Colin, but you can't change my clothes with a flick of your hand?"

Colin's lips thinned and he shook his head. "Never could pull it off." His expression lightened. "But the good news is the MacLomain's are verra familiar with time-travelers, hence my Ma, so you've nothing to fret over."

"Fret over? Are you kidding me? If you talked more like Trevor that'd be helpful. Try "worry about.""

"You're just nervous." he shot back, a glimmer in his eyes. "It's all good. Just relax and follow my lead, eh?"

Hearing him talk like they were back home threw her off. "No," she exclaimed. "Don't talk like Trevor, keep talking like a Scotsman. It doesn't seem right to do it any other way."

He shrugged and held out his hand. "Come on, you're not the first twenty-first century woman to arrive here. Remember, Ferchar was laird of this castle when Caitlin arrived."

She couldn't wrap her mind around that. But he made a good point. Caitlin must have arrived in twenty-first century clothing. Probably not a tank top and booty shorts, though. Why did she have to pick today, of all days to wear something sexy? Right now she'd be happy if the ground opened up and swallowed her. She couldn't be that lucky so she grabbed Colin's hand and started walking.

As they got closer to the castle her feelings of dread were replaced by an unexpected sense of contentment. There was something magical about this place. Not just because she was in Scotland, though that in itself was amazing enough, but there was a mystical power, a draw that she couldn't quite explain.

She should have been super tense. But she wasn't. Even with all the curious glances thrown her way she didn't feel uncomfortable. She actually felt like she belonged. In some weird way it was as if she was being welcomed into the family. The clan. Everyone greeted them with warm smiles, and the genuine love and respect Colin received helped put her at ease.

But she still had to meet his mother.

By the time they reached the first drawbridge several warriors walked alongside them, chatting with Colin, proud it seemed to escort him home. While she wanted to study each and every Scotsman it was impossible. She was actually walking over a genuine moat and beneath a well-kept portcullis for the first time. She was so excited that she wanted to jump and down. But that wouldn't be appropriate. She could hardly contain herself. All she could do was gaze up and take in every single detail, then store it in her memory for use in a future novel.

Now *this* was what she called research. Scots dialect echoed around her, both in English and Gaelic, and the castle loomed taller than ever. How completely astounding! She'd been given a front row seat into every Scottish historical ever written.

Colin stopped dead right in front of her. She'd been too caught up in her own thoughts to notice, and almost trampled him. What the ...? When she looked up, she saw an old woman standing beneath the next portcullis. With long, streaming white hair, a functional dress and the MacLomain plaid wrapped over her shoulder, she eyed Colin. McKayla's heart clenched when she saw tears welling in her eyes. The woman maintained her composure and notched her proud chin. "Are you home then, son?"

As he moved forward McKayla released Colin's hand. Mother and son stared at one another for a long, drawn-out moment before he dropped to his knee and lowered his head. "I am home, Ma. Will you have me back then? Will you forgive me?" He grasped her hands. "I am so verra sorry for the heartache."

Again breathing became impossible. Arianna trembled as she looked down her nose at him. It was obvious that she wanted to teach him a lesson. Wanted to be strong, and dish out some tough love for what he'd done, but her body language was betraying her, showing her true feelings. It wasn't long before she cracked. She closed her eyes and bowed her head. Heartbreaking didn't begin to describe the relief in her voice.

"In every lifetime would I forgive you. In every lifetime would I take you back, my lad."

McKayla teared up when Colin wrapped his mother in his arms. Their grieving was a distant memory. For their son had come home. It spoke highly of the kinship they possessed, and their ability to forgive.

Forgiveness. What a foreign concept. It was something she wasn't particularly familiar with. Though Caitlin didn't know it, after McKayla's parents split up she'd spent a few years in foster care. When her Dad took off her Mom went through a dark period, leaving no one to care for her. Thank God she'd met Seth. He was an anchor in an otherwise stormy sea. He had been going through something similar, and they could relate. Because of that time in her life she became slightly more reclusive. Seth always said she'd crawl inside herself or develop a more assertive nature.

Clearly the former prevailed. The only positive was it suited her love of writing.

McKayla stood awkwardly on the bridge fully expecting to find her way into the castle alone. But again, she was surprised when Arianna pulled away and headed in her direction. Heart thumping heavily up into her throat she almost took a step back. Her apprehension was unnecessary because Arianna smiled and took her hands. McKayla looked into eyes as stunning as Colin's.

"Welcome, McKayla. 'Tis so good to finally meet you." The older woman looked her over from head to toe. "I know how scared you are right now. Lord, do I know! I was naught but a youngling when I traveled back in time from 1799 to meet my Iain." Her eyes grew distant. "Hard, terrible, glorious, unforgettable times they were." Then her eyes once more met McKayla's. "But worth every moment."

McKayla was unsure of what to say, so when she started to speak, she snapped her mouth shut and stopped.

"No, no," Arianna said, kind eyes urging her to speak. "Say what you will."

I have a tremendous amount of respect for you. By the way, you have a pretty great son. But she didn't say that at all. Nope, instead she said, "Sorry about the outfit, especially the short shorts."

What the heck? She'd just spoken with Trevor's...um Colin's mom for the first time and she'd said 'sorry about the outfit'? *The shorts?* Way to go, McKayla.

It didn't bother Arianna any because her smile widened. "You'll do just fine." She took her hand and they started to walk. "Though I like the shorts we shall get you into a dress straight away." When they reached Colin, Arianna grasped his hand. "McKayla will need a tour of the castle, and you'll both need some food. Which would you prefer to do first?"

"Whatever is most convenient," McKayla said. "Thank you."

Arianna nodded and looked at Colin. "She will stay in your chambers. You fled one bride and come back with another. The

MacLomain's are an easy crowd but gossip travels. 'Tis imperative that when it hits the MacLeod's they hear a reasonable explanation, aye?"

"Aye," Colin agreed, clearly smitten with seeing his mother again.

"The MacLeod's?" McKayla asked, unable to stop herself.

"Aye." Arianna shook her head. "'Twas their laird's daughter left at the altar three years ago."

A MacLeod? And not just any Macleod. The Macleod's *daughter*? What was going on? Colin knew she'd written about a Colin MacLeod! For God's sake, he'd helped her write it. There had to be more to the story. Something he wasn't telling her. Because this was all becoming too uncanny. It took everything she had not to confront Colin about it, but she wouldn't ruin his homecoming. It certainly wasn't for his sake but for Arianna's. She seemed wonderful.

A light breeze passed over the bridge and as if it told her something, Arianna stopped short. "What is this pain you suffer from, Colin?" Arianna pushed up his tunic and touched the circle on his abdomen. Startled, she pulled back her hand, fear clear on her face. "Tell me, son."

Colin shoved the tunic down and shook his head. "'Tis nothing."

"Nothing is always something in this family," she murmured. "We will talk of this later."

"Aye, later, please." Colin kissed her on the cheek. "Promise."

"At long last, brother, you return," came a deep, even voice.

He has a brother? When she turned, McKayla almost tripped over her own feet. A man even more arresting than Colin, if that was even possible, approached them. With white blond hair, he was as tall and muscled as Colin, though his skin was tanner and his eyes a jaw-dropping Emerald. With darker slashed brows and a chiseled face his looks were the sort that kept drawing the eye.

Her eyes were glued to his dimples as he bowed in front of her. "So nice to meet you, lass. I am Bradon and you must be his…" Clever eyes flickered to Colin before landing once more on her. "For now."

Chapter Seven

"What happened to his hair?" Colin sat on the stairs leading up to the castle and frowned as Bradon escorted a willing McKayla around the courtyard. "It used to be much darker."

Sitting next to him, his mother shrugged. "Only the good Lord knows. He came home with it one day and we didnae question him. You've got to understand when you left 'twas terrible for him."

"It looks magically induced," he mentioned, which would be no surprise. Beyond impulsive, Bradon always acted without thinking first. Aye, the same could be said about Colin but gods save his parents, their youngest son was crazier than their oldest.

His Ma sighed, her eyes locked on the castle's tower. "There were others hurt by your departure."

Colin didn't have to ask. He already knew. His sister Torra. "Should I go see her now?"

"Nay," his Ma said immediately. "You need to give her several days to watch, learn, understand. No other felt the loss as deeply as she did, my sweetling. Surely you must know that."

Oh, he knew it. And it had eaten at him more so than everything else. Torra had always been special. The youngest of Iain and Arianna's children she spoke only sixteen words a year, four at each solstice and four at each equinox. A recluse, she hadn't come out of the main tower since she was twelve, ten years ago.

His Ma's expression was admirably resilient when she said, "I have not laid eyes on her since you left. Nor has your Da. She willnae allow it."

Colin put his arm around her frail shoulders and pulled her close. "You have been so verra strong, Ma. Because of me, you've had to be more so." He rested his chin on the top of her head. "I will make this right. All of it."

Long minutes passed before she said. "If you love her truly, then you shall."

He didn't need to ask who she spoke of. Besides his mother, McKayla and Torra were the most important women in his life. "I love her truly, and so I shall."

They sat next to each other in silence for a long time until Bradon led McKayla up the steps. With his wit and charm he'd made a project out of showing her the armory, stables and kitchens. But his lass looked better off for the time spent away from him, and he more than needed the time with his Ma. But when his brother offered to show McKayla the castle innards, Colin shook his head. "Nay, brother. Now she is mine."

They hadn't exchanged an embrace on greeting and Colin understood that Bradon didn't intend one now. McKayla said, "Are you sure? He's a fabulous guide."

Fabulous? In more ways than one if he had his way. But Colin banked the thought. He knew his brother was lashing out. With a quick kiss on his Ma's cheek he stood, smiled and held out his hand to McKayla. "If I may? You have not seen the half of it yet."

For a fraction of a moment, he knew she was tempted to say no. She wanted his brother to show her. But the ever evasive ability to tell others exactly how she felt hadn't quite kicked in yet. And he fully intended to take advantage of that right now. Soon enough, medieval Scotland and the consequences of time travel would transform her into an entirely different creature. Not by choice but by design. It happened every time.

After saying goodbye to Arianna and Bradon, they walked up the stairs toward the front door of the castle. Instead of mentioning how incredible everything looked, McKayla said, "He reminds me of Trevor."

Colin flinched and worked at a grin. "No surprise, Bradon's a forward thinker."

They'd no sooner walked through the front door when a female voice rang out, "Guess I won that wager, Malcolm. She's walking in with the traitor instead of Bradon."

While he knew she'd be faced with a lot when meeting his clan for the first time, Colin wasn't prepared for how trivial his cousins would act. And though he tried to keep in mind that he'd hurt them with his departure, he'd only allow so much. With a hand on the small of her back, Colin introduced McKayla to his rude brethren. "McKayla, as you didnae meet them properly before, allow me to introduce my cousins, Malcolm and Ilisa."

Face impregnable, Malcolm sipped from his tankard and offered no greeting. Ilisa only narrowed her eyes. Bloody blackguards. While he might deserve their wrath, his lass certainly did not.

Instead of subjecting her to more of their callousness, Colin focused on giving an uncomfortable McKayla a tour of the great hall. As he suspected she soon became less aware of them and more intent on her surroundings. It almost seemed that through her eyes he saw the hall in which he'd been raised for the very first time. She questioned him on everything from the massive nautical tapestries to the classic medieval architecture.

"*This*," she said, impressed. "Has got to be the most amazing thing I've seen so far. And that says a lot because this whole place and everything in it is way beyond impressive."

Colin grabbed two tankards from a passing servant and handed one to McKayla. The object of her admiration was the mantel perched over the great fireplace. Though he'd not explained as much the many faces carved into its smooth, thick surface were generations of MacLomains.

He enjoyed watching her sample the mead. Her lips pursed and brows rose slightly. The MacLomain's didn't water down their drink. "This mantle has been here as long as the castle itself. The verra heart of the beast some say."

"I could see this being the source of all magic," she murmured, eyes roaming over the varying expressions that stared back.

"Would you like to sit? Enjoy the fire and your drink before continuing on?"

She shook her head. "No way. There's still too much to see."

Her eyes slid to his cousins. "And it wouldn't hurt to take a break from them. I don't need to hear what they're saying to know I'm the subject of their conversation."

With a nod, he took her hand and led her up one of two long sets of stairs flanking either side of the hall. "They'll be dealt with. You won't have to suffer through this much longer."

"Dealt with?" she mumbled. "What's that supposed to mean? I'm not sure you should be *dealing* with anyone. As far as I can tell they're hurt. They believe this treatment is what you deserve. And I'm a target by default. They obviously cared a great deal for you."

Observant. As always. Regardless, while he might deserve it she certainly didn't. They reached the top and started down the first torch-lined hallway they came to.

"You've a kind heart, lass. I will deal with my cousins with discretion. You need not trouble yourself over it."

"Oh, stop talking to me like we've only just met." She ran her fingers along one of the torch brackets. "I get that you're sliding back into old habits which probably means a level of formality I'm not used to…but still…it's weird."

He couldn't agree more. But despite himself, being here again was forcing him to recognize the man he'd left behind. The man he was *supposed* to have become. "You've the right o' it. But chances are neither of us will be able to avoid a few minor changes in my personality. The way people expect me to act here is far different than how they did in the twenty-first century."

"Obviously." She glanced down one of many long hallways before they climbed another set of stairs. "But that doesn't mean you have to get all rigid when we're alone."

Colin grinned. "Choice words."

He didn't miss the grin she buried in a sip of mead. Once they'd reached the third level he steered her out onto a wall walk. As expected her eyes went wide and she put a hand over her mouth. This view was the best in the castle. It overlooked the field, rolling green forest and a sparkling loch majestically spanning out on either side.

It took little time for her to brace her hands on the rampart and lean forward, face to the wind, a wide smile on her face. She shook her head. "My writing doesn't do Scotland justice. In fact, I don't think the right words even exist to capture it."

"I didnae think you did too bad considering you'd never been." He leaned against the rampart, preferring to watch her rather than the countryside. Absolutely breathtaking were amongst the many words he could use to describe her. He'd always likened her to the Fae because of her pale sparkling blond locks and slightly tilted silver eyes. With sweeping green fields and sapphire waters beyond, his musings seemed more the true now.

Though McKayla's eyes never left the view, she said, "The way you're looking at me isn't conducive to that whole 'let's focus on the friendship' end of things, Colin."

Nor did he intend it to be. Though he knew their friendship would always remain impregnable and cherished, she would be his again in all ways possible. He hadn't risked everything to walk away now. Besides, the idea of being with another woman had turned his stomach since the moment he'd laid eyes on McKayla. "I made it clear I'd earn back your respect. Never once did I say I'd discontinue pursuing what we had before. Besides, as Ma made clear, the clan expects it."

She turned a frown his way. "I meant to talk to you about that."

"I'm sure you did."

"Your mom is clearly a kind woman so I didn't want to say anything but I'm not too comfortable pretending I'm married to you. And I'd say the same thing if you looked like Trevor."

He moved his hand a fraction closer so that it rested against hers on the rampart. A shiver ran through her body and though he knew she itched to snatch her hand away she didn't.

"It might be easier than you think," he murmured.

"Oh, I'm sure it'd be incredibly easy," she replied, frowning. "But that's not the point. I don't intend to fall back into your arms in a few shorts hours and forgive you just because you've decided we're starting over. As far as I'm concerned, I'm as single here as I was at home. Besides—" She held up her hand and twisted the Claddagh ring. "This won't allow it."

Colin ignored a flash of irritation and kept his tone light. "A few short hours? Of course not. I'll give you a day or two."

And that bloody ring didn't threaten him in the least.

She crossed her arms over her chest. Though what he said might sound like a jest to most, she knew better. "If this is your way of earning back the right to call me Kay, you're doing a terrible job."

No doubt. A terrible job didn't even begin to explain it. He was making a complete mess of things. His emotions were getting the best of him. That was something he'd have to control if he was going to face everyone waiting downstairs. But it was damned hard not to throw her up against the wall, and take her now. He had no desire to go forward without knowing she was firmly in his corner. *His* lass.

McKayla's expression softened. She sensed his thoughts. Could almost feel the insecurities he tried so hard to mask, insecurities that held no place in the life of a MacLomain.

So instead of exasperating her with honeyed words he shared his concerns about what he'd left behind. "Gaining the forgiveness of my parents and William was the easiest. Bradon and Ilisa I'm sure willnae be easy but they'll come around. Malcolm, however, is the most affronted by my actions and by far the least likely to budge on his misgivings."

McKayla exhaled and her shoulders relaxed. It seemed she appreciated both the topic switch and his desire to share his concerns. "What was he like before you left? Was he jealous that you were to take control of the clan when based on birthright it should have been him?"

"Nay," Colin said. "'Twas never like that with him. We were closer than brothers and developed an unbreakable bond. At least I'd always thought it to be such. He knew in time he'd lead as well and as far as we were concerned we'd all but rule together. We've always seen things the same way, shared the same vision for the clan. Our unerring faith in and love for the MacLomains is mutual."

"If that's the case he's more likely to forgive than you think."

He winced. "You would think but nay. The verra pacts we made when bairns, the verra devotion we had to this clan built the strong kinship we shared. For such a Scotsman, 'twould be near impossible to ken the actions of a brother who turned away from all he'd promised to protect."

"Let me ask you this then," she said softly, tucking hair behind one ear. A gesture he hadn't seen in some time. "You've gone through life-altering changes in the past three years, so why is it impossible to think that perhaps he has too? Maybe the man you left behind has changed. You're basing your opinion on someone you once knew. It seems rather narrow minded."

"Naturally, I dinnae doubt he's changed, lass. But 'tis bitterness and resentment that he's allowed to eat away at him, making the chances of an amiable truce even less likely than before." He shrugged. "I cannae see it being any other way."

"Then coming home seems to have clouded what used to be a pretty clear head. Do you imagine he only wanted everyone to *think* he resented you? Could his actions all be for show? If you two are so similar, then who's to say he's not regressed but progressed. Did he know the misgivings you were having before you fled? Did you talk about anything you were going through?"

He'd always appreciated her optimism. It helped under the weight of such heavy thoughts. "There was little I didnae share with Malcolm."

Though there were a few things he hoped he'd never have to share with anyone.

McKayla grinned, a smile that to this day caught him off guard. "There you have it, then. Sharing with him now might help break the ice."

She'd always been able to lighten his mood. A smile. A word of encouragement. But lately her grin came less and less despite the start of a successful new career. Deep down he'd always known why and no doubt exasperated it by 'staying in touch' with her when he 'moved across the country'. He'd broken her heart and hated himself for it. It didn't matter that it was for her own good.

When the hair she'd tucked behind her ear broke free, he tucked it back... like he'd always done before. His hand lingered, unable to pull away. Their gazes caught as always, in the unmistakable draw the two shared. Her smooth skin all but glowed in the low hung sun. Her soft locks a halo. And her lips, full, moist, tempting.

"Ah, there you are."

McKayla pulled back.

"Aye, here we are," Colin acknowledged, doing his best not to sound aggravated with Bradon. He fully expected his brother to make an appearance before they made it to their chamber. Some things didn't change. And seeing his brother made it impossible not to cast a disgruntled glance in the direction of her ring...a ring whose stone just happened to match the color of his brother's eyes.

"Good to see you again, lassie," Bradon said to McKayla.

She offered a warm smile and nodded. Colin was pleased it wasn't a blush. Because while she might think she was still single, she bloody well wasn't.

"The men are meeting in the great hall to discuss your homecoming. Ma will be up shortly to finish showing McKayla around."

Just then Arianna appeared on the wall walk. McKayla seemed all too happy to see her and vanished with a small wave and a nearly audible sigh of relief.

"She's nothing like the doe-eyed lovelorn lass you left at the altar, aye brother?" Bradon remarked as they walked down the hall. "Mayhap this time you'll be less inclined to leave the poor wee one to tear up on the rest of us."

Colin did well not to flinch. He deserved that. Let's see how much his brother would divulge. "And what became of the MacLeod lass?"

"Married off to another MacLomain of course."

No sooner had Bradon said it when the lass they spoke of exited a chamber just ahead. Startled eyes locked with Colin's. As he lived and breathed and as she'd vowed, Nessa MacLeod still stood within MacLomain walls. What the hell?

Bradon chuckled when the lass curtsied then vanished to whence she came. "Well, what did you imagine would happen?"

Not this. But he understood the importance of marriage pacts and one with their longtime enemy, the MacLeod's, was needed. "Dare I ask who she married?"

"Need you? Only one lad would have made sense without you here."

"Malcolm," he said slowly. A new sense of dread settled over him.

"Indeed," Bradon confirmed. "God knows *he* wouldnae let down his countrymen."

While he hoped McKayla's assessment of Malcolm's distain might be right, merely a show for the clan, now he knew otherwise. They had spoken at length about Nessa MacLeod. Though stunning, with smooth dark looks, never was there a more vicious, manipulative and cunning woman to be had. It was hard to imagine his cousin thriving beneath her clever ministrations. And now it was even more impossible to hope Malcolm would ever forgive Colin for handing him such a fate.

Though the words soured his tongue he asked, "Have they any bairns then?"

"Nay." Bradon's interested gaze shot to Colin. "But not for lack of trying."

Whether or not his brother believed him, any feelings he'd once harbored for the lass were long gone. He would have thought leaving her at the altar would make that clear.

Nothing more was said as they joined the others in the great hall. Colin didn't need to use magic to know who would be waiting. William and Malcolm sat at a trestle table. His Da, plaid wrapped over his shoulders, sat in a chair before the fire. When his sons arrived, Iain made his way over and joined them at the table.

This meeting would be held so all could look him in the eye.

William sat at the head of the table, Malcolm and Bradon to his left, Colin and Iain to his right. Tankards were plunked down and even after the servant left, a heavy silence settled over the abandoned hall. No MacLomain clansman or woman need bear witness to such a crucial and no doubt unsettling family reunion.

As laird of the clan, William was first to speak. "As you all know Iain and I have forgiven Colin for leaving us three winters ago." His gaze settled on Malcolm and Bradon. "Never would I force you to do the same. I do, however, expect a show of acceptance. Though it need not be when you're alone it most

112

certainly will be when around your clan. We have always stood united and that willnae change now."

Arms crossed over his chest, Malcolm sat back, his steady gaze locked on Colin. Not put off in the least, Colin stared right back. As expected he saw no flicker of compassion in his cousin's eyes. In fact, he barely recognized the man he once knew. He realized that there stood a very good chance that Nessa MacLeod had not only made his cousin bitter but corrupt.

Though Malcolm responded to William, his eyes remained on Colin. "Verra true, Da. *We* have always stood united. But *he* has not."

Colin didn't need to respond. His cousin spoke the truth. But he'd not cower and ask for forgiveness ... again. Both Malcolm and Bradon possessed magic. They knew he meant what he'd said. If nothing else, they could see it in his eyes.

"Colin," William said. "A good laird knows better than to assume and never gives up when it comes to keeping his clan as one."

All eyes shot to William.

It seemed his uncle had read his mind. But why had he said such?

"You cannae mean to make him laird," Malcolm said, eyes narrowed.

"Aye, 'tis exactly what I intend. This verra eve I'll give him the clan for all to bear witness. 'Twill be done before the wedding."

Colin sat up a little straighter. "Wedding?"

"Aye." William took a sip of whiskey. "To the Broun lass from the future. Straight away."

Oh, she wasn't going to like that. Colin, however, wasn't so opposed to where this discussion was heading. Except, that is, about becoming chieftain so soon. It wasn't deserved in the least.

Before anyone could say a word William continued, "Which leads us to the actual reason for this meeting. Why Iain and I brought you and the lass here when we did."

A slither of hair-raising trepidation raced up his spine.

"Do you really ken the clan you became involved with when away, lad?" Iain asked.

"Aye," Colin said softly. "The Hamilton's are little known in these parts but I've come to ken them well over these past few years."

"Never could you have aligned yourself with a more dangerous sept," Iain said. He shook his head and sipped from his tankard.

"And 'tis just that, a sept," William agreed. "Like you, a small group of them broke from their kin, those who delegated themselves worthy enough to assassinate their own countrymen. They have always been their own judge, jury and executioner."

Colin never felt like he'd betrayed his father more so than when William's words were uttered aloud. Iain, ever the contemplative warrior and former leader, remained silent. But Colin knew he felt the impact of the words, the simple and brutal picture they painted of his firstborn son.

"Unfortunately," William continued. "One of those who broke away from the Hamilton's was son to their chieftain. That in itself wouldnae be so bad if of course—" His troubled gaze settled on Colin. "You hadn't killed him."

And so it began. Colin knew what would happen the moment he ran that blade across his mentor's throat. War. Vengence. Revenge. In any order. The Hamilton's were for lack of a better word, vicious. A thriving clan to the north, they'd never been amongst the MacLomain's enemies but they'd never been allies either.

Malcolm took a long pull from his tankard but remained silent, choosing to glare at Colin, instead. Bradon, however, spoke up for the first time. "Do we share any allies with them? Is there middle ground to be had?"

"Verra few and those who are we'll not draw into this," William said. "Keir Hamilton is well-known for his ruthlessness and his unorthodox use of both light and dark magic."

That was an understatement. Colin had met the man once. It was safe to say he had no desire to do so again.

Bradon appeared to contemplate William's words a few moments before something occurred to him. Incredulous, he asked, "He's not *the* Keir Hamilton, is he? The one they say can summon a *deamhan* to do his bidding?"

"Aye," Malcolm said, eyes churning with contempt. "Some even say he allowed his son to be possessed by one for no other reason than the power it gave him." Turning his cup one fraction at a time on the wooden surface his eyes remained locked on Colin. "And if that was the case, what's to say the *deamhan* didnae make its way into our lad when he murdered its host."

So now his cousin thought to accuse him of being possessed by a demon? What a preposterous approach to discrediting Colin's ability to rule. If the Scots were nothing else they were a superstitious lot and such a claim would sway the clan.

"Dinnae be ridiculous," William said. "If your cousin had a beastie locked in him we'd know it."

"Would we," Malcolm stated, not particularly interested in an answer as he continued to study Colin. "None of us here possess enough of the dark magic to see one of its minions."

"Nay, but Ferchar does," Colin countered.

"Ferchar," Malcolm murmured. "I'm curious. You traveled back and forth to the future for years. I find it interesting that Ferchar never mentioned seeing you there. Could it be he never really knew who you were?" His cousin tilted back his head in further contemplation. "And if that is the case, cousin, then your powers have indeed grown. Tenfold I'd say. Enough so that you've the ability to hide whatever you wish to be hidden."

Malcolm was trying hard to discredit him. But this way? Colin could barely believe his ears. *Possessed.* Who would have thought he would come up with something so far-fetched to keep William from turning the clan over to him. He was grasping at anything and everything hoping to change their minds. If they weren't discussing such a serious matter he might have laughed in Malcom's face. But he refrained. There was no way in hell that Malcolm believed his own accusations, but it stung Colin nonetheless

115

He took a deep breath and kept his voice even. "Aye, my powers have grown. And aye, I learned a lot from those with whom I traveled. I have a better understanding of both light and dark magic. But as we both know, a MacLomain wizard is pre-destined by the verra gods themselves to draw one type of magi toward us. Mine, as you know, is light magic." Unable to help himself he leaned forward and cocked his head. "And what again is yours, Malcolm?"

They both knew he attracted dark magic every bit if not more than Ferchar.

"Enough," William said, his less-than-patient eyes skirting between the two. "If there was ever a time that you two need to stand together, 'tis now. As you know the summer solstice has just past. When it did Torra muttered four words, passed from a servant's ears to ours."

The three younger men waited for William to continue; anxious to find out what prophecy Torra had foreseen. Since the moment she'd gone into seclusion, every word she spoke came to be.

It was not William who spoke but Iain. "Colin. Death. Keir. *A-bhos.*"

Very rarely did Torra mix English with Gaelic. "The last word was "here."" Their plan was clear. Colin took a deep breath and blew it out. He didn't like this at all. "So you mean to bring Keir Hamilton to our doorstep."

"Aye, laddie," William said. "Because as we see it Torra's words could be interpreted one of two ways. Either he'll kill you or you'll kill him. The fourth word is the only one we can control."

"But why rush me here? And why McKayla? What aren't you telling me?"

"They sent a message," Malcolm growled. "Shortly after you killed their kin."

Colin looked from man to man. What was he missing?

"Coira," William said hoarsely.

Coira! His aunt, William's wife. He stood, truly frightened. "I assumed she was visiting Annie. Where is she? Have they hurt her?"

"Nay, she lives," Iain said. "But they've barred her from returning home. She is trapped in the nineteenth century with Annie and Arthur."

Colin slowly sat. Deemed a wizard by the gods of Ireland several decades ago, his aunt Coira was now stuck in the very era in which she was born. While he might be relieved that she was well, he understood the pain they were suffering being barred from one another.

"So verra few know how to time travel. This cannae be," he murmured.

"But 'tis," Iain said. "The last mental connection William had with his wife was severed by Keir's voice. He warned that he now controlled all passage through time. We were verra lucky that we got you here at all. We had no such luck with Coira. You should know that he vowed blood revenge on you, Colin and the lass whom was always meant to die, who *had* to die, McKayla."

"I'll be curious to learn more about that last bit," Malcolm said. "It almost sounded as if she'd been here before. Has she then?"

"Only once when I brought her back to keep her safe from the brotherhood. The verra moment I killed my mentor." Colin looked at William. "I cannae begin to tell you how sorry I am for what has happened. I will figure this out. But it cannae be here. I must travel north and face Keir Hamilton on my own. Find a way to protect this clan from danger."

"You'll do no such thing," Iain snapped, his weary yet firm eyes on his son. "You've been gone long enough. I'll not have your Ma or sister suffer more. By the grace of God, we brought you home so that we might work together as the clan we once were, with the strength we've always had. Out there alone you will be slaughtered. Here..." He looked pointedly at Malcolm and Bradon. "Is where your true power lies. The three of you have always battled better together than apart. You've years of both physical and magical training. Use it to defeat this undefeatable Hamilton. Use it to remind the whole of Scotland what made the MacLomain clan such a formidable power to begin with."

The fire roared and spit on the hearth as if in response to the declaration.

"Aye," William said, steely reserve in his voice. "'Twill only be a matter of time before Keir realizes you and McKayla are no longer sitting ducks in New Hampshire. When he does he will come. And when that happens the enemy he wishes dead will sit as chieftain of the MacLomains, with the lass he wishes dead as the laird's wife. You two will unite your clan and renew their spirits before the hammer falls."

Malcolm was about to speak when William shook his head, razor-sharp eyes covering the three younger men in one pinning gaze. "In front of your clan you will show nothing less than comradeship. Forgiveness given by all, you will be as you once were. Because if you dinnae, even though I might not be laird after tonight, I will personally see you drawn and quartered. Dinnae think otherwise so serious am I about this."

"And you used to be the jokester," Iain muttered. "But he has the right of it. We'll see you all done for, laddies. Each and every one. Not only is Coira's safety at risk but all of those we've come to care for from the future."

"Especially Arthur," William commented.

"Especially," Iain said. "Bloody bastard's only aged a few years our time. Still in his forties while I'm in my seventies! Ballocks."

"Time travel and its idiosyncrasies," William agreed.

Colin, Malcolm and Bradon listened to the two of them banter and Bradon realized by his cousin's expressions it was something that hadn't happened in a while. Most likely since he'd left. Again, he cursed himself. The consequences of his actions were far reaching. At one time all had been far more light-hearted. Hell, they were Scotsmen! Even with the Sassenach oppression they'd always managed to find humor in life.

Malcolm stood. "There is much to think about but for now I believe I will spend some time with my wife."

Again their eyes locked. If Colin wasn't mistaken, he saw a hint of triumph in his cousin's regard. What was that about? He recalled with pin-point accuracy their many conversations about

Nessa. It had been made clear what sort of woman she was. Aye, he'd had a fondness for her, mostly beneath him if he could manage. But never was there a time that he'd felt, never mind declared love for her, especially not to Malcolm's knowledge.

When Bradon stood and made his excuse to leave, Colin was surprised to see something other than scorn in his brother's eyes. Could it be he welcomed the challenge? Or could it be he'd simply been looking for a valid excuse to forgive without seeming weak?

Colin rose. He couldn't wait to get back to McKayla.

"Nay, lad, not you," Iain said. "Sit."

So he did without question. After all, three years was a long time, and he had a lot to answer for.

"Though 'tis hard to believe, there's an even greater reason why we forced you and the lass home," William said.

What greater reason could there be than wanting Coira returned safely?

"When did you intend to tell us?" William asked.

Uneasy, Colin said, "Tell you what?"

"This, son." Iain put a firm hand against his side. "When were you going to tell us the magic of the rings and the Highland Defiance had come together to create something so powerful even we dinnae ken yet its sole purpose." Iain pressed. "The circle. Stamp of the gods. I cannae help but call it the Mark of the Highlander."

119

Chapter Eight

For the first time since she'd arrived, McKayla was finally alone.

No way around it. Her senses were in overdrive. One astonishing thing after another had been thrown at her today. Yes she should be out-of-her-mind scared but the truth was she wasn't...well maybe at first but not now. Between Bradon, Arianna, and of course Colin, she felt welcome and far more comfortable than she probably should considering she'd traveled back in time nearly eight hundred years.

Now she sat on what would be equivalent to a California King sized bed. A four poster behemoth, it was the only opulent thing in an otherwise unassuming chamber. The room was huge with tapestries, bearskin rugs and skins on the windows but damn did it all seem to dull in comparison to the bed.

If her surroundings weren't enough to keep her heart racing her new attire certainly was. Fingering the silky white dress, warmth flooded over her. She hadn't realized women from this time period dressed so fancy. The long, elegant sleeves tapered to triangular points that fell over the hand and stopped at the base of the index finger. Beyond this point were circles of petite pearls meant to anchor the sleeve in ring fashion. The same pearls ran along the low neckline and the deep point where bodice met skirt.

Parallel to every polished line of pearls was a glorious stream of glistening diamonds. Right before the pearl rings, the ends of the sleeves were exotic and mysterious with their unusual star shapes woven with even more diamonds. According to Arianna, every single pearl was hand selected from oysters born of the North Sea long ago by a woman named Iosbail MacLomain.

Interesting. The very name she'd used as her heroine's subconscious voice. Yet another bizarre connection between her book and this place. But she had to suppose it was merely coincidence. Or was it?

Unable to resist the urge, she stood and spun. What she wouldn't do for a mirror!

"I dinnae think a lovelier creature ever existed in the whole of Scotland."

McKayla stopped twirling and a blush bloomed on her cheeks. Colin leaned against the doorjamb, his eyes roaming over her with unabashed appreciation and stark desire. Her knees went weak at the sight of him. With black boots and a tunic, he wore the MacLomain tartan in what appeared to be true regalia fashion, with a shiny emblem at his shoulder. His dark hair shone in the torchlight, a few small braids still interwoven.

Wide-shouldered, he nearly filled the doorway as his pale gaze continued to admire her.

"You don't look so bad yourself," she returned softly, pretending to brush away a non-existent fleck of dust from her sleeve. *Remember he's Trevor, McKayla. You don't need to be so nervous. You've known him for years!* But the moment their eyes met, all logic fled. He was so bloody hot and way too sexy. Staring into those thick-lashed hungry eyes she couldn't remember if she'd ever written about a man with so much sex appeal. Surely. Maybe. Doubtful.

"McKayla," he said gently. The deep rumble of his voice locked her feet to the floor.

"Yeah," she whispered then shook her head when he moved closer.

But he didn't stop. No, he strode right over and caught the ring of flowers perched on her head moments before it slipped off. She lifted shaky fingers to her hair. Why was she so nervous? Tossing the flowers aside, he took her hand and brought it to his lips. Though chivalrous, the gesture did nothing for her frayed nerves. Now he stood so close, so tall and so darn handsome her legs were starting to tremble.

"McKayla," he whispered, putting her hand against his cheek. "'Tis just me. Your best friend. The lad who offered you cake via Skype just yesterday morn."

"That seems like a lifetime ago," she murmured. McKayla looked into his eyes. "It's almost as if *that* was a dream and *this* is reality. I must still be in shock, huh?"

"I'd imagine in some ways we both are," he acknowledged. "But based on how I feel and by what I see in your eyes when you look at me 'tis the best sort of shock there is, lass."

Strong hands cupped her cheeks and his eyes reeled her in further. "You. Me. This…is life altering. 'Tis what should have always been, McKayla. Dinnae be frightened or embarrassed by it."

Thoughts of what she'd said earlier surfaced. That she intended to stay single. At least as long as it took to figure everything out. The way he looked at her now told her that he'd never considered the statement anything but useless words. As far as Colin MacLomain was concerned she was his. Always had been and always would be.

And he didn't think he was arrogant. Ha…

"It's hard," she whispered. "When you act so different than the man I know."

His thumbs brushed over her cheeks. His eyes studied hers. In a flash she watched determination bordering on domination filter down to confusion then regret. It was impossible not to see the war going on inside him. One, it seemed, between the man he once was and the man he'd become.

Warm hands abandoned her cheeks to cup her neck and then her shoulders. His eyes dropped, interested in where his hands traveled. "I have always loved touching you," he said, eyes still downcast. "So petite, fragile, but with such underlying strength." His eyes shot to hers. "But I couldnae break you if I wanted to."

Though she knew his statement should alarm her, it didn't. He worried over just how much she could take. "No," she replied evenly. "You couldn't."

She knew what he saw in her eyes…unwavering determination. Because she had no intention of buckling beneath all that was thrown her way. And though he thought she was strong, which she was, it was partly because of him. However upset she might have been, if she had to travel through time she was glad Colin was with her. The castle, the people, they gave her a renewed sense of confidence she'd not experienced at home.

When Colin looked at her now he not only saw, but sensed her fortitude. He didn't move away but instead remained close, his hands touching, cherishing. There was a poignant chemistry between them that never existed before. Or perhaps it needed this land and time for the desire to sharpen into this unavoidable magnetism.

"Formalities must be observed this eve. I must go down to the great hall before you," he said at last.

"Of course," she replied, caught in the strange almost otherworldly attraction sizzling between them.

When he leaned close her breath caught. He tilted his head until their lips were inches apart and whispered, "I will see you down in the great hall. Know when I do 'tis with a greater love than even you can fathom."

What sizzled moments before now burned and blazed between them. Still, his lips didn't touch hers. His muscles flexed and his body seemed to vibrate, even tremble, before his kiss finally fell on her cheek. Then, without another word, he was gone.

After he'd left, McKayla released a deep gush of air. When had she stopped breathing? Her body felt like liquid when she nearly stumbled, grabbed a bed post and sank down onto the cushioned spread. McKayla twirled the ring on her finger. Trevor never said he loved her. *Ever*. It was only after they decided to be friends that he said I love you, but it had always been strictly platonic. They were friends and nothing more. Or so it'd always seemed.

"M'lady, when you are ready."

Startled, McKayla stood, grateful her legs had steadied. Malcolm stood in the doorway. What the hell was he doing here? Intensely good-looking, he seemed part lion, part panther with pale brown, almost bronze eyes and raven black hair. Though his jaw was as chiseled and his frame just as muscular and honed as Colin's, this MacLomain kept pent up a little something extra. What it was exactly she couldn't be sure. She suspected emotions…repressed, exacting and alarmingly patient emotions.

And now she had to walk with him.

Alone.

Colin might've shared exactly *who* was to escort her down.

Then again, had he, she probably wouldn't have gone. Malcolm? Truly? Why not Bradon. Now there was someone she could spend hours with. She felt a kinship with Bradon, had liked him almost instantly. Flirty, fun, informative, he was incredibly easy to get along with.

Malcolm, not at all.

He seemed exasperated by her mere presence. Though it was about the last thing she wanted to do, McKayla took his arm and allowed him to lead her down the hall. Kilted and intimidating she'd never been more aware of an individual in her life. Torches spit and hissed on either side of them and smoke filled her nostrils, but she only to heard the heavy thud of his boots, and the whispery dusting of dagger against wool as he walked. Oh, she'd seen the weapon.

"I dinnae intend to bite you, lass," he said, voice so soft she barely heard it.

"Don't you?" she replied. "I know you don't want me here."

Did I really just say that? McKayla clamped her mouth shut.

If possible, he stiffened further. "'Tis not you I find fault with." He seemed to hesitate but then continued. "But you are correct. I dinnae want you here."

Did he not realize he contradicted himself? Annoying.

"Then clearly you do find fault with me," she enlightened.

"I find fault with your situation. You dinnae belong here. Nor does he."

Bristling she said, "*He* being your cousin, Colin? I'm pretty sure he belongs here." They stopped before descending the stairs. "And while I agree that I don't fit in here, heck I don't even want to be here," McKayla exclaimed. "But you're going to have to deal with it, and me. If I have no choice, neither do you."

Seth would be proud. She was finally standing up for herself.

Then she noticed how jam-packed the great hall was. Night had fallen, the doors were thrown open and it appeared a celebration was most certainly taking place. As they walked down the stairs, McKayla couldn't help but smile. Pipes trilled, people danced, some on tables. Trays upon trays of food were laid and the smell of roasting meat, smoked fish and baked bread permeated the air.

More eyes than she was comfortable with turned their way as Malcolm steadied her. Walking down the stairs in a gown was going to take some practice. Soon they rounded the last step and he pulled her forward. As they moved into the great hall, she became aware of a tall, gorgeous woman with long, black curling hair. Her cutting sky blue eyes shaved McKayla from head to toe in one damning appraisal.

Thankfully they weren't near her for long.

McKayla and Malcolm had just made it through the crowd and over to the great hearth when the pipes ceased and William's voice rose above the mayhem. "MacLomains, my kin, my clan, the time has come!"

The hall fell silent. All waited with baited breath. Malcolm never released McKayla's arm as Iain, Bradon and Colin joined William in front of a low fire. Their tartans wrapped proud, they were an impressive sight.

William looked over the crowd for a long minute, eyes locking with several clan folk before speaking, "For many years now you've done me the honor of calling me laird as you did Ferchar before me and—" He placed a tender hand on Iain's shoulder. "This great man before that."

Many smiled, nodding at Iain.

"But I am no longer a young lad and this clan, as it has many times before, once more faces new challenges." When several people looked concerned he said, "We have always been and will always be a strong clan. One of the mightiest. Not because of who led us but because we are as one. So now let me be as every great laird has been before, honest. Honest because you deserve it. Honest because it would be a disservice to you if I wasnae, aye?"

"Aye!" someone yelled back.

Most nodded, mumbling their agreement.

"As you all know we welcomed home Iain's son, Colin." He grasped Colin's shoulder as the crowd grinned, many yelling out their approval. "Though he might've left for a time it doesnae matter because he is home now, aye?"

"Aye!" most yelled. A round of cheers filled the room.

Malcolm stiffened. McKayla glanced up. His face was steely as he eyed Colin.

"With Colin's homecoming comes undesirable news from the north. A battle looms," William said, his voice challenging as he gazed around the room. "What say you to that?"

McKayla thought for sure there would be murmurs of dissent. Instead she nearly had to cover her ears when the room roared to life. Some cried, "To our doorsteps with the swine!" Others yelled, "Down with the bloody blackguards!"

It seemed the MacLomains liked a good fight.

And on it went. William, who certainly seemed to be revving up the crowd on purpose, raised an arm in the air. All fell silent. "We do love a good battle," William yelled, but then his grin fell away altogether. "And while I might still be strong, my wits and magi would serve greater purpose giving council to the next generation of MacLomains, to men with more endurance on the battlefield."

The hall grew silent, a hair raising eerie silence. They all sensed something big was about to happen.

"'Tis time to do what our beloved Adlin MacLomain wanted. Though gone from us, his wishes remain. Never doubt that his vision for the clan will always be what is best. The things he foresaw...that when the time was right, Iain's son would rule." William squeezed Colin's shoulder. "*Now* is that time."

McKayla sensed the clan's willingness to accept Colin as their Laird. She saw proud nods between the men, awed looks on the faces of children, and warm smiles shared between the women.

Even Bradon wore a look of admiration when he glanced at his brother.

William faced Colin, hands grasping his shoulders. It was hard not to stare at them, at something she never thought in a million years she'd witness. Trevor...Colin...becoming chieftain of a Scottish clan. William said nothing for a long moment, just stared into Colin's eyes, before he nodded. Something passed between

126

them, an air of recognition, an understanding that only those of the Maclomain clan were aware. Because in that moment all the men surrounding the outer rim of the room snatched weapons off the wall and raised them high in the air.

With a mighty roar they cried, "*Ne parcus nec spernas*!" three times.

Even Malcolm.

What she wouldn't give to know what that meant. McKayla didn't like being in the dark, but didn't dare ask the man on her arm. William and Colin raised their joined hands in the air. As a loud crack of thunder rumbled overhead, so too did a huge round of hoots and cries from within.

It was impossible not to smile…especially when Colin looked her way. Sweltering summer heat had nothing over the fire in his ravenous gaze. In fact, his regard held her so enthralled that she nearly missed it when William said, "But what would a new MacLomain laird be without a new MacLomain wife?"

Even as Malcolm walked her away from the crowd and toward the men before the fire, McKayla still didn't process what'd been said. Well, partially. There was a niggling of dread that Colin was to be married. Right now. Had he not left another at the altar? Would it not make sense that he made up for that? But tonight? She felt sick. How could he? She knew how. To make up for all the wrongs he'd inflicted on his family and clan. No sacrifice was too great. Not even her. It was his duty, she understood that, but she didn't have to bear witness to it? Did she?

When Malcolm released her, Colin took her hand. Her knees almost buckled. Oh God, he was going to tell her how sorry he was that he'd have to marry another right here, right now in front of the entire clan. She would die from humiliation. Why did they bring her here, just to shame her? And where was the next MacLomian wife? She wanted to see her, to look her in the eyes. She didn't know why. But she had too.

The thought of being trapped in the past having to watch Colin with another woman made her physically ill. She searched the faces in the crowd for his bride. But she saw no one. Something wasn't right. Then it occurred to her that there were no other women standing nearby. The next thing she knew she was being pushed before a man in brown robes. William, Iain, Bradon and Malcolm flanked them. Frowning, she looked over at the four of them. What the hell?

Bradon winked.

Malcolm scowled.

Iain and William grinned.

The crowd seemed curious.

What was everyone so damn happy about? She didn't think it was too funny having to watch the man she lov…, Colin marry another, but the rest of them sure seemed to be enjoying her misery.

Colin leaned over and whispered, "This is just for show, lass. The clan needs to see unification."

McKayla frowned and whispered back, "I don't understand."

The man in robes spoke but his brogue was so thick she barely caught a word. Her frown deepened when he wrapped a bit of plaid around her and Colin's entwined hands.

"Again, just for show," Colin assured with a whisper before he said aloud, "I, Colin MacLomain tak thow McKayla to my spousit wyf as the law of the Haly Kirk schawis and thereto I plycht thow my trewht and syklyk."

Now Colin's brogue was so thick she could barely make sense of it. What the heck had he just said? Her name was in there somewhere. The man in robes looked at her kindly, expectantly, as he said a whole slew of undiscernible words.

Colin leaned over and whispered yet again. "Just say yes. Even a nod will do."

McKayla shook her head, beyond confused.

Colin grinned. "Nay, dinnae shake your head lass. Nod."

Her brows came together. "Tell me why."

"Do you want to help save my clan? Do you want to get home safely?" he said softly.

She nodded. "Yes, of course."

The robed man made the symbol of a cross in the air, smiled and removed the cloth from their hands. The room burst into another round of cries and shouts. Oh shoot, she'd nodded and said yes.

But what had just happened?

The next thing she knew Colin was surrounded by clansmen and she was wrapped in Arianna's warm embrace. Kind eyes assessed her when she pulled away. "You've not a clue what just happened, do you lass?"

McKayla continued to frown. "Uh, no, I don't."

Arianna sighed but smiled regardless. "It went much the same way for me. Tricked right into it I was. Never was I more furious! But thank the good Lord it happened." Her loving gaze went to Iain who had joined them. "Or I wouldnae have had so many wonderful years with my husband."

Iain pulled her close. "Please dinnae be half as harsh on Colin as Arianna was on me, aye?"

"When *what* happened?" she asked, feeling almost foolish. Because what she thought happened couldn't have possibly. There was no way. There better not have been.

Before she knew it Bradon pulled her in for an embrace and said, "Welcome to the family, sister. If I had only found you first."

Eyes wide, she jerked back. "Sister?"

"Aye." A crooked grin erupted. "Are you not married to my brother then?"

"What…say that again?" she stuttered.

"Oh dear." Arianna shook her head.

Iain shrugged and looked skyward. "He's in for it now, he is."

"In for what?"

Colin's voice came so close to her ear that she jumped. How had he ended up behind her? Turning, she frowned. "What are they talking about? Because I never agreed to marry you, Colin. You never even asked! How…how…" She started to trip over her words again.

Before she could argue further, Colin scooped her up, made his way through a well-meaning crowd and brought her outdoors. The air was only slightly less oppressive. Though thunder rumbled across a dark and brooding sky, no rain fell. Not saying a word he carried her down the steps, banked a sharp right and went down a small arched hallway connecting the main courtyard to a much smaller one. About halfway down, he finally stopped and sat on a bench tucked in an alcove. Torches burned along the way but their nook was hidden from curious eyes.

McKayla was about to freak out but he put a finger to her lips. "Please, lass, hear me out. Aye, what happened in there was a wedding but it doesnae mean anything. They were useless words said to show unification to the clan before what is going to be a verra difficult time. I'm sorry that I didnae ask first but it all happened so fast."

Fast? Was he kidding? But his heart was in his eyes so when he removed his finger she didn't lash out. She looked down and realization hit. "This dress." Her eyes met his. "A wedding dress. You knew when you saw me upstairs."

"Aye," he replied. "William seemed to think our being wed was imperative to rally the clan and I wasnae inclined to argue with him after everything I've put them all through."

"So it wasn't your idea?

"Nay."

McKayla was surprised to feel a nugget of disappointment.

"Not to say I wasnae eager to see his idea through...even without your knowledge."

Though she knew she should be more upset, she wasn't. Because Colin was right, once she went back home her marriage to him wouldn't exist. They'd been married...eight hundred years in her past, for God's sake. No court of law would recognize it or even understand it for that matter!

However, it was impossible to ignore that he'd lied, *again*. "Colin, I think you'll be an even harder man to trust than Trevor. That, I suppose, is the saddest part of all."

"Did you really have no clue whatsoever about what was happening, McKayla? None at all?"

Was he trying to turn this around on her?

"Don't you dare try to make this my fault." McKayla raised her voice. "Sure, I might've started catching on but what was I supposed to say in front of all those people? Stop! I don't want to marry you!"

A couple slowed when they heard raised voices but continued on when they realized it was their new laird and his wife.

"Sure," he responded, adjusting his legs so she nestled more firmly on his lap. "I think if the idea truly turned you off you would've handled things differently."

Much like when they'd been on her bed back home, McKayla tried to ignore the feel of his firm thighs, large build, and earthly male scent. More than that, she tried to ignore how much sense he made. "Despite what a complete jerk you've been since the start of all this—" She made a gesture at his wide chest. "My best friend's in there somewhere and there's nothing I wouldn't do for him. Especially considering what he was facing…*is* facing."

Sensing victory he took her hand. "Though it might not have been tonight I did ask you to marry me."

McKayla choked on emotion. Yes he had. "Then you ran and ended it."

When she went to get off his lap he pulled her closer. "I didnae bring that up to slap you in the face with it, lass. I brought it up because I want to right all my wrongs. I have many regrets and that is the biggest one. I never meant to hurt you. I never should have asked you to begin with. 'Twas my fault not yours. I knew we were from different worlds, and I knew I could never give you the life you deserve."

His voice grew more impassioned. "When I told you just yesterday at Stonehenge that I loved you more than anyone, anywhere at any time, they were not words from one friend to another. Nay, they were words said by a man who loves you deeply; who would've married you had the circumstances been different."

"Now they are," she whispered.

"Now they are," he whispered. He ran his fingers through her hair, cupped the back of her head and sat forward until their lips were mere inches apart. "And here, not only are you my love but every inch my wife."

His free hand caressed her thigh, its heat a burning brand through the thin material of her dress. Lightening crackled and seemed to electrify the suddenly sparse air. Colin's hooded gaze relished the slight quiver of her expectant lips, the sharp rise and fall of her chest. "There will always be one truth between us McKayla and that is my love for you. 'Tis strong and wicked and wholly yours. And mark my words, 'tis something that cannae ever be taken from you."

McKayla almost said, "Fool me once shame on you," but couldn't seem to push the words past her lips. Everything about Colin MacLomain bespoke risk. As much as she sought only truth now she knew better. Here in Scotland he'd led a very secretive life. After all, he'd said as much. To truly let him into her heart meant embracing tolerance. But how different would that be for her anyway? Trevor had always been difficult to understand.

Yet she allowed them to grow closer over the years. Why? Plain and simple. She loved him. And as it turned out they didn't need a physical relationship for that love to grow and strengthen. Did it make her weak to give into him now? To allow him the benefit of her compliancy? Perhaps. But as she gazed into his eyes, with a summer storm rolling in and the sound of pipes and celebration all around, McKayla knew she would've said yes had he asked her earlier to wed him.

Understanding that she needed him to ask the question, he set her on the bench and dropped to one knee. "Will you marry me then?"

"So backwards," she murmured when he grinned and kissed her. Long, slow, so languid her body ignited in white hot delicious desire.

"I'll marry you," she whispered.

Never before had her skin felt burned, fevered, enflamed like this. Tongue exploring the deep recesses of her mouth, Colin pulled her back onto his lap and repositioned her so that his rigid, steel length pulsed eagerly against her swollen center. Rain started to pour, sending a soothing mist of wind down the hallway.

"Eyes," she murmured into his hungry mouth.

He groaned and banged the wall by his side.

His lips only left hers long enough to say, "Come," when a small panel slid open to their right.

Before she had a chance to be impressed by the hidden door, he sidled through with her still on his lap. With an impatient thwap he hit the wall and it slid shut. Just like that they were sitting on a bench on the opposite side of the wall in a tiny stone open-air room covered by the steep edges of the castle. McKayla only had a split second to notice rows and rows of Heather, Bluebells and a variety of other sweet-smelling flowers before Colin yanked up her dress enough so that she could straddle him.

The contact between her already swollen flesh and the rough wool of his tartan made her whimper in near release. Issuing a harsh breath against her neck, he ran his hands up her thighs and grasped her backside.

"Too bloody long," he murmured against her aching skin, sucking then licking then whispering words she couldn't hear.

While she knew he was talking about the last time they'd been together, to her it was all feeling very much like the first time. His body was, well, *different*. Even the way he touched her felt new, unique, way beyond incredible. And as for 'too bloody long' she suspected that would soon be proven true. His impatient shaft pulsed against her, restless for freedom.

When his lips found hers again he offered another round of heart-thumping kisses, his tongue exploring, tempting in ways that had her rocking back and forth. Head flung back, she cried out when ripples started to fan out, clenching her stomach muscles from where she ground against him all the way up to just beneath her rib cage.

Rain started to gush from the sky. Her eyes shot open when an icy drop hit her cheek and rolled down her neck. Colin leaned his head back against the stone, his predatory, near crazed gaze trailing the drop in the torchlight. Inch by slow inch it rolled. He watched as though it was all that kept him alive in an otherwise parched world.

McKayla's throat went dry when he licked his lips.

Lightening flashed seconds before thunder crashed. Still he watched, motionless, mesmerized. Then, as frozen as the moment seemed, a fresh round of wildness entered his eyes. A yelp escaped her throat when he stood and slapped her up against the castle wall.

133

She couldn't breathe. A frantic, under-used heart pounded in her chest.

When he came to her this time his plaid was aside and nothing kept him from pressing against her entrance. *Oh sweet Jesus.* He lifted her higher, spread her legs further, all with a determined, near desperate look on his face.

She dug in her nails and bit her lip when he pressed forward. Considerably larger than Trevor, she felt stretched, full. A small moan escaped her throat. She'd never felt so *hot. Searing.* She was losing control, free falling in a mass of sensations she couldn't explain or understand. One thing was for certain this was better than any encounter she'd ever had with Trevor, and she never wanted it to end.

Mckayla could barely hold on. She clawed at the wall like a caged animal, then grabbed Colin, making a trail with her nails down his back and chest. She needed him. His strength, his body, his mind, *his soul.* She wanted to crawl inside his skin. He was relentless, sliding in and out in a steady mesmerizing rhythm, watching her every reaction. His eyes never left hers. Not once did he slow his ruthless pursuit of filling her body. Possessing her. There were no sweet murmurs urging her to relax as Trevor had done the first time they were together. But this time he wasn't dealing with a virgin.

And this time he wasn't Trevor.

A new spike of sensation tore through her. McKayla screamed out. Pleasure didn't ripple through but burst wide open when he thrust hard and filled her completely.

Sweet, stinging pleasure washed over her as she watched Colin from beneath lazy lashes. He was feeling her throb around him, cherishing the moment, the tight, stroking grasps and clenches.

As the rain fell, the summer storm mixed together the poignant smell of flowers with the musky scent of desire. Colin, chest rising and falling as rapidly as hers, released a low, primal growl. His steady rhythm, his intoxicating scent, his soul connecting with hers, she couldn't take anymore, it was all too much.

Her body was alive with sensation, but she didn't have the strength to hold herself up. Sated, exhausted, she went limp in Colin's arms. He used brute strength to hoist her up. When she flailed, he grabbed her wrists against the wall and executed a jaw-dropping display of strength and agility. Tossed by the thrust of his hips, she slid up and right back down his rigid length. Every muscle in her body locked and sucked him closer. Sure, steady, even, he forced her into a rhythm that had the muscles in her legs turning to jelly.

"I can't," she tried to say.

Never stopping he nipped her earlobe, his hot breath tickling her ear. "You can, lass."

Only a sheer bit of her dress and Colin's hands kept the harsh abrasion of the stone wall from scraping her vulnerable skin. McKayla bit her lower lip and closed her eyes. He did nothing to protect her from the elements, but did everything to force her to feel *him*, their surroundings, the harshness combined with the passion. Everything. Every last bit came alive, had *life* and *feeling*. This is what it felt like to be possessed by someone. To not just have sex, but to truly make love with your mind, body and soul.

His thrusts came faster, deeper, with a drive and challenge she found herself eager to meet. Renewed, invigorated, she grabbed his shoulders and pulled her legs up high, forcing him deeper still. As fast and wild as the storm, they rose together, thrust after delicious thrust until a throb started deep inside her womb. With a roar, Colin thrust one last time and fell against her. Crying out in response, her whole body seemed to both implode and explode at the same moment. Her belly cramped then burst, pleasure zig-zagging everywhere. Even her teeth tingled when sensation after sensation blew through every last unmapped corner of her being.

Time ceased. Immeasurable, unending, it just stopped.

There was only him and her and...this.

When she returned to awareness it was to find him kneeling, forehead against the wall beside her. She turned her face to him and licked the rainwater from her lips.

"I don't think your clan will think too highly of me for doing this out in the open."

135

Colin turned his head and chuckled. "Lass, you're with the MacLomain clan. 'Tis a wee bit o' good gossip you just created. And naught is more appreciated."

Her face heated. "How can I go back in there? Look at me. I'm soaking wet. They'll know exactly what happened out here."

A devilish twinkle entered his eyes. "These walls have eyes, lassie. You'll not escape a good tale around a campfire. In the right crowd of course."

McKayla leaned her head back against the wall and sighed. "You know, I would've written what happened exactly like this. Only I don't think I could have done it justice."

"Aye." He grinned and leaned back. "You do have a gift for portraying us highlanders, but this that just happened was extraordinary. 'Twill be hard to recreate it. But have no doubt, I will."

She smiled, wholly aware of their intimate position. "Do you really think I have a gift?"

"Aye, you know that I do."

Her smile widened as he pulled her closer.

"As much as I would like to stay like this forever," Colin said, lifting her into his arms. "We need to get back to the celebration."

"I can stand on my own two feet you know."

Colin winked. "That's doubtful."

Cocky! But right now it was half his charm. "So you can't change my clothes with magic. What about *drying* them."

Colin sat on the bench and hit the wall. The door slid out. He eyed the damp dress clinging to her skin. "Nay. 'Tis not a gift that is mine." He tilted his head to the side and smirked. "Besides, I'm enjoying the view."

"Colin," she admonished. "I can't go back in there looking like this. You have to do something!"

Rubbing her fingers together, she frowned and looked at the Claddagh ring.

"What?" he asked, concerned.

"I was just thinking…" She raised her eyes to meet his. "About what Seth said about the ring."

Colin took her hand. "'Tis of no concern. Seth is not part of the MacLomain, Broun connection. He couldnae create something that would interrupt it."

She stared at it, unsure. "It burns a bit."

Colin went to touch it but stopped. "His magic protects it somehow but it willnae harm you. I would sense it otherwise. Knowing Seth, he's probably attached something to it that gives you a little sting when you're with me."

Now *that* would make sense.

"Should I try to take it off again?"

"Nay," he said without pause. "Seth is trying to protect you. And somehow the ring is doing just that. That is one thing I'll give the lad."

McKayla didn't want to discuss it any further. Right now, she was more worried about trying to make herself look somewhat presentable. Talking about Seth and Trevor would only give her a headache. No good would come of it. Not now anyway.

They left the hidden garden and stepped out into the torch lined hallway. Colin walked around her, tucking and smoothing. "Almost perfect."

"Almost?"

It was hard not to feel giddy. With his wet hair slicked back, he appeared as handsome and fit as ever, *way* too attractive. "Oh aye," he reported. "The dress that is. If I remember correctly, you're a wee lass who will always look better with nothing on at all."

A blush warmed her cheeks.

He inhaled deeply and looked back the way they'd originally come. "Though I'd rather head directly to our chamber I suppose we must join them."

Their chamber. Right. That would take some getting used to. McKayla nodded. "I suppose so."

Hand in hand they walked a few steps before he stopped, clearly uncomfortable about something. "This has been a lot. How are you lassie?"

McKayla looked toward the hallway's exit then at him. "Actually, I'm doing okay." She tucked hair behind her ear, more aware of him than ever. "Really okay...in..." Her whole body was still tingling from their time together. "A super good way." She tucked hair behind her other ear and worked to keep her eyes locked on his. "Epic sort of good."

God, I'm acting like a teenager!

But he'd brought out the magic in her.

"Good." His brows arched. "Great!" They continued to walk and nearly reached the courtyard when he stopped again. This time he was frowning. "There's more, McKayla."

"Okay," she said and waited.

Colin cleared his throat. "As it turns out when I left a lass at the altar all those years ago she wasn't quite...left at the altar."

A strange sort of trepidation slithered over her skin and she wasn't sure she liked it. "Okay," she said slowly. "Where was she left then?"

"Well, technically at the altar. But as it turned out not alone for long." He glanced outside and sighed before his eyes met hers. "She ended up marrying Malcolm. Nessa MacLeod lives right here in the MacLomain castle."

Chapter Nine

McKayla put her hands on her hips then by her side then back on her hips, staring outside then back at him several times before she said, "Are you serious?"

"Verra," he said solemnly, waiting for her to get upset. While he knew he should've told her earlier so much was going on. Then when it wasn't…it was again. Between becoming laird, marrying the love of his life then having sex with her for the first time in this form, telling her about Nessa was the last thing on his mind.

Even now when he knew he should feel guilty for not telling her, all he could think about was how bloody amazing she'd felt against the wall, in his arms, surrounding him. Her dainty little body had suffered for taking this version of him but she'd done it. All of him. He'd never know how but they fit. And they would until the day he died. Over and over and over again.

"Colin?"

Hell. She'd been saying something. Shutting out visions of her open, panting lips and fluttering eyelids when he thrust into her, Colin said, "Aye."

"Aye, what?" McKayla shook her head. "You were a million miles away."

"Nay, right here. Just mulling things over."

McKayla shook her head. "No, you were thinking about something else. How could you drop a bombshell like that then ignore me?"

He was about to respond but she cut him off. "You did that at home too. I'd be talking to you and you'd drift off. Where do you go? I always thought it was a techie thing…" Her voice trailed, caught between the past and present. After a few deep breaths, her bonnie light gray eyes settled firmly on him. "Were you ever really a techie? Did you create that kilt-wearing flashlight with your hands or with your magic?"

"Hands," he responded, insulted. "I might be a wizard but in the twenty-first century I enjoyed creating things. Loved the challenge."

Her eyes narrowed slightly. "I'd like to think so. A person's passions in life make up a great deal about who they are and without that…"

Oh no. McKayla only rambled like this when she was upset. Nessa must have hit her harder than he thought. Colin pulled her into his arms and murmured in her ear, "She means less than nothing to me or I would have never left her at the altar. You need to know that."

McKayla shook her head and pulled back. "You misunderstand. I don't give a damn about Nessa. The thought of you not being a techie really bothers me. I don't know why. I can't explain it, but it bothers me. I guess it's who you *are* to me. I know it sounds silly but I guess I want to know that something about you, something about *us,* was true. That the person I fell in love with and the things we shared weren't all based on a lie. That you were real, *we* were real. Does that make any sense? I hadn't thought about it until now."

"Aye, lass. It makes perfect sense. *We* were real. It was all real. And if I lived in the twenty-first century, with or without my magi, I would love technology. And you."

So she wasn't upset about Nessa? By the way she nodded, took his hand and continued back it seemed not. Just when he thought he had his lass all figured out she surprised him.

They'd no sooner returned to the courtyard when Ilisa appeared. Dazzling in a deep green dress, her long red hair flowed around her shoulders. Firstborn to Arthur and Annie who now resided in the nineteenth century, Ilisa had chosen at ten winters old to return to medieval Scotland. Though it broke her parent's heart it was the best option. Their daughter was far too wild for New Hampshire, especially the day and age in which she was born.

"I *wondered* where you two had got off to," she all but bellowed across the courtyard as she sauntered their way. Colin had to hand it to her, she walked as well in a dress as she did when she threw on trousers and wrapped herself up in as many daggers as she could find.

"Ilisa," he said in greeting. "As always, nice to see you cousin."

"It is, isn't it?" She turned a confrontational eye McKayla's way. "And what think you, foreigner, is it good to see me?"

About to have issue, he was cut off by his new wife.

"Are you drunk?" Mckayla asked, eyes narrowed as she peered at Ilisa. "I've been meaning to ask you that since we met."

Colin ran a hand over his face and tried not to laugh. But he wasn't doing a very good job of it. It took almost more restraint than he had.

Ilisa stepped nearly nose to nose with McKayla. In truth it was really more nose to top of head with the height difference. His cousin stared long and hard at his wife. And Kay, bless her heart, didn't bat a lash. After too long for his taste, Ilisa raised her arm in the air and made a come-hither motion.

Arms crossed over his chest, Colin watched a stable boy run forward with a stool and place it behind his cousin. What was she up to? Knowing her, it could be anything. Some said she was crazy. He knew she was crazier.

When at last she made a move it was to finger one of McKayla's locks. "The way you have your hair cut."

McKayla eyed the woman's hand in her hair then met her eyes. "Yeah. What about it?"

"I like it," Ilisa declared and promptly sat on the stool. Reaching into her ample cleavage she pulled out a small knife and handed it, hilt first, to McKayla. "Cut mine like yours."

Colin pinched the bridge of his nose and shook his head.

McKayla took the blade and looked from Colin to Ilisa. "Um."

His cousin cocked her head then swiftly rolled her eyes. "Now here I thought you've a set o' ballocks on you girl." She snapped her hand in the air and the stable boy came running again. He handed a flagon to McKayla then scurried off.

Confused, McKayla looked from the flagon to the redhead.

"What?" Ilisa nodded at it. "Go on. Drink now. Seems you need some courage if you're to see through what I asked of you."

Colin twisted his mouth. Ilisa had a good dose of both her Ma and Da in her to be sure.

"Well then?" Ilisa said.

McKayla eyed the flagon, knife, and then Ilisa. "Have you no shears?"

"Wouldnae matter." She pointed at the dagger. "I want it cut by that. Have you the ballocks?"

After a surprisingly long pull from the flagon, his wife handed it to him and said, "No, I've not the ballocks, only tits and a blade I'm afraid."

Before Ilisa could approve or disapprove, McKayla grabbed a long chunk of hair and made a clean, if not yanking cut. His cousin's eyes went wide and a smile blossomed. "Bloody hell, that hurt my scalp nearly as much as an arrow's graze!"

Colin chuckled along with quite a few others who had come around despite the drizzle and mud and retreating storm. Why should that surprise him in the least? Highlanders, Scotsmen, *his* clan, loved a good show.

Ilisa offered him a wink when she took the proffered flagon. After a deep swig she tried to hand it back to McKayla. His little wife shook her head no and continued cutting off what was by far the most bonnie fire-red hair on this side of Scotland.

The crowd gathered and pipers brought their music outside. As the moon slid free from the fleeting cloudbank, logs were carried into the courtyard and a bonfire was lit. Still, McKayla cut, working the blade at an impressive angle. One it seemed that no longer hurt Ilisa and made the hair less frazzled. When the stable boy ran back out to gather some of the hair she said, "'Twill be for my lassie."

Colin didn't need to ask who she meant. He knew.

Torra.

It took everything he had not to turn and look up at her. Because without a doubt his sister watched from high above, taking it all in and seeing things from this night that would echo far into the future.

"Well, look at that. Who knew she had a face under all that hair?"

Bradon joined them, arms crossed over his chest as he watched. Colin had no way of knowing why his brother had decided to reach out to him but he wouldn't let the gesture go unappreciated. "And who knew McKayla had it in her to cut it all away."

His brother arched a brow at him. "Ah, so you thought I spoke of Ilisa."

Two years his junior, Bradon had seemed such a child when he left. It appeared he'd grown up since. And he was right. McKayla did appear to be blossoming here. "Aye, but what do I know."

"More than you did when you arrived home. Hopefully more than when you leave again."

Colin's chest tightened. He didn't blame his brother for assuming the worst. "'Tis not my intention to let you down."

But his brother had no chance to respond.

McKayla was finished.

With a quick flick of her wrist, she offered the blade to Ilisa, hilt first. Looking at the knife for a long moment and then at McKayla, Ilisa finally took it and tucked it back in her cleavage. Never had he seen a stranger sight than his wife in her white wedding gown standing in a pile of red hair. Not nervous in the least, she stared down at Ilisa as the Scotswoman felt her short locks for the first time.

Like him, the wide crowd waited with baited breath.

Even the pipes stopped.

Ilisa felt first the left side, then the right. Frown in place, her hands traveled slowly to the back of her head. *Tick. Tick. Tick.* If there'd been a clock, the sound of its small hands clicking forward would have blasted through the courtyard.

"Well," McKayla said, her voice firm and curious.

Colin repressed a grin. God he loved her.

Ilisa stood up slowly and took another long swig from the flagon. "Well," she said, her unreadable eyes on McKayla. "It seems my head feels a whole lot lighter!"

McKayla grabbed the flagon, her voice soft when she said, "Good, because I'm pretty sure it needed to be."

But her words were lost in the cheers and hoots. The clan loved Ilisa's new locks almost as much as she did. With a swagger only his cousin was capable of, Ilisa was off enjoying the admiration and praise for being a forward thinker. After all, she battled alongside the men. She *should* have shorter hair. It only made sense.

McKayla took a long swill then fanned her breath, pointing at the flagon. "This is *strong*. What *is* it?"

With a chuckle he took a swig. "'Tis Highland whiskey, lass. The best of the best."

"Best of the best, eh?" She shook her head, obviously shaky and still coming down from the pressure Ilisa had put her under.

"Had you drank whiskey back home you'd better ken how good this really is."

"He's the right of it, lass," Bradon said. "At least I assume."

McKayla watched Ilisa flirting with several men. "So what can I expect from her next?"

Colin smiled. "You never know with that one. She might be your best friend now."

"Or…" Bradon laughed. "You might deal with more situations much like this."

Colin shook his head.

"What?" Bradon shrugged. "We all know Ilisa's a wee bit touched, aye?"

"You don't need to protect me, Colin," McKayla said. "Any fool can see she likes to test people." She glanced at Bradon. "You might call it touched but I doubt it. She knows exactly what she's doing."

"Aye, she does indeed," a low feminine drawl came from behind them.

Nessa MacLeod.

If Colin had hackles they'd be going up.

Goblet in hand she meandered to his side, her sly blue eyes on his though she spoke to McKayla. "We MacLomain lasses always know precisely what we're about." Her slightly narrowed eyes shifted to his wife. "Dinnae doubt it for a moment."

"I'm starved," McKayla said, clearly not wanting to engage Nessa. "Any chance we can eat?"

"Aye." Colin took her hand and turned to Bradon. "Will you join us brother?"

Bradon looked between Colin and Nessa. "Nay. You go. I'll keep current company."

Nessa, obviously unfazed by Colin's brush-off, smiled at Bradon. "Shall we dance then, cousin?"

Colin and Mckayla didn't wait to hear Bradon's response, but kept on walking.

Once out of earshot McKayla glanced over her shoulder at the twirling couple. "That woman seriously creeps me out. Rude too. Looking at you like that. Doesn't she know we just got married?" She shook her head and frowned. "Who is she anyways?"

"Sorry I didnae introduce you. Mayhap next time." Colin hoped not. Now to tell her the last thing she'd want to hear. "That, lass, was Nessa MacLeod."

Her eyes went saucer round. "No."

"Aye, I'm afraid so."

"Poor Malcolm." She looked at him, unsure. "Or do all Scotswomen act that way?"

"Nay," he scoffed as they walked up the castle stairs. "Nessa is a poor example of my kinswomen. Never have I seen a MacLomain act so poorly. But then she was a slippery sort when she was a MacLeod."

McKayla eyed him as they walked into the boisterous room. Colin knew what she was curious about and prayed he'd not have to answer more questions about Nessa until later...because he'd promised to be truthful. It seemed for now he was safe from revealing anything unsavory as she was caught up in the merriment of the clan. No doubt the spirits she'd imbibed helped. With a soft glow to her cheeks and bright eyes, his wife had a wide smile on her lovely face.

"Come, you need to eat before you play." He sat and pulled her onto his lap.

"You like me in this position, don't you?" she commented with a twinkle in her eye.

"You've no idea." He fed her a few berries then some bread.

Dutiful for the first few bites, she eventually shook her head and laughed. "I can feed myself."

Colin smiled and ate a few scallops. It did his heart good to see her happy. And though he knew it wouldn't last, tonight he intended to keep her laughing.

Puckering her lips she said, "There's no real make-up here. How do my lips look stained with red berry juice?"

Not willing to miss an opportunity he pulled those very lips to his. Sweet, receptive, she kissed him with vigor. Sugary, delicious, he wrapped his tongue with hers and enjoyed what he considered the appetizer. Because when he had her in his bed later true fervency would begin. He fully intended to sample everything she had to offer. Too many years had passed and he wanted far more than what he'd had in the garden.

They may have kissed for days had someone not cleared her throat. "Well, are you going to dance with me or not?"

Colin pulled back and smiled. Ilisa stood over them, hands on her hips.

"If you'll have me," he said.

His cousin shook her head. "Just like a lad to think I'm speaking to him." Her gleeful, devious eyes turned to McKayla and she held out her hand. "Nay, me thinks a spin with yer new wife would be great fun!"

McKayla grinned and shrugged, taking his cousin's hand. "Sorry, *lad*." She smirked at Colin. "Looks like I've had a better offer."

It was impossible not to laugh. Ilisa winked and the women wrapped elbows. Before he knew it, they were swept away in a Highland jig. After he received a fresh mug of ale from a passing servant, Colin made his way through the crowd, greeting everyone for the first time as their laird. It was downright humbling how graciously they'd forgiven him for leaving. No better clan existed and he intended to devote the rest of his life to protecting them.

Colin had the sudden feeling that he was being watched.

And he was.

Malcolm stood on the landing above. Watching. Asessing. Gooseflesh rose on Colin's skin. His cousin looked every bit the dark overlord. Their eyes met. There was fury in the connection. His cousin had developed deep-seated feelings that though Colin suspected were not hatred, were certainly close. And it was hard not to blame him. After all, he had suffered the most. A mother lost in time. A wife meant for his cousin. A position of authority now denied him.

"He'll come around," Bradon said, falling in beside him.

Colin was pleased his brother had sought him out once more. "And have you? Come around? Or is this simply the show of support promised?"

Bradon glanced up at Malcolm. "I've not the mind or inclination to fume as he does. But you must remember you were not the first to leave him. That said I tend to think you will take the wrath for all other betrayals."

Colin frowned. They'd been but bairns when Malcolm's younger brother vanished. It was assumed to this day that he'd died. Still, it'd taken a toll on his cousin and had left a huge void, one which Colin helped fill. Nearly the same age, he and Malcolm had forged a strong bond shortly thereafter. They'd been like brothers.

Malcolm's eyes soon slid away from Colin, intent on the door. Nessa entered. "Wish you'd kept her entertained longer," Colin muttered and drained half his mug.

"She aims to create more problems between you and Malcolm," Bradon provided.

"Aye." With a heavy frown he said, "That look on his face now says as much."

"He's besotted. She's wrapped him good and tight she has." Bradon grabbed a chunk of bread off a table and took a bite.

"So he loves her then?"

"As much as I've seen any lad love a lass," he said around a mouthful. "And up until you arrived she's been well behaved. But now…" Bradon again gave him a curious glance. "I see trouble brewing to be sure. What was it between you two?"

147

Lust mostly. Never love. At least not on his part. "Not much. We were thrown together to help lessen the never-ending feuding between the clans. There was little time to know the other."

"A whole summer she spent at this castle." Bradon took a swill of ale. "How long did it take for you to love your McKayla? I'll wager less time than that."

Less than a minute. But that was beside the point. "'Twas never a match, Nessa and I."

"Mayhap not for you," Bradon conceded.

Their eyes met and his brother shrugged. "Move forward verra carefully. For Malcolm is always watching."

And he was. When Colin looked up his cousin's gaze was narrowed and flickering between him and Nessa. Bradon was right. Jealousy was debilitating. If Colin didn't watch his every move, it would disintegrate whatever thin tie might remain between him and Malcolm.

Bradon chuckled when McKayla and Ilisa twirled by, their faces flushed and merry. "Ah, but she's a bonnie wee lass. I think mayhap I would've sacrificed the whole of my clan for her as well."

Not offended by the fondness he saw in his brother's eyes when he looked at McKayla, Colin assured, "You're not nearly modern enough for her, lad."

"Speaking of..." Bradon pinned him with one of his infamous grins. "Tell me about this time she comes from. Are there more there like her?"

Colin thought of Sheila and Leslie. The idea of his brother meeting them didn't seem so implausible. Sheila maybe. Leslie never. She would crucify him with one look. "Nay," he replied easily. "McKayla's one of a kind."

"Too bad. So I suppose both you and Ferchar are just lucky in love."

His brother was no fool. Where there were two, there were bound to be more. He downed the last of his drink and received another, looking around the room. "I see more bonnie lasses here than I ever did in the future. Have you not had a love then?"

Bradon shrugged, bored. "A few. But none that warm beyond my bed."

Colin eyed him. "Tell me about your hair. 'Tis a strange thing that."

This topic brought life to his brother's eyes. "You wouldnae believe me if I told you."

Interest peeked. "Share brother."

"I cannae." But Bradon had a spark in his eyes he'd never seen before. "Not yet."

"And whatever this is turned your hair near white?"

"Aye, in one single moment."

"Great magi," Colin murmured.

"The greatest."

A strange, otherworldly tingle raced over his skin. "Are you in danger?"

"Nay," Bradon assured, his gaze somewhere far away.

Though he didn't sense danger around his brother such mystery made him uncomfortable. Too long had he abandoned Bradon. Now it was time to change all that. "I expect you to tell me eventually."

As if sensing the shift in Colin's demeanor, Bradon's brows lowered. "Mayhap. When I'm ready."

Not particularly interested in crossing swords so soon after what seemed an amiable reconnection, Colin nodded. "Aye, brother."

Like a hellcat come to wreak havoc, Ilisa stopped short next to them. A ripple of laughter escaped McKayla as she was flung to the side.

"Now you!" Ilisa demanded.

Colin didn't have a chance to refuse before Ilisa was swinging him around. And then before she could catch her breath, McKayla was twirled away by a more-than-willing Bradon.

When the music slowed, Ilisa wrapped her arms around Colin's neck. "She's well-worth the sacrifice, laddie."

"Is she?" Colin said, pleased by her approval. "And what makes you say so after she cut off all your bonnie hair?"

"That she had the stones to cut off my bonnie hair, of course," she said with a wink. "You owe me for that."

"I do?"

"Aye!" Ilisa grinned. "Look how well she's doing. The clan likes her. She showed courage."

Realization hit him like a bolt of lightning. Ilisa sacrificed her hair. For him. For them. So that they could be happy. He didn't know what to say. Or do. He was shocked. But Ilisa was right, the clan was accepting McKayla.

"You never wanted your hair cut, did you?"

"Oh, I didnae say that. Mayhap a wee less o' a trim." She shrugged, not overly concerned. "But the lass had something to prove."

"Thank you," he whispered. "You're a good lass and I'm so sorry for any hurt I've caused you over the years."

Ilisa's expression grew serious. "'Twas a great harm you caused us all." Her chocolate brown eyes met his. "We...*I* missed you something fierce."

"Aye, and I you, lassie." He pulled her closer. "Never again will I leave you like that. You have my word. I intend to prove that my word is worthy of you," Colin promised. "Of everyone."

Though her eyes didn't water, Ilisa blinked a little too rapidly as she studied him. "Then I will stand by you, my laird. As I support my clan, I will support you." She looked around the room, seeing something even he couldn't. "We are entering a new era. I can feel it. The Sassenach grow braver and we Scots..." Her voice lowered to a sad whisper. "Grow tired."

Unlike her, he knew their history. He knew what would happen to Scotland over the generations. At only ten winters, the age when she'd returned to the clan, she'd been told nothing. Arthur and Annie had spared her. No doubt, they longed to keep her fierce spirit intact.

But now he saw it weakening.

And it scared him.

Ilisa had never been one to hint at sentimentality yet it was there. In the way her words caught in her throat. In the less than direct gaze she gave those who passed. It seemed even his fiery cousin was not the same lass he'd left behind. Still, the jut of her chin was the same and the defiance in her stance unwavering.

"Now we go forward together. As one. As MacLomains," he said firmly.

"Aye," she said, her eyes holding his, voice stronger than moments before. "We go forward together."

Soon after, she kissed his cheek and vanished into the crowd, her voice once more rising and her stride strong. In her and Bradon, he had confirmed allies. Now if only he had Malcolm. When he located his cousin he was dancing with Nessa. Close, clearly disregarding the rambunctious crowd around them, the two swayed. Colin could admit they made a striking pair. Both tall, both attractive, they seemed a centerpiece to the clan celebrating around them.

Speaking of centerpieces.

Easy to find despite her small stature, his gorgeous wife stood near the great hearth, deep in conversation with both his Da and William. The men seemed enchanted, their expressions saying more than mere words.

Colin was about to head McKayla's way when a firm voice stopped him. "Not quite yet, son. A dance with your Ma first."

With a warm smile, he pulled his mother into his arms. "How are you, Ma?"

White hair shining in the torchlight and skin soft and more supple than most her age, Arianna smiled. "Happy that you're home and well. Happy to see a renewed gait in your Da's step because of it. But mostly, happy to see you've found true love."

He grinned. "Then you're happy. 'Tis good to hear."

"Aye," she confirmed.

But he saw something else in her eyes. "Yet."

They danced closer to the fire. Even on a warm night he knew she grew cold. "Yet." Nostalgia entered her eyes. "The mark on your abdomen means the start of big things. 'Tis a sign." Her gaze turned sharp. "And the mark is on *my* son's body."

"Aye," he confirmed, voice tender. "But 'tis just a mark, nothing more."

Her gaze narrowed. "A mark that burns. A circle that closes ever more when you travel through time. What is it, Colin? What does it mean?"

Colin wondered how much Da had told her. Everything most likely. Best to be honest. He owed her that much. "'Tis a mark that will eventually seal me in one era. When the circle is complete I will no longer be able to travel through time."

"Who did this?" Her regard grew curious. "Was it Keir Hamilton? He bars Coira from coming home. Has he such power when it comes to time-travel?"

"I dinnae think so," he replied honestly. "There is no evil in this mark."

"Yet it causes you pain."

"Great pain...at times," he conceded. "But I dinnae feel controlled by the enemy when it happens." Colin shook his head and murmured, "'Tis something else entirely."

"Your Da told me he feels old magic in it, that of the Highland Defiance and the rings." Quizzical she said, "Though never part of my experience coming to Scotland I know the Defiances were time-travel gateways created by Adlin MacLomain. 'Tis a strange thing they'd be connected to this mark when the verra opposite is implied, dinnae you think?"

Before he could speak she said, "And the rings with stones to match the wizard's eyes, bringing true love together. Such different things."

"But all related to Adlin MacLomain," Colin said softly.

"Aye." Her turquoise eyes met his. "All related."

"What was Adlin truly like?"

A fixture around campfires Colin's entire life, tales of Adlin MacLomain had been vast and varied. All recanted with respect and of course, all with an air of mystery. Colin didn't kid himself when it came to the revered chieftain. He knew the clan's patriarch had ended up in the twenty-first century.

"'Tis why you went there to begin with. You wanted to meet him."

His Ma's observation caught him off guard. He nodded. "Aye, I did."

"But your path swayed when you sensed McKayla. You could have found a way to meet him but once you saw her you didnae want to risk it." She touched his side gently. "Because of this. Because she meant so much."

"Aye," he whispered.

"True love. 'Tis so good." Arianna's eyes glistened for a moment. "Worth it all, Adlin MacLomain would say."

"Would he?"

"Oh, aye!" She smiled. "Adlin was a believer in love. And he was a good man. The verra best." Arianna pulled back and took his hands. "He brought many great loves together including me and your Da's. Many would say it was the rings and the Irish gods and Lord knows that was part of it. But it took a verra meddlesome MacLomain wizard to make sure all the dots were connected."

"What of him as a leader though?"

"Och, son, look around you!" Arianna squeezed his hands. "He birthed this clan. Born of a Celtic king and a Druidess, he was immortal until he was no more. Those tales around the fires are true. All of them. Even those about the Defiances...*especially* the tales about those."

"All gone now," he said.

"As far as we know." The corner of her lip inched up slightly and a renewed sparkle lit her old eyes. "But mayhap not. Mayhap 'tis like your Da says and both the magi of the Defiances and rings culminated somehow in your mark. I cannae ken why or how but what if? It could mean something truly great."

The very idea that the burning mark determined to bar him from the future was a good thing seemed impossible. Then again, the only thing that seemed threatening about it was the possibility that it might keep him from McKayla. That would be devastating.

Arianna's wise eyes seemed to follow his every thought and a mother's concern soon overrode. "Enough with heavy thoughts this eve, my son." Her slender hands cupped his cheeks. "It will all fall into place. It always does. Now 'tis time to be merry for your clan and merry with your wife, aye?"

Colin could think of nothing better. Kissing her soundly on either cheek, he pulled his Ma close and said, "I do love you something fierce."

"Aye," she whispered. "And I you." Arianna nodded toward McKayla, eyes a little more determined. "Go on now. Quick like."

When Colin turned he understood the new urgency in his Ma's voice.

McKayla was standing with her back to the wall.

Nessa MacLeod, arms crossed over her chest, stood in front of her.

Chapter Ten

"Not sure I need to answer. I suspect you know exactly where I'm from."

Nessa looked McKayla over once more. "You've barely any breasts, pegs for legs and that hair. 'Tis unsightly to say the least. Obviously you are not from around here."

McKayla was becoming more and more irritated by the second. "My breasts are a decent B cup and my legs are long enough to get me around." She fingered her locks and shrugged. "As for the hair, it's a lot less maintenance. Not such a bad thing."

"B cup?" Nessa frowned. "What does that mean?" She stood up straighter, showing off her ample cleavage. "It doesnae matter. What does matter is—"

"Is what?" Colin appeared through the crowd so suddenly even McKayla didn't see him coming.

Loch Nessa, as McKayla had taken to calling her, cocked her head in Colin's direction. "What matters is that she's here, aye my laird?"

Summer heat prevailed and it was hard not to notice that he'd removed his tunic and tied back his hair. *Sweet Jesus.* Though his plaid was still wrapped over his shoulder, muscles rippled everywhere. Over his wide shoulders, down his arms, chiseled and well-defined right down his chest to his washboard abs. Mouth desert dry, McKayla tried to keep it from forming a wide 'o'.

"It does make quite a bit of difference," he conceded and wrapped his arm around McKayla's lower back, reeling her in closer. His fingers brushed just beneath her breast. "'Twas pleasant to see you, Nessa. Good eve."

Colin scooped McKayla up and headed toward the stairs. This time when he did, the whole room exploded with applause and cheers. The laird was officially carrying his bride off to bed. She didn't need to be from the medieval period to gather that much. Thankfully, he moved fast and in no time they were down the hall and traveling up the next set of stairs.

"Let's go outside for a bit," she suggested.

This time when they returned to the wall walk, Colin sat her on the ledge high above the ground below.

"Good thing I'm not afraid of heights," she commented, peering down. "It's a long drop."

Colin pushed her dress up so that he could stand between her legs and wrap his arms around her lower back. "I'm a shifter. I'd sprout wings and catch you if you fell."

It was hard to imagine him shifting into anything other than Trevor.

Still miffed, she pulled at the top of her dress.

With a tepid frown, he said, "Now I know you didnae let Nessa get to you."

McKayla peered down at her cleavage. "She's no more than a high school bully. I get that you left her at the altar. I'd be mad too. But did she have to attack my poor boobs?"

"There's nothing poor about your *boobs*, lass." A shit-eating grin crawled onto his face. "I mean *breasts*."

It was hard not to grin in return. "I said boobs. You can too."

"Now who's in high school?"

No doubt. Loch Nessa only dragged her down for a few minutes. Before that the night, however short lived, had been beyond wonderful. McKayla bit her lip and tried to ignore how masculine Colin looked as she fingered his tartan. "William and your Da are pretty amazing men. I learned a lot about them tonight. About Coira, Malcolm's mom. I still can't believe she was from the 1800's. The colonial period! And lived in my house. Just like your mom did. It's all so surreal." She shook her head. "All of it. The rings, the love, all remarkable stories."

Colin watched her, his eyes never leaving hers. "Aye, they are. I'm glad you think so as well."

"Of course I do. Why wouldn't I?"

"'Tis just a lot to take in all at once. How are you...really?"

That he cared meant so much. "I'm good." She paused and then said, "Better than I thought I'd be."

"You amaze me," he murmured, his large hands covering her thighs but not initiating anything further. It seemed worry prevailed over lust.

McKayla shook her head, sharply aware of her surroundings. The warm summer wind. The lap of waves in the distance. The echo of bagpipes off the castle walls. "I wish you would have swooped me back here the day we met." She leaned back, trusting that he'd hold her. "I wish we would've skipped all the years in between and went from the threat of a sandy laptop straight to this. That would've been perfect."

"Would it have?" His warm hands held her tighter. "But what of your novel? Words that will touch so many?"

She stared into the star flecked sky. "Somebody else would have written those words, eventually." McKayla closed her eyes and let the wind brush over her. "Besides, I've always believed that all great ideas exist in a constant stream of energy that runs over us all. Those who are meant to receive them, will. Another writer would have come up with the same idea and written it just as well."

Yanked forward but still held tight, McKayla had no choice but to look at Colin. "That is where you're wrong, lass. While I agree with your theory that ideas are out there in the universe for the taking, in fact I know it to be true, what you did with your novel could have only ever been done by you."

Writers always struggled with the idea that someone else could write their story better. But right now, looking into his sincere, concerned eyes, she had no desire to let him down. "And it will be a best seller."

"Aye, it will." His grasp shifted, allowing one hand to wander. "As will everything you write."

Now *this* was Trevor territory. A discussion she'd only ever had with him. Yet it wasn't him she wanted to talk with right now, because what he implied meant she'd be going home. An uncomfortable sensation rolled through her. *Fear.* "When I go home, will things be as they were…with Trevor I mean?"

Colin's eyes remained hidden in shadows, his answer vague. "Unlikely."

Before she could respond he shook his head and pulled her closer. "Nay, I promised you truth." Silence fell as he gathered his words. "My home is here now. I willnae be going back to the twenty-first century lass. 'Tis too risky."

It felt as though her limbs started to freeze over. "What do you mean?"

"This," he murmured, touching the circle tattoo. "Keeps me here. I cannae explain it save to say 'tis a good thing, something of my ancestors."

Now her limbs were all but frozen. She whispered, "This is all part of what I said on Skype. What Leslie heard. His is the circle that never connects. A means to let me in. If ever it closes, we are forever lost."

"So it seems," he said softly. "'Tis true. Somehow the Claddagh rings of the past symbolize the circle and the Defiances make up the time-travel aspect."

Eyes wide, she said, "Your Da and William told me about both. All of it." She shook her head. "Complicated, interesting, even I couldn't come up with…"

"With what?" he asked, hands on her thighs now. "Because what you wrote in your novel rivals all of it."

"Does it?" she asked. "I don't think so." But she wasn't beyond being curious. "Colin, why did my hero have your name? And why MacLeod as a last name, one that clearly correlates with your abandoned marriage to Nessa?"

McKayla expected him to hesitate, to try to make sense of things, but he didn't. "My guess is because your subconscious was trying to pull you closer to me. I've no other explanation."

"Isn't that a little too hard to believe?" she asked.

Now Colin looked to the sky, the mountains in the distance. "If there is one thing I've learned, lass, nothing is too hard to believe when it comes to my clan, or when it comes to the magic that is part of my verra upbringing."

Caught in his sudden melancholy she stared. Not at the majestic castle looming ever taller beyond his substantial height, but at his face. A face chiseled and formed by the choices he'd made. While she knew him to be in his twenties, his face was already that of an early thirty-something. A face pre-mapped by harsh decisions and regrets. He was about to enter his prime but if Colin wasn't careful, he'd be middle aged by tomorrow.

And yes she heard him say he wouldn't be returning to her century but for now she chose not to believe it. If things were really as magical as he said they were, there stood a very good chance he was wrong.

Speaking of magic.

With everything going on she'd pushed what Caitlin told her to the back of her mind. Yet it was time she understood more, no matter how much it frightened her. "Caitlin said I was a witch. That all of us are." She cleared her throat, afraid to ask. "What exactly does that mean?"

"I wondered how long it would take you to ask." Both his tone and expression were compassionate. "'Tis nothing you should fear. It willnae hurt you." He tapped her forehead above and between her eyes. "It resides here." Then he touched her abdomen. "And here. Yours, while not overly powerful yet, is rare."

"How so? And what do you mean *yet*?" she whispered.

"It seems you may have the power to not only take away pain but mayhap heal. As to *yet*, I suspect your power will grow, especially now that you're here."

"The ability to heal," she murmured. "That doesn't seem so bad. A little unnerving, maybe."

"Nothing for you to worry overmuch about," he assured. "You will need to be schooled in your gift so that you learn to better control it."

She thought of the circle tattoo. "So that's why your pain faded when I touched the circle."

Colin nodded. "Verra likely."

She leaned her head against his chest. This was, as he said, a lot to take on. However, she felt more ready to handle everything now than she had been before. She could do this, *had* to do this. But for now, she wanted to step away from all of it for a little while. Whether legal or not, this was her wedding night and she wanted to enjoy it. Theirs was a story she had no doubt would unravel soon enough.

159

It seemed he was of a like mind because he murmured against her ear, "I've had refreshments brought up to our chamber. What say we go enjoy them?"

She nodded and started to pull away. But Colin, as usual, was having none of it. Before she knew it he'd once more scooped her up, determined it seemed that she not walk tonight. But McKayla wasn't about to complain. Nope. The truth was being carried around by this strapping highlander was starting to become her preferred method of travel.

Not surprisingly, their chamber was a welcome romantic oasis. Fresh cut flowers were scattered about and the skins over the windows pulled back, allowing a warm summer breeze to blow through the room. A few wall torches flickered, just enough to cast a low, seductive glow over the mammoth bed she so admired. When he lowered her, it was not to the bed's all-too-tempting surface. Instead her feet met the floor. He spun her around and started unfastening the dress.

McKayla held onto the bedpost that'd supported her earlier. Save this time, Colin hadn't left the room. No, this time his nimble fingers were working ever so efficiently. Then again, so were his lips. One gentle kiss at a time he made his way down the side of her neck. It was impossible not to shiver with awareness when he pushed the dress down over her shoulders.

When he lowered his body along with the dress, she grasped the post tighter. Eyes closed, McKayla focused on every subliminal touch, every manipulative caress of the man kneeling behind her. One hand tenderly rode up her now exposed hip bone, tracing the curves of her pelvis then stomach, while the other hand worked the material down her legs.

She groaned when he flicked his tongue, trailing down her spine and gasped when he nipped the upper right hand side of her behind. Biting her lower lip, she began to melt when his hand abandoned the dress and rode up her inner thigh. The touch was powerful and effective if for no other reason than that it was done ever so lightly, as if a feather brushed against her.

With an almost desperate grasp on the post she leaned back slightly when his agile, talented fingers dusted her clitoris. To turn into his touch became impossible when he stood; locking her into position, one hand still manipulating below while his other hand caressed first one breast then the other. Again his lips met her neck, hot breath fanning her sensitive skin.

Moaning, ready, she pushed back against him.

Aware of the hitch in his breathing and his burning chest against her back, she ground against his thick erection. Both aroused and frustrated by the material between them, she almost sighed with relief when he tore away his plaid.

Astonished, McKayla yelped when she was spun and tossed across the bed, landing square on her back. Yes she was small but he'd handled her as though she weighed nothing. There was no time to scramble into what she hoped would be a more enticing position before he spread her legs and came over her. Like earlier, he had that same wild look in his eyes. Desire, yearning, desperation.

McKayla's eyes rounded as his nude form rose over hers. Outside in the storm it'd been too dark to see everything. Now by firelight every glorious well-defined muscle was visible, most especially the muscle that mattered most. *Dear Lord!* There was little time to admire him before his lips came down on hers. Now when they kissed it was needy, ravenous, synchronized. She pressed her hands against his chest and felt the hard contours before curving her fingers over his broad shoulders.

"You've no idea how long I've dreamt of this," he murmured against her lips. "To have you here in my chamber, in my bed."

A response trailed away on a gasp when he spread her legs further and pushed forward. The ache from taking him earlier bit back for but a second before pleasure washed over her. A long groan lodged in her throat when he wrapped one arm beneath her back and pulled her up, seating her even deeper. Somehow with one of his master maneuvers he managed to kneel back. Now she straddled him, her legs wrapped around his torso.

This gave him all the control.

Which it seemed this Scotsman liked when it came to intimacy.

Head titled back, she wrapped her arms around his neck when he cupped her backside and began to thrust. Deep, full, she was consumed by the rolling sensations and building pressure between her thighs. Her heart started to hammer then catch as if even it was losing ground to the power he had over her.

In and out, over and over, he brought her ever closer until her body started to let go. All the little muscles that made up her abdomen started to spasm. Holding on became impossible. But she didn't need to because he wrapped his arms around her and thrust one last time, his shudders matching hers, their bodies trembling endlessly.

Later, after their bodies had relaxed and she lay by his side with one arm and one leg draped over him, Colin said softly, "We're taking lots of chances with you not on birth control."

"I know," she murmured. Of course he knew she'd stopped taking the pill. She told him everything. But what had been the point when she wasn't sexually active? "And it should alarm me. Yet it doesn't."

His eyes met hers, emotion thickening his brogue. "Are ye wanting a wee bairn then, lass?"

A warm smile curling her lips, McKayla bent her elbow and propped up her head. "Honestly, I hadn't given it much thought until now." Their gazes held while she considered something she should have before sleeping with him. "And it was irresponsible not to." She frowned. "How could I...we, if I'm not here and you're not there."

He stroked her hair, eyes guarded. "Will you be wanting to go back, McKayla?"

How could it be any other way? The idea of never going home frightened her. But then, as she continued to stare into his eyes, the idea of leaving him scared her even more. "Oh God," she whispered.

Did she actually think that she'd love him any less in this form? Better yet, had she actually ever fallen out of love with Trevor to begin with? No, it was clear in the tightness of her chest when she looked at him, thought of him, that she loved this man

162

with all her heart. More so, perhaps, because she now knew all he'd kept from her.

Saddened, but inherently eager to appease, Colin said, "'Twill all work out as it should, as it was meant to be. Dinnae fear."

Suddenly, that's all she could do. "I can't stay here," she blurted. "I don't belong. And I've got a book coming out," she added as an afterthought.

Colin nodded. "Aye, you do. But remember, though the day may already be here that I cannae travel through time, it should always be an option for you."

"Should it?" She shook her head. "Somehow I can't see that. Not without you."

"There are others who would travel with you. Ferchar often travels back from your time. You wouldn't have to be alone."

"How easily you assume this will all work out with Keir Hamilton. Have you forgotten you've got an evil time-travel gatekeeper blocking everything right now?" She sighed. "Yes, I know about Keir. William shared. When were you planning on telling me?"

"I wanted to give you one eve free from more concerns. Keir is but a bump in the road," he replied and winked, sounding like his twenty-first century self. "We MacLomains are not held back long."

"So you say."

"So I know," he assured, tucking a bit of hair behind her ear. "Do you remember the first time I did this? Tucked your hair behind your ear?"

She smiled, resting her chin on his chest. "Hurricane Sandy. In the basement. Our last time together as a couple. Or should I say a slip up long after we'd split."

His eyes grew distant as he rubbed a strand of her hair between his fingers. "It'd been longer then, windblown. I knew if I touched it...if I touched you, I wouldn't be able to stop. So bloody beautiful."

"You always made me feel that way." She traced a small pattern on his chest. "Beautiful. Other men don't do that. Not like you."

"'Tis a shame because you are."

"Not like my cousins. Despite what you might think I'm pretty average in the looks department."

A hint of amusement glinted in his eyes. "Now you're just fishing for compliments."

"Am not!" she said. "I'm too pixie-like. And these legs." She shifted just enough to brush what was fast becoming his renewed arousal. "Like stubs so says Loch Nessa."

He chuckled. "Like the monster? Clever." He grabbed her beneath the knees and rolled her beneath him. "And these legs...are they not long enough to wrap around me? Because as far as I'm concerned, that's the only requirement necessary."

He held her leg up in the air, looking it over. "As to the pixie aspect, I dinnae ken. Aye, you're a wee thing but it suits me well. "Tiny." He thrust forward and she cried out. "Tight." With a jerk of his hips, he had her against the headboard. "And all mine."

She gasped sharply.

Eyes closed, he groaned deeply.

Ravenous, eager, their desire for one another consumed. Time fell away and McKayla was unable to do anything but feel...*want*. Their yearning and need was so great, so thorough. No words existed to describe the carnal sphere they entered. It wasn't merely love but worship and something else, something that made one's eyes water, heart flip, teeth clench, and jaw drop.

It was beyond bliss.

"Gods, I love you," he whispered sharply when he pressed forward.

"Colin!" she cried when he brought her to another excruciatingly perfect orgasm.

Hours later, so spent she could barely move, McKayla stared at him while he slept. Lord, he was beautiful. And though she'd dozed on and off, the things they'd talked about weighed on her mind. Mostly how it seemed as if a very large part of her wanted to stay. Or so it seemed based on the amount of unprotected sex she'd been having. Even *after* discussing it!

Unlike Leslie, she'd always loved children. The idea of having them with Colin literally made her heart hurt. And would it be so bad raising them here, protected by a clan who would love them. True, the medicine in this time wasn't nearly what it should be, but what if she had the ability to heal, wouldn't that be something?

McKayla cuddled closer to him, more content than she'd been in a long time. Eyes drifting shut, she first thought the distant singing was merely the wind. Soon though, the sound found more clarity and she sat up. Drawn to the eerie tune she slipped into a dress and stepped into the hallway.

The castle was quiet. Only a few torches burned low leaving most of the long hall to shadows. She traveled to the end of the hallway then up a set of curved stairs. Yet the singing grew no louder. Still, she knew where to go. As she climbed she realized it was leading her up into one of the towers.

There was a lone room at the top and as she approached the doorway the singing stopped. Afraid to breathe, she put her back to the wall and sidled close enough that she could peer in unseen from the doorway.

A frail girl sat on a bench in the middle of the room rocking back and forth.

It was impossible to make out anything save her small frame and long streaming hair. Was she crying? When she inched forward the girl stopped rocking and her body went completely still.

"Are you all right?" McKayla asked.

Drizzle turned into a driving rain and pulled her attention to the window. Flat on the bottom and rounded on the top, she swore for a split second an old man stood there, his long white robes and hair blowing in the wind. But it must've been the mist from the rain because when she blinked there was nothing there.

Face still veiled by thick hair, the girl once more started to rock.

Concerned, McKayla took a step forward then froze when a fire flared to life on a hearth against the far wall. Trembling, the girl started to rock more adamantly. White knuckled, her slender hands grasped the bench and she began to moan.

Determined to go to her, McKayla took another step into the room.

This time the fire roared, angry, spitting sparks so high they sizzled across the ceiling. Petrified, she screamed, "Come, take my hand! We need to get out of here!"

But the girl didn't listen. And no matter how scared, McKayla refused to leave her behind. Unwavering, she took another step then another.

Now the girl was shaking her head, back and forth, back and forth.

The fire curled over the ceiling and heated her face.

"Now!" McKayla yelled. "Come on!"

Still no acknowledgement from the girl.

This was crazy! What was wrong with her?

"McKayla. You owe me a debt."

Ice water trickled through her veins when the voice rumbled out from the fire. A raspy, broken sound made up of crackling flames.

The girl froze. Her head turned in the direction of the fire.

McKayla shook her head and stared wide-eyed as the flames ever so slowly crawled over both the ceiling and floor toward her. Entranced, lulled, she heard the voice change, became more masculine. "Dinnae you know who I am?"

Again she shook her head, eager to understand, compelled to drift closer.

A face formed, once made of flame and eyes so dark they seemed to cut right through her. "'Tis me, lass. It has always been me. Colin MacLeod."

Confused yet caught up in whatever spell he weaved, McKayla reached out her hand. On cue, he did as well, one of fiery hotness.

A roar rose up so loud and screeching it rumbled the floor. Stumbling back, she looked at the girl...but not a girl at all. What came at her was ferocious, fierce and impossible to look away from. Terrified, McKayla screamed at the top of her lungs.

Eyes squeezed shut she screamed again and again.

Even after she fell to the floor and was scooped up by Colin, *her* Colin, she screamed.

"Nay, lass." He sat and pulled her head to his chest. "You are well. 'Twas just a nightmare."

The screams turned to gasps and she blinked against the harsh but dull light coming in through their chamber windows.

"What the bloody hell?" came a voice from the doorway. Bradon, sword in hand, stood both groggy yet alert. Right behind him were Malcolm and Ilisa, daggers in hand.

Ilisa sidled past the men and stood, legs splayed, sharp eyes scanning their chambers. "What happened?"

Still shaking uncontrollably, McKayla struggled to take a deep breath, more than mortified they were here to witness this.

Colin ran his hands over her back and arms, trying to comfort her. "Just a nightmare."

Malcolm frowned. "Och."

That's all it took for her to pull herself away from the stark terror she'd felt moments before. Though wobbly, she pulled back from Colin but didn't dare stand. Not quite yet. "It was more than that. *Had* to be." When she looked at the others she wasn't surprised to find Malcolm scowling, Bradon compassionate and Ilisa dubious but relenting.

"There was a girl in the tower," McKayla started to explain. "She had long, dark hair, very slender."

This got their attention.

So she stood, grateful for Colin's steadying hand. McKayla grasped the material of the dress, more sure by the moment it had been no nightmare. "I put this dress on then walked up there when I heard singing. It was the girl. Possibly an old man in white robes. But most importantly there was a face in the fire."

Bradon's eyes grew very curious, though his expression was guarded. "A girl in a tower?"

"Yes, here, just down the hall."

She didn't miss the look Bradon and Colin exchanged.

Even Ilisa now wore a pensive frown.

"What scared you so?" Colin asked. "Was it the face in the fire?"

"No." She shook her head, unable to look him in the eyes. Petrified by how drawn she'd been to the otherworldly visage. "Though that in itself was strange."

"How so?" Malcolm asked, his eyes flickering to Loch Nessa, who drifted up beside him.

"It...*he* seemed to know me." She wrapped her arms around her midsection. "Stranger than that, he called himself by the name of the hero I wrote about." Her wary eyes met Colin's. "Colin MacLeod."

"'Tis impossible," Loch Nessa gasped.

Everyone looked her way. Malcolm took her hand, concerned. "What?"

Loch Nessa pulled her hand away and crossed her arms over her chest. "'Twas nothing."

"'Twas clearly something," Ilisa bit back.

McKayla was surprised at the animosity between the two. Loch Nessa, chin notched up a fraction repeated, "'Twas nothing."

But a shiver raked over the picturesque woman. One not unnoticed by Colin. "Out with it, lass. If there's yet another threat, we need to know about it."

Not bothering to look at Colin but at Malcolm instead, she sighed when he nodded.

"Fine then." She looked toward the window, out at the dismal sky. "I have an older brother. He's in line to take the position of chieftain when 'tis time. Or at least he was." Her dark gaze then settled on Colin. "But like you, he abandoned his clan years ago. As you all might have guessed, his name is Colin MacLeod."

Chapter Eleven

Less than an hour later, all but Malcolm and Nessa sat down in the great hall. The celebrations had lasted far into the wee hours, so very few were meandering about and those that were didn't seem at their best. As he stood before the fire, hands clasped behind his back, Colin stared up at the faces in the mantle and tried to assimilate all he'd learned.

The most daunting by far was that a Colin MacLeod really *did* exist.

Then there was McKayla's exchange with his sister, Torra.

If all that was not enough, what his wife said Torra changed into kept him frowning.

"You never told her we had a sister?" Bradon asked quietly so that McKayla and Ilisa, would not overhear.

"Nay, I'd not had the chance."

"You've had nothing but chances," Bradon said. "But for some reason you kept her a secret."

Colin frowned. "McKayla had enough to deal with."

"Or *you* had enough to deal with."

"Or I had enough to deal with," he conceded with a sigh. "What do you make of all this?"

"Many things. Some good. Some bad."

They received goblets of mead from a passing servant, and Colin took a long swallow before he said, "Nothing good can come of a Colin MacLeod existing. Especially since Mckayla wrote about him. I think 'tis good that Torra allowed McKayla to get near her. But what do you make of what she said our sister became?"

Colin watched his brother's face closely and saw what he expected, secrets.

"I think she saw our sister as a beast only because she was pinned beneath a spell, one of MacLeod's making. As to there being another Colin out there, 'tis something worth paying attention to. I dinnae like how he parallels your circumstances,"

169

Bradon said. "What are the odds that both you and he would abandon your clan? And both of you tied together through marriage?"

"'Tis a strange coincidence and I dinnae believe much in those," Colin said. "I did notice one strange thing though and I've not the heart to tell McKayla how becoming I find it."

Bradon's unwavering eyes met his. "Aye?"

"Aye, did you not notice?"

Guileless, Bradon shrugged. "She's as bonnie as ever, brother. *That* I noticed."

Colin sipped his mead, amused and ever more curious. "The white streak in her hair was not there hours ago. 'Twas not there until she awoke on my floor screaming."

Bradon, much of his old charm and mischief surfacing, grinned. "Must have been a bloody good night of rollicking."

"Better than ever," he acknowledged easily. "But that's not my point and well you know it."

"Do I?" Bradon shrugged. "A lass can age quickly when met with enough stress."

Colin eyed his hair. "As you so obviously did."

A look of relief was evident on Bradon's face when Ilisa and McKayla joined them.

With a tepid glance upward, Ilisa said, "Nessa knows more about all this than she's saying." She put a hand over her chest and issued a mock gasp. "I have a brother named Colin MacLeod and it's just occurred to me to mention him!"

Bradon chuckled. Colin and McKayla did not.

"I never did ken what Malcolm saw in her," Ilisa said.

"Something he saw the moment she arrived," Bradon reminded.

Colin frowned. What was he talking about?

"What, you didnae know?" Ilisa asked, her eyes cutting.

"Nay, it seems not," Bradon said.

Apparently even McKayla would not let this topic rest. "What am I missing?"

Colin looked at his brother. "Pray tell?"

Bradon's brows lowered. "You didnae know Malcolm loved Nessa the minute he laid eyes on her?" Now he frowned, but the expression bespoke deviousness. "Even I could see it and God knows I dinnae often notice such things."

The very idea that his cousin loved his betrothed upon first sight nearly made him laugh. Were they serious? "Impossible."

Ilisa shook her head. "Just like a lad not to see what was right in front of him."

McKayla looked at Colin. "He does seem pretty into her. Any chance you missed that?"

Her question made him feel stupid. Besides, how could Malcolm possibly have felt that way after everything he'd told him? "I dinnae miss much so I'd have to say no. Nessa is contriving. Could she have reeled Malcolm in without him ever having seen it coming? Aye."

"Reeled him in?" Ilisa guffawed. "Nay. She didnae have to try in the least with our lad. She had him long before you even left. Not physically but certainly mentally. Are you so daft that you truly didnae see it?"

"Clearly." Bradon's eyes narrowed on his brother. "But those were troubling times for you, were they not?"

"I left her at the altar and abandoned my clan," he replied dryly. "So, aye, they were *clearly* troubling times."

"Well, she recovered soon enough after you left and everyone is with who they want to be with," Ilisa said. "So why dinnae we skip the old news and get to what really weighs on my mind."

"Because what weighs on your mind matters most," Bradon offered.

"Exactly." Ilisa looked at Colin. "What will the clan's next move be?"

"Oh no," McKayla said softly. "While that might certainly weigh on your mind it's not what's weighing on mine."

Colin wasn't sure he wanted to continue with either conversation.

"You have a sister. When did you plan on telling me that?"

Even as he cleared his throat she shook her head and continued. "I want to meet her. Please."

171

"Oh, nay," Bradon said. "'Tis impossible. Torra will see none of us. Not since Colin left."

"Why not?" She looked at them all. "Something's wrong, isn't it. Has to be. Aren't any of you worried about her especially after what happened to me last night?"

"As Bradon said, she willnae let us see her," Ilisa said. "But aye, we will always worry about her."

"What if she's up there fried by fire as seemed the case?" McKayla crossed her arms over her chest. "I think you're all nuts for not running up there right now." Wide eyed, she looked at Colin. "For not running up there the minute I told you!"

"We dinnae disrespect her," Bradon said, sterner than he'd ever heard him.

"Disrespect her?" Unconvinced, McKayla looked at Ilisa. "Really? And you agree with this?"

Ilisa's lashes might've issued an uncharacteristic flutter but her direct brown eyes and the unyielding reserve in them didn't. "You dinnae ken the way of the MacLomains. We dinnae question the actions of our kin. We trust them." Her eyes went to Colin then back to McKayla. "That should be clear by now."

While he would have been surprised by her actions a scant forty-eight hours earlier, Colin wasn't now. His wife spun on her heels and proceeded to walk up the stairs. He swigged down the last of his drink and watched her go.

"Where's she going?" Ilisa asked. "Off to have a temper tantrum?"

Colin shook his head and opted for a mug of ale. "Nay, she's off to find Torra."

Just as he suspected, Ilisa and Bradon went wide eyed then scrambled after her. Good. If he couldn't learn from their words, he fully intended to learn from their actions. He followed them up the stairs. McKayla had barely made it down the first hallway before they caught up.

Bradon on one side, Ilisa on the other, they tried to stop her first with words.

"'Tis never good to disturb her," Bradon said.

"She is ill, lass. For some time now," Ilisa added.

McKayla shook her head and plowed on, head held high. "She's afraid and alone." She glanced at them both. "And way too overprotected."

Though both might've slowed a bit in response neither let up when she reached the stairs leading to Torra's chamber. Bradon barred her progress with an arm against the wall, a solid gate keeping her from going up. "I willnae allow it."

"Nor I," Ilisa agreed, leaning against the wall on the opposite side. "You dinnae have the right."

"Yes I do," McKayla said firmly, looking between them. "Am I not a MacLomain now?"

Colin leaned against the wall, crossed his arms over his chest and watched.

"'Tis not as simple as that," Bradon argued.

"He has the right of it," Ilisa assured. "'Tis complicated really."

"Apparently nothing about this is simple," McKayla said, then slipped beneath Bradon's arm and ran up the stairs.

They stumbled like fools after her, nearly tripping over one another.

McKayla arrived seconds before them. The door gave no resistance when she raced into the room. Everyone froze.

"She's not here," Bradon said. "Where is she?"

The worry in his voice did not go unnoticed.

"Fools."

They turned to find Arianna on the landing below. Hands on her hips, his mother looked at them, expression damning. Eyes narrowed and voice barely tolerant, she said, "These walls have ears. Did you think for a moment I would let my daughter be subjected to any of you?"

Colin couldn't help himself. "But I thought she would see no one."

"Then you thought wrong," Arianna spat. "We gave her no choice. With the four of you behaving such as you are, we had no option but to protect her." His mother huffed as she walked away, voice trailing down the hall. "From her own kin no less!"

There was no point chasing down his Ma when she was in a foul mood. But what had they done wrong? There had to be more to the story. What was really happening with his sister? That was a mystery he intended to solve. But first he'd have to deal with Mckayla. Colin stepped aside when Bradon and Ilisa passed, apparently off to brood.

But when McKayla tried to pass, he blocked her path.

Wide, gray eyes stared at him. "Don't think for one second that I'm happy with you."

"I won't." he replied, not put off in the least.

"You deceived me yet again."

"Aye but 'twas not with ill intention. My sister has always been different and I've always protected her. Am I sorry I didnae tell you about her? Aye. But not so much that I'll grovel now. There was no way to know she would reach out to you as she did."

"No, I suppose not," she said, a bit too compliant as her eyes held his. "You let me down again, Colin. I knew you had secrets and I know you still have more." McKayla stood up straighter. "I guess I just keep hoping that you'll share them with me." She shook her head. "Isn't that the whole point? To close the gap between us?"

When she pushed forward he let her go.

There was nothing easy about letting this era unravel for her. Right down to his ill sister. While he tried to break her in slowly it seemed everything was determined to do otherwise. He'd no sooner slumped down on the stairs, head in hands, when the last person he wanted to talk to seemed to come out of nowhere.

"Where is she then?"

Not bothering to look up at Malcolm, he said, "Wherever Ma put her."

"Does Arianna know about Colin MacLeod?" Malcolm asked.

Not really wanting to have this conversation but aware he didn't have a choice because Malcolm wasn't budging, Colin raised his head. "Better yet, did you?"

His cousin's steely eyes looked down. "It doesnae matter whether I did or not. All of this is on you, Colin."

"Mayhap some but not all." He shook his head and turned the conversation to what he felt mattered most. "Did you love Nessa right from the start?"

Taken aback, his cousin's gaze went from the hallway back to him. "Would it have mattered? You had so many opinions. All was figured out in your eyes."

Baffled, Colin said, "I told you what I knew of her. How was I to know you felt so strongly?"

Malcolm peered down as though he'd been waiting a millennium to do so and replied, "It never surprised me that you didnae see my desire for her. So caught up were you with the need for freedom from all this." He made a gesture that while small encompassed the castle. "We were not good enough for you. *She* was not good enough. I'd loved her always and you saw her as nothing. All of us as nothing."

Colin was quick to reply but his cousin was quicker.

With a sharp shake of his head, Malcolm said, "This clan, our kin, might be quick to forgive you but never think for a moment I will. You are harmful to those you love. If even now they have not figured it out then may the gods watch over them evermore." He paused, as if to gather his thoughts. "No matter this revelation about Colin MacLeod, I will stand by Nessa. Dinnae think I willnae."

Before Colin could reply Malcolm was gone.

He closed his eyes and lowered his head. Never once had he realized that Malcolm desired Nessa. What had it been like for him to see them together that summer? Because though not yet married they'd been amorous and open with their affection.

Until the night he realized what she was.

Or better yet what she wasn't.

Faithful, amongst other things.

While she might not have held his heart, she'd certainly held his attention. In truth, he didn't find fault with her for taking another to bed. It had been around the time he'd met McKayla. Colin suspected Nessa sensed another woman had captured his interest. Because, as it turned out, the lass had a way with black magic. Not just dark magic but one step further…a form of magi that went far deeper and was exceedingly dangerous. He'd shared all of this with Malcolm, from the dark spells she weaved, to her taking a lover while they were betrothed.

Malcolm had been equally disturbed by the information. Or so he thought.

Restless and intent on leaving, Colin never imagined Malcolm would pursue Nessa. Not after he'd told him who she *really* was. He'd been so sure William would have had her packed up and shipped home.

But his cousin had fallen in love. And no one knew better than he did how love could make you do crazy things.

It made him sick to think of how easy it was for Nessa to turn from one MacLomain to another. Did she truly love Malcolm? He could only pray that if she didn't, it wouldn't destroy him. For that would only add to his regrets.

With a heavy sigh, Colin walked up the stairs and into his sister's chamber. Hands braced against the eave of the window he stared out over the trees and thought not of Malcolm and Nessa but of his sister. He still remembered standing outside this very room the night she arrived. Never had a child come into the world so silently.

It seemed almost a sign of what was to come.

But Torra had not always been silent. There was a time…

"There, Col!" A peel of laughter rippled across the room. Colin turned and watched through the eyes of time as Torra ran across the room into his waiting arms. He scooped up his three year old sister and kissed the bridge of her nose. Though only ten winters, he was tall and strong, so he sat her on the window sill with ease.

"And what are you up to today, my wee bonnie lass?" he asked.

With huge sage green eyes, she tossed her black hair and said, "Building castle *all* mine."

"Oh, aye?" With a chuckle he asked, "And how many rooms will it have?"

Torra held up one finger and smiled.

"Just one then?"

She nodded, quite sure of herself.

"But where will everybody sleep?"

"Just me." Then she seemed to consider that and held up two fingers. "And room for you."

"Well what about Ma, Da and Bradon?"

After giving this a moment of thought she issued a grin that reminded him of Iain, crooked and mischievous. "Stables."

Colin laughed, shook his head and kissed her cheek. "Well, I'm glad I get to sleep inside your castle."

Her little arms came around his neck and she held on tight. Sad, he once more turned and looked out the window. That little girl was long gone and the connection they'd shared lost...or so it seemed. Even after she turned twelve-winters and had changed, forever locked inside her own mind, she still allowed him to visit. But though they sat for hours, silence reigned. The young, bright happy girl she'd been had vanished. In her place someone who almost seemed an oracle.

How else could they explain her uncanny foresight?

"This room was the only part of that summer that I didnae especially like."

Nessa MacLeod.

Colin gritted his teeth. "Naturally, 'twas not about you."

"Aye, true 'twas the only place that was *not* about me."

He shook his head. "There was no love betwixt us, Nessa." Colin turned and frowned. "But for what it's worth I am sorry that I left as I did. Despite your indiscretions, no lass deserves such."

Though he knew she *did* deserve it, Colin was determined to make things right with everyone he'd wronged. Even her.

Nessa leaned against the doorway. "You dinnae mean a word you say, Colin MacLomain. You didnae then and you dinnae now."

He made to speak but she continued. "You know as well as I that love blossomed." Her tone grew bitter. "Until you met *her*. What else was I to do when I found out about it?"

"How did you know about her, Nessa?"

"I could *smell* her on you," Nessa hissed. "How did I know? My magi of course…and your actions. One day you'd have me in your bed, the next no more."

"You were not without company to keep you warm," he replied caustically. "Ours was never a love match, even you knew that."

"I didnae!" she replied harshly. Upset that she'd reacted so strongly, she inhaled deeply. "I loved you verra much. 'Twas my magi that turned you away. I knew it then." Her eyes, almost desperate for a second, met his. "And I know it now. We dinnae have a choice about the gift that is ours. You know that better than anyone. "

"Nay, but we always have a choice about how we use it," he ground out. "And you didnae use it for good then, and I suspect you haven't used it for good since. Tell me then, if we had such a great love what heartache did you suffer when turning your attentions to Malcolm?" He crossed his arms over his chest. "It must have been a terrible feat indeed."

Nessa stood up straighter. "Malcolm has been good to me. I would never hurt him."

"Do you love him?"

"Enough so."

Colin's stomach soured. He didn't have to ask to know she'd already been unfaithful to his cousin. She knew nothing of love. Malcolm deserved better. Nessa took what she needed from whomever she needed it. Why hadn't Malcolm listened to him? Was love truly that blind?

Whether or not he'd wanted to, Colin said he was sorry. That was all she would get from him. More than done with the conversation he made his way toward the door. Nessa, of course, didn't budge an inch.

"Think what you will of me," she whispered. "But I was not the first to betray." Her eyes roamed over him. "'Twas you all along."

Physically no, but mentally yes. In truth, he'd not lain with McKayla until after Nessa had been unfaithful. But he'd already given away his heart. So aye, he had betrayed Nessa first. But

178

regardless, none of it mattered now. She was married to another MacLomain.

"Colin."

Nessa rolled her eyes and glanced over her shoulder. "Your new wife doesnae like me being alone with you, my laird." She smirked. "Does she not know I am married?"

"You might be married, but you don't act like it," McKayla said, halfway up the stairs. "It's clear enough that you've angled yourself so Colin will have to touch you to exit the room. And then there's the passion in your voice when you speak to him."

A trickle of laughter escaped Nessa's lips but fizzled away when Malcolm appeared at the bottom of the stairs. His eyes went from Colin to her. "Come, lass. Something is happening."

Colin stemmed out his magic and muttered, "Bloody hell!"

"To say the least," Malcolm replied, his tone dry.

"What?" McKayla asked Colin after Nessa and Malcolm left.

He shook his head. "Ferchar has come."

Startled, she looked down the stairs then at him. "How do you know?" She frowned. "Never mind. Magic right?"

Colin nodded and took her hand. "There's more."

"Okay," she said slowly as he pulled her down the stairs. "Care to share."

They stopped at the railing overlooking the great hall. "He didnae come alone."

Chapter Twelve

"Oh my God!" McKayla waved her arms and yelled. Was this an illusion? A trick to lull her into a false sense of security? Because right now, she couldn't believe her eyes. And only God knew how bad she wanted this to be real. With them here, she knew everything would be all right. Because together, there was nothing they couldn't handle.

"Seth, Sheila, Leslie, up here!"

Nearly tripping on her dress, she held up the obtrusive material and flew down the stairs. They all seemed stunned but were waiting for her at the bottom of the stairs. McKayla flew into Seth's arms.

"Do you have any idea how worried I've been?" Seth asked.

She nodded and squeezed him tight before pulling her cousins in for a group hug. They held onto one another for a long time, afraid if they let go they might slip back through time leaving someone behind.

"I can't believe you're here," McKayla gushed.

"Neither can we," Sheila replied, wide-eyed as she looked around. "It's still kind of hard to believe."

"It might be for a bit," McKayla said. "But it's okay. Everyone is really nice."

"So it seems." Leslie frowned, her sharp eyes taking in everything from the medieval men, many of whom were already staring back with appreciation, to the castle itself. "Where exactly are we again?"

"Ferchar's old castle," Seth said, eyes bright, not a shred of fear in his excited regard. "Thirteenth century Scotland!"

"Though I'm totally thrilled, *why* are you here?" McKayla asked, unsettled.

Her concern didn't lessen any when she realized the hall was being cleared out save immediate family. She didn't have to turn to know Colin stood behind her. Seth's narrowed gaze gave it away.

Seth stared down Colin. "I'd like to know the answer to that myself, Colin. Why are we here?"

"We'll soon find out," Colin said, promptly kissing the back of Sheila's then Leslie's hands. Both stared as he urged them to follow.

Sheila pulled McKayla close and whispered, "Wow, sweetie! He looked great back home but something about this place seriously agrees with him." Her eyes lowered. "And check out your dress. *Love* it!"

If only she'd seen her dress last night. But that conversation was better left for later.

McKayla had to hand it to her cousins. They seemed to be taking all of this in stride.

But like her, what choice did they have?

Though she felt so much better with all of them here, McKayla couldn't help but be worried. If Ferchar brought them to medieval Scotland he had a very good reason for doing so. What had happened? Were they in danger? Without doubt. Nervous, she watched as Colin stood with Ferchar, Iain, and William in front of a fireless hearth. The air became so oppressive even the low flames had been doused.

The younger men and Ilisa sat at a trestle table.

Colin urged all to join them.

When he sat at the head of the table she naturally assumed the men would sit alongside him, but that wasn't the case. "Come, lass, next to me."

So McKayla's family ended up on one side of the table and Colin's family on the other with Ferchar sitting at the opposite end. Tensions were impossibly thick as Seth sat to her immediate right flanked by his cousins. The only one who appeared at ease was Bradon, his interested gaze sliding over Sheila and Leslie. Sheila looked right back and smiled. Leslie, however, was less than impressed as her critical gaze traveled over each and every one of the MacLomains.

"What has happened affects us all," Ferchar began.

Seth being Seth didn't hesitate to ask, "What exactly *did* happen? Typically I like to be asked first before being yanked through time."

When Bradon arched a brow at Colin, no doubt wondering about Seth's forward behavior, her husband simply shook his head.

Seth *had* to be the last person he wanted to see here.

Well, he'd just have to get over it.

Ferchar's response was directed at Colin. "A magical wall has formed. One so strong I've never seen the likes of it. I had but two choices. Keep them there or bring them here. Gods know Caitlin can protect our son." His less than impressed eyes grazed over the others. "These three however will better serve here and will be far safer."

"Better serve?" Leslie said. "Who precisely are we serving? Because I don't recall being asked."

"No," Sheila agreed, her eyes swinging to Leslie. "But you could focus on the scarier thing he said…we're safer here."

"Was it Keir Hamilton then?" Colin asked.

"Aye, 'twas the name given."

Colin exchanged a look with Iain and William.

William had already filled Ferchar in on what was happening. "His interest lies with McKayla and those she surrounds herself with. They are future MacLomains and ending them is a fervent goal."

"Excuse me but I am no MacLomain," Leslie informed.

"Not yet," Iain said.

"Pardon?"

"What he means is that if you're here then you'll someday be one, lass," Bradon informed, a twinkle in his eye.

Leslie squashed that twinkle with a few select words. "Over my dead body."

Bradon cocked a brow.

"I've been dead, it's not fun," Seth muttered. But McKayla could tell he was enjoying all of it.

Leslie only frowned.

"But why is Seth here?" McKayla asked. "I can assure you he'll never be a MacLomain."

182

"Can you?" Ferchar asked. "Did Seth never tell you about his encounters with Adlin MacLomain? Did he not tell you that he descends from the Broun lineage?"

Both Colin and Iain looked at him. Waiting.

Iain, eyes narrowed, looked closer and whispered, "You're of Calum's kin."

"Who's Calum?" McKayla asked.

"Arianna's cousin." Iain looked at Ilisa. "He's your uncle's distant offspring."

Ilisa and Seth looked at one another, surprised. She spoke first. "Bloody hell, we're a good looking lot!"

Sheila stifled a small burst of laughter.

Seth grinned and nodded. "We are, eh?"

"So it seems we are stronger in numbers?" Colin said.

"Most assuredly," William said, his gaze shifting to Ferchar. "But I still dinnae ken how you managed to move all of you through time when Coira is closed off."

Eyes softening, Ferchar said, "He barred your wife first. The magic he used gave me forewarning. Now we will stand strong with more power than he can even imagine. He cannae beat us. And once he falls, so too does this gate he has erected."

"We believe he made an appearance last eve," Iain said.

McKayla looked at Colin, confused.

"All know of your nightmare, lass," he explained. "And while we've only recently learned Colin MacLeod exists, we aren't sure he was the one who met you through the fire."

"Colin MacLeod?" Seth asked, taking her hand. "The guy from your book? Are you serious?"

"I think the word you're looking for is hero, not guy," Leslie corrected.

"Does it really matter?" Bradon asked.

Her eyes cut to him. "Proper terminology *always* matters. At least where I'm from."

"Long story," McKayla murmured to Seth then looked at Colin. "So you think it might have been Keir Hamilton in the fire?"

"We cannae rule it out," Colin said.

William frowned at Ferchar. "You have much faith leaving your family alone. I wish I shared such confidence."

"Unwavering faith," Ferchar said. "As should you, my friend. Between Coira, Annie and Arthur, no enemy would dare tackle such a front."

"But you've just a wee bairn and wife."

Ferchar's chest puffed up some. "Och, but he's a bloody special bairn."

"Is he ever," Seth muttered.

"What do you mean by that, lad?" Iain asked Ferchar.

A fatherly pride lit his eyes. "There's something special about this next generation. Though we are the last of the four original great MacLomain wizards, I suspect Adlin was just feeding our egos. It seems our bairns are stronger and better equipped to deal with this ever changing Scotland and all its in-betweens."

"What of my wife?" Seth asked. "Is she in danger?"

"Nay, not in the least. If she were, I would know," Ferchar responded. "As I said, the MacLomains are at the heart of this. Keir Hamilton's eyes have turned our way and his wrath is formidable."

"Which brings us to why you are here," Colin said.

"Aye." Ferchar's eyes locked on the younger clansmen, Malcolm, Bradon and Colin. "Without warning, his armies will come as a swarm upon our land and shores."

"How do we best defend ourselves?" Colin asked.

"Position those with mediocre magic on the borders alongside half of the clan's strongest warriors," Ferchar responded.

"The rest of the warriors will surround the castle. The strongest wizards will stay inside the walls," William added.

"It makes no sense to put the most important of the MacLomain lineage in one place," Malcolm said.

"Assuming we're the most important." Bradon looked at his father. "Where will Torra be?"

McKayla looked at the MacLomain men. Colin's sister was very important. That much was clear, and though she was upset he hadn't told her about Torra, she felt the same pang of urgency Bradon seemed to have.

184

"In the dungeons below," Iain said, his eyes meeting Seth's. "With him."

Ah, perhaps the real reason Seth was here. But it made her heart skip a few frightened beats. "Why?"

"Because there is dark magic, then there is downright evil," Colin said softly.

Seth snorted. "You must have loved saying that."

The corner of Colin's lip inched up a fraction but fell when McKayla shook her head.

"No way, not going to happen." She plunked her and Seth's entwined hands on the table. "He's my friend." When everyone looked at her with resolve she stood her ground. "As wife to the MacLomain laird, I assume I have some say in this." She made a point to look at all who mattered. "Am I wrong? If so, can we call Arianna down and see if she disagrees?"

Iain and William chuckled.

"What?!" Seth, Sheila and Leslie said simultaneously.

Seth snatched his hand away from hers. "You're wife of *who*?"

"Oh, right," she muttered and shrugged. "I'm married." McKayla glanced at Colin then the others. "To him. Last night. Sort of."

Sheila's eyes rounded and a wide smile broke over her face. "Really?"

Caught up in the joy her friend offered she couldn't help but grin. "Yeah, so it seems." But then she saw the dark looks on Seth and Leslie's faces and felt the need to explain.

"Just here..." she trailed off. "But not at home."

"You know I wasn't happy with what Trevor pulled but wow, sweetie. He married you here? That says something!" Sheila nodded, grinning.

"Yes, that he's a master manipulator," Leslie remarked.

"And a total douche," Seth added.

Oh heavens. McKayla eyed all three of them, not sure how to respond, but then Colin's eyes narrowed on Seth. "Why dinnae we get back to why Mr. Evil is going to protect my sister."

"I'll bet my evil beats your good any day," Seth challenged and then looked at Iain. "So I'm a warlock. That's clearly why I'm here. As long as I know my wife is safe, it's all good. Tell me how to protect your daughter and I will."

Iain nodded his thanks but it was William who spoke next. "Colin's mentor fled from a great darkness."

Colin's frown deepened. Iain's eyes locked on his son and he said, "Whether or not you knew, your mentor fled from a man born of pure evil. We suspect 'tis the verra reason he joined the assassins who execute in the name of good. You see his Da raised him on death and black magic. And while your mentor might have been strong in the magi, he could not touch his Da. For Keir Hamilton possesses the strength of our founder and brethren, Adlin MacLomain, with one difference." His eyes once more turned to Seth. "He is a warlock."

"I never did ken the difference between a wizard and a warlock," Bradon said.

Leslie's expression was nothing less than smug. "Does it really matter? Both titles sound ridiculous."

McKayla looked at her cousin. What in god's name was she doing? Baiting Bradon? It most certainly mattered but it seemed Leslie was determined to retaliate against Colin's brother.

Instead of flirting like McKayla fully expected him to do, Bradon sat back, crossed his arms over his chest and said, "Are you not sitting in a castle surrounded by medieval Scotsmen who are indeed wizards? One would think you sharp enough to keep your thoughts to yourself, instead of verbalizing them."

"*Verbalizing*. Wow such a *big* word." Leslie folded her arms over her chest as well. "If I knew you understood such words I never would have—"

"Enough," Colin interrupted, and tossed them a disappointed look, before focusing on Ferchar. "Aye, Seth might be a warlock, but I dinnae think he's strong enough to be at the heart of this…to protect our sister."

"Nay, he's the right of it, son," Iain said. "Seth needs to be with her."

"Aye," William seconded.

Clearly frustrated and reluctant, Colin turned to the younger men. Malcolm seemed oddly complacent. He disagreed with his father. But because of the animosity that existed between him and Colin, he said the opposite of what he felt. "I tend to think our elders are right."

Colin sighed and looked at Bradon.

"I would never second guess Da. Nor would I question William or Ferchar," Bradon exclaimed. "How can you, brother?"

As chieftain, Colin had the final say. It was his decision to make. McKayla only prayed it would be the right one. She was pretty sure he wouldn't base his decision on her fear for Seth. And she could only hope it wouldn't be because of the friction that existed between them. She had to trust that Colin would put his personal feelings aside, and that he knew exactly what he was doing. For everyone's sake.

Colin looked across the table and took a deep breath before he spoke. "Ferchar and William will protect Torra when the time comes. Not Seth."

"Fool," Iain muttered and frowned.

All went quiet. Colin's face remained unreadable but she knew his father's remark must've stung. Seth's expression was nothing less than puzzled. Colin ignored everyone and looked at Ferchar. "When do you expect they will arrive?"

Ferchar didn't appear the least bit put off by Colin's decision. In fact, it seemed he had expected it. "Verra soon."

"Then we must alert the clan and be ready."

William stood. "Verra good."

When everybody made to leave Colin shook his head. "Malcolm, Bradon, Ilisa." He looked at McKayla. "You and yours as well. Stay. We must talk."

Iain, Ferchar and William looked at one another then at Colin before nodding.

The door to the hall blew open. Wind whipped and tossed the rushes.

No matter how much she loved the castle, McKayla had a strange feeling that they'd be better off outdoors. Less imprisoned by what might prove a too-heavy discussion. "How about we sit outside? Get some fresh air."

"Sounds absolutely reasonable to me, lass," Bradon agreed.

"Me as well," Ilisa seconded.

"I'd rather not," Malcolm said. "Be part of any of this."

Seth, Leslie and Sheila were equally neutral.

"Too many ears," Colin said.

"Not everywhere," she responded and shot him a pointed look. Understanding her implication he nodded.

So with drinks in hand they made their way to the castle's hidden garden. The MacLomains sat on one side of a veranda, while Mckayla's friends and family sat on the other.

She and Colin sat on the outer curve, his large body close, protective.

And though the wind picked up it remained warm. If it started to rain they were all covered.

"This is where it begins," Colin said once they'd settled.

They all looked at him as though he'd lost his mind. Any tension he displayed earlier seemed to vanish. "We're the leaders of the next generation. We're missing Torra and Ferchar's bairn, Logan, but otherwise we're all here." His indifferent regard flickered over Seth. "And that includes you too, or so it seems."

"I'm here because you ordered it, not by choice," Malcolm said, not hiding his disdain. "As is Seth. And while we might not be allies, 'tis not the MacLomain way to make guests feel unwelcome."

"And I never meant to do such." But Colin's tone was lukewarm. "I remain curious to see if he will be as important as Ferchar seems to think."

"*He* happens to be sitting right here," Leslie remarked. "Though you speak as if he isn't."

Sheila, clearly eager to change the subject, gazed at their surroundings. "I still don't know how you managed to be Trevor back home after growing up *here*. Why on Earth did you ever leave?"

"It seems quite obvious. Is McKayla not your cousin?"

Everyone was surprised by Malcolm's question.

Sheila looked at him, not put off by his brooding demeanor. "Last I checked, yeah. And who are you again?"

"Malcolm MacLomain, first born son of William MacLomain and Coira Broun," he replied as if amazed she didn't already know. Sheila didn't have a chance to respond.

"Can we just get to the point of this little meeting," Seth said, clearly annoyed.

"Agreed," Bradon said, sipping from a mug. "Far too many lasses are wondering where I am."

"Even with that God awful hair?" Leslie said.

McKayla chuckled, and all eyes swung her way. "What? It was funny." Good Lord, granted these were trying times but everyone was way too uptight.

"Aren't you supposed to be *the laird's wife*? All proper like," Seth asked. "And don't think you're off the hook yet, because I'm still dying to find out why you married him so fast. It's a bunch of shit that he couldn't wait until we were here."

"Shit? Is that like horse and cow manure? I believe we say shite?" Ilisa grinned then looked at Colin. "You abandoning your clan all those years ago was total *shit*, Colin."

Seth smiled and nodded. Ilisa winked back.

Colin and everyone else shook their heads.

Bradon, in good form, waited his turn to respond to Leslie. "The hair was an unfortunate mishap." He leaned back casually, legs spread, plaid covering just enough. "But have no doubt, lass, all else is as it should be and in good working order."

Leslie's eyes widened.

Sheila busted out laughing.

Malcolm scowled.

McKayla tried not to laugh. She was sure Colin was more than frustrated and she didn't want to add to that. This was serious and it was time they all acted as such. Seth's eyes met hers with encouragement before he redirected the conversation back to where it needed to be. "Okay, Colin. I'm as eager as the next to hear what you have to say."

Colin squeezed her hand as he looked at Leslie and Sheila. "It pleases me that you're here if for no other reason than to lend support to McKayla. You are amongst many I've not been honest with over the years and for that I'm sorry. I hope you can forgive me."

Sheila's eyes softened, Leslie's hardened.

"Rest assured that you will be well protected here," he promised.

"Aye," Bradon added, amused as he looked at Leslie. "Even the sharp tongued lassie."

Leslie's eyes narrowed a fraction before she glanced dubiously up at the castle. "Something tells me I'd be safer protected by one of the many fleas that must infest this place."

"Leslie!" Sheila shook her head and said to Colin, "*We* accept your apology. We just need time to get used to everything."

"Oh, I dinnae think your flea-loving kin accepts his apology at all." Bradon's gaze flickered to Malcolm. "But at least she's not alone in her discontentment, aye lad?"

"You have my thanks," Colin said to Sheila, apparently not worried about winning over Leslie just yet. "I only wish you could have come under better circumstances. I'm afraid it will be an unusual welcome for all of you. Preparing for war of any sort puts the clan in a rare mood."

Interest peaked, Leslie asked, "How so?"

Ilisa chuckled and looked her over. "While the whiskey might not be well served, the lust certainly will be. Where there's battling there's mating."

"Aye," Bradon agreed and winked at Leslie.

Appalled, her eyes met McKayla's. "Is she serious?"

Before she could respond Sheila piped in, "I could think of worse things."

"No doubt you could," Leslie muttered, as though she couldn't work a room full of men as well, if not better, than most women.

"Cut to the quick," Malcolm said, his eyes on Colin. "I grow weary of this conversation."

Sheila shot him a grin. "So I guess talk of lust doesn't appeal to you."

"Mayhap if my wife was sitting here, aye."

McKayla's cousin offered him a loose shrug. "Good for her then."

Despite Sheila's gracious response, Malcolm's frown deepened.

"As we speak the clan takes up arms. But it will not appear so to outsiders. Instead, they will see only celebration. A fire will be lit on the field and all will seem as it should be," Colin continued.

"Won't that make it a whole lot easier to see what they're aiming for?" McKayla asked.

"They willnae get so close as that." He eyed the sky. "And the gods favor us now with an incoming storm. A hurricane in fact."

Seth looked up. "Really? In Scotland?"

"'Tis rare but not unheard of," Ilisa said. "And it will make it far more difficult for our enemy."

"Aye." Colin shocked McKayla when he looked at Seth and said, "Though 'tis unlikely our lack of fondness for one another will change, while here stay close to me and learn."

"Learn from *you*?" Seth crossed one leg over the other. "I thought this time around I had one up on you being a warlock and all." The corner of his lips inched up. "Evil understands evil, right?"

"What do you know of handling a claymore? A bow and arrow? Can you ride a horse?"

Seth's lips flattened. "I see your point."

McKayla couldn't help but grin. "It'll do you good to work as a team."

Clearly neither agreed but Colin seemed resolved when he looked at Bradon and Malcolm. "You will accompany me while I teach him. You both are seasoned warriors and he needs to be trained quickly. This will also give us a chance to learn from him. Malcolm, you better ken the dark magic. Mayhap you can glean something from this warlock that Bradon and I cannae."

Seth glanced at Malcolm, intrigued. "So your magic must work something like Ferchar's."

"Something like," Malcolm said, dark gaze still settled on Colin.

Colin addressed Sheila and Leslie. "McKayla and Ilisa will show you to your chambers and find you something appropriate to wear."

Ilisa sighed but smiled nonetheless when she looked at McKayla. "But then I'm off to sword practice."

"Of course." McKayla glanced at the girls. "Maybe we'll join you for a bit. Great for research."

"Then let's make haste." Colin stood and pulled her into his arms. "The sooner we are prepared the sooner I can spend more time with my new wife."

Not concerned in the least by the others he pulled her close for one of his long, knee-weakening kisses. And while she might've thought to keep it brief, once it started she certainly wasn't able to end it. Hand tangled in her hair and free arm snug around her waist, his kiss was as thorough as any other. It was impossible to say how much time passed before he pulled back and cupped her cheek. "This will all be over soon."

McKayla ignored a swell of emotion. He was right. It would be…one way or another.

When he and the men left, she continued to stare after him.

"*Damn*," Sheila murmured, eyes wide and a silly grin on her face. "That was one hot kiss."

"Aye," Ilisa said. "Highland men dinnae mess around."

McKayla's cheeks burned but she couldn't help but agree. "No they don't."

A light drizzle began as they made their way back to the castle. Leslie shuttered, her disgruntled gaze looking out beyond the courtyard. "Will they really light a fire with a hurricane coming? It seems pointless."

"Aye." Ilisa shrugged. "The weather isnae here yet. There's time enough for a burn."

"I assume we won't be standing out in it," Leslie quipped.

"Afraid you might melt?" Sheila shook her head. "I love the wild weather. Don't mind getting wet in the least."

Within a few minutes they'd been shown their quarters which were close to McKayla's. Each were given appropriate clothing before Ilisa made true on her promise and vanished to go practice her swordsmanship.

"We'll join you soon," McKayla assured. The MacLomain lass, all-to-eager to be with the warriors nodded and waved, not overly concerned as she vanished down the hall.

Leslie and Sheila grabbed their clothes and joined McKayla in her chamber.

"Look at this room," Sheila said, awed. "It's immense. And that bed!" She winked at McKayla. "Well used already I'll bet."

Leslie looked out one of the windows. "So much land."

McKayla joined her. "Beautiful isn't it?"

With a loose shrug, her cousin said, "You know me. I've always been more of a city girl."

But there was a level of appreciation in her terse reply.

Sheila thumped down on the bed and giggled. "Bounces a little too. Not such a bad thing."

Leslie shook her head. "Is there no end to your tactlessness?"

"Not really." Sheila continued to smile. "But better to be fun and tactless than miserable and annoying."

"Sheila," McKayla chastised.

"What? She is."

"Please don't bicker. I'm not in the mood."

Startled, they looked at McKayla.

"I don't think you've ever been so straightforward with us, cousin." Leslie said,

"Probably not." She sat on the bed next to Sheila. "Sorry. I'm just a little edgy."

"No surprise," Sheila said, compassionate. "This is all totally crazy. You must've been so frightened when you traveled back. At least we knew what to expect. Ferchar has been awesome."

"Did Caitlin talk more about our magic?"

Leslie nodded. "Enough so. Though I still find it hard to believe."

Sheila's brows drew together. "You'd think traveling back in time would've made it all more real for you."

"To a degree," Leslie murmured. "But it will take time to process I suppose."

"You're allowed to be off kilter," McKayla said. "I certainly was. It's been one unbelievable thing after another." She patted Sheila's hand. "Our Sheila's always been good at new things. It's a gift."

"Speaking of good things." Sheila grabbed McKayla's hand. "How or should I say *why* did you agree to marry Trev…I mean Colin so quickly? I know you've always loved him but still, big move. If it wasn't for the heart-melting way he's constantly looking at you or that super steamy kiss outside, I might be more concerned." She hesitated. "Should I be more concerned, sweetie?"

"No, it's okay." Her heart kicked up a notch as she shared. "Yes, it was unexpected and sure I wasn't too happy at the beginning, being tricked and all, but you both know he's the only man I'd ever want to marry."

"The same man you wanted to marry years ago had he not left you," Leslie reminded.

"We've since worked through all that," McKayla said softly. "And now you can see with your own eyes why. *This* is his home and time. We were worlds apart."

"I might be able to forgive him for lying to you, even leaving you," Leslie said. "But now he's put you in extreme danger with his foolish actions. That I can't forgive."

They stared at one another. Though she knew Leslie loved her it was hard to see that such anger remained. Though it might be a lot to ask she wanted them to care for him as much as she did.

"Well, as I told Colin, I'm all about forgiving," Sheila said. "We all make mistakes. I like to think that if we at least make an effort to right our wrongs it should be rewarded. And I'd say it's clear he's making the effort." A warm smile blossomed. "And it's obvious he's in love with you. He pushed you away to protect you. That's pretty darn selfless."

"If he wanted to protect her he should have stayed away from her to begin with," Leslie remarked then sighed. "No matter. What's done is done." She sat on McKayla's other side and took her free hand. "I won't pretend I like him but I *will* be cordial for your sake. You deserve to be happy and me being difficult works against that end."

194

She squeezed their hands. "I love you both and am so glad you're here." McKayla bit the corner of her lip. "Which doesn't mean I'm not wicked worried about you and would rather you be safe at home…if I really thought it was safe."

"We'll be fine," Sheila said. "Did you see the size of the men around here? Especially Colin and his family? They're taller than Seth! At 6'4, he always looked pretty huge to me."

"And they all seem…" Leslie cleared her throat. "Strong enough."

"Do they ever," Sheila agreed. "Muscles everywhere. Gorgeous faces. And those eyes. All of them!"

"I doubt pretty faces and stunning eyes will do much to protect us," Leslie said dryly.

"What do you suppose Ferchar meant about us becoming MacLomains?" Sheila asked, interest apparent. "I can't imagine pairing up with Malcolm or Bradon. But maybe one of the others around here."

"Malcolm made it clear he's married," Leslie reminded. "So he shouldn't even be on your radar."

"Pretty sure I just said both of them were off the table."

McKayla worked hard not to sigh. "I'd say Bradon's free for the taking. But definitely steer clear of Malcolm. He's got a wife that will kill you before she'd look at you."

"And like I said, good for her," Sheila huffed and stood.

Both stared curiously after her. Sheila didn't typically get snappy.

"Well, Bradon might as well be married for all his availability," Leslie remarked. "I strongly suspect he's likely already fathered multiple children from multiple women. Total player."

"You're probably right about that," Sheila said, studying her dress.

McKayla slid a glance at Leslie. Honestly, she was surprised her uptight cousin had noticed Bradon at all. She typically focused on a man with nothing but financial success in his future. But the more she thought about it the more she realized Bradon had made a point of targeting Leslie several times. It seemed her cousin had not been oblivious.

"I can't believe we're getting ready to put on these dresses." Sheila held hers up to her chest. "They're magnificent."

McKayla eyed what they'd been given. Not as simple as what the women wore for day dresses but not nearly as extravagant as her wedding gown, they were lovely.

"I've been paying attention," Leslie said as she began to undress. "I think you did a great job describing medieval Scotland in your book. Yes, there are some noticeable differences, ones I think we should address during edits, but most of it is very similar."

"I totally agree," Sheila said as she started to get ready.

In little time, all three were dressed.

Her cousins looked beautiful. Stunning. Sheila with her thick curling dark auburn hair and soft blue eyes was in a dress that matched. As if hand-picked to draw out her wide, oval eyes, the color was perfect against her ivory skin.

Where Sheila was stunning with her carefree almost princess-like looks, Leslie was her dark, magnetic counterpart with luxurious black hair. The tallest of the three, with a willowy yet curvaceous figure, they'd be hard pressed to keep any hot-blooded Scotsman away from her. The dress she'd been given was such a unique shade of green that it enhanced and magnified her pale green eyes.

"You two are breathtaking," she said, smiling.

"Not nearly as much as you, cousin." Sheila shook her head, eyes as wide as ever. "That dress…you… look incredible."

Even Leslie stared. "Whoever picked this out for you knew exactly what they were doing."

Though the pale crème dress felt sumptuous she knew they humored her. They'd always been more attractive. "You guys are sweet."

"And I love the white streak in your hair. Great highlight!" Sheila said.

"What highlight?" McKayla asked, fingering her hair, cross eyed as she tried to look at it.

"It's just a sun streak," Leslie clarified. "But I agree. It looks fabulous."

Unsure, she started to question more but she was cut off.

"She's always been clueless about her looks," Sheila said to Leslie.

Leslie nodded. "Yes." She took McKayla's hands. "Every single man you've ever allowed to get close has absolutely loved you. The rest wanted too, but couldn't get near enough. When are you going to realize how beautiful you are?"

"Yeah, okay." McKayla blushed. "Whatever you say, but thanks."

Sheila touched her hair. "You've always had fairytale looks. The sort the rest of us can only dream of. If your face and hair aren't enough, you have that perfect little body."

Embarrassed, McKayla pulled away and changed the subject. "We really should head down. I'm eager to see some swordplay."

She conveniently set aside the fact that it soon might not be play.

It was late in the day when they arrived downstairs. Though the drizzle had stopped the skies roiled black, brooding and angry over the highland mountains. Wind whipped and flipped their hair even before they made it to the door.

Nearly every man who passed stared. She was surprised to realize that even though she'd married their laird, none were above admiring her just as thoroughly as her cousins. Leslie and Sheila appeared to be handling themselves accordingly. Sheila grinned, allowing one or two men to walk alongside for a bit. Leslie, not entirely opposed to the attention smiled, especially when a particularly handsome Scotsman winked and put his hand over his heart in passing.

Despite the looming storm and upcoming battle, the courtyard teemed with activity. The kitchens and most especially the stables were busy. The smell of freshly baked breads and roasted meats permeated the air, mixing with the scent of hay and ocean. A smith sharpened blades, the screech of metal against metal constant. Horses with heavily armed warriors trotted by, the clank of hooves creating a deep rumble across the drawbridge.

"This place seriously blows my mind," Sheila said as she looked around.

"Completely," Leslie agreed. "Better than any movie or book has portrayed it." She nudged McKayla's arm. "Except yours of course."

It was an odd yet refreshing thing to see Leslie playful, if only for a moment.

They'd nearly made it beneath the second portcullis when she stopped short and her breath caught.

"Holy hell!" Sheila said.

"Now there's something you don't see every day." This from Leslie.

Seth and Colin raced horses hard and fast toward one another. Horrified, she watched as one whipped a blade at the other. For her it seemed everything went into slow motion. In truth, the weapon flew fast and true, right through the heart of the other.

And one man fell.

Chapter Thirteen

Heart in her throat, McKayla ran. Please don't let him be dead! She'd never forgive this. They'd always had issues with each other and now the worst had happened.

Falling to her knees, she pulled Seth's head into her lap, frantically looking for the knife that should be protruding from his chest, the blood that must be spilling. But there was nothing. Instead, Seth's eyes popped open and he sputtered, "Friggin' awesome!"

Colin chuckled and she looked up with a frown. "What the…"

Her husband, once more shirtless and glistening with sweat grinned down from his steed. "Now, lass, you didnae think I'd kill him just yet, did you?"

Seth sat up and coughed, a wide smile on his face. "Love this whole horse riding thing. And the medieval weapons. Unreal. Leathan will never believe this."

McKayla thought of his Scottish cousin and fellow paranormal investigator. "Nope, he probably won't." Irritated but used to dealing with Seth's near death escapades, she shook her head and eyed his chest. "By the way, what happened to the blade that should've taken you out?"

There was no need helping him to his feet. Seth stood in an instant, a grin still splitting his face. "All magic. Mock practice."

Sheila and Leslie were as winded when they looked from Colin to Seth.

"I think he's wanted to do that to you for years," Sheila commented.

"You've no idea." Colin said.

"As I said, all the men you've allowed to get close have loved you," Leslie said so softly she barely caught it.

It occurred to McKayla they were referring to Seth. He'd heard because his unwavering gaze met hers. "Once upon a time," he murmured. "But then I met Alana." He winked, his blue eyes warm, encompassing. "And I had to let you go."

Leslie and Sheila exchanged a triumphant look. How long had they been sitting on this tidbit of information? She supposed it didn't matter now. The love she and Seth shared was right where it belonged…as close friends.

When Colin shifted his horse, Seth was forced to take a step back. He held out his hand to her. "Come, my love, allow me to enlighten you a bit more."

McKayla stared up at her highlander. Eyes wild, victorious, he waited. All along he'd known of Seth's feelings. No wonder the inherent dislike. But somehow in the time they'd spent out here battling, maybe even because of the blade he'd just thrown, the last of his frustration was spent. Or maybe he'd finally seen the love in Seth's eyes when he spoke of Alana.

She reached up and took his hand. Easily over sixteen hands tall, he pulled her up effortlessly onto his impressive horse. Plunked down not in back but in front of him, he adjusted her skirts and pulled her neatly back against him. A sharp thrill shot through her. Hands against the blazing heat of the steed, pure power flexed beneath her as Colin steered the horse away from the others.

"I've never been on a horse," she whispered, heart thudding heavily.

His deep voice rumbled against her back, warm breath close to her ear. "I know."

And he had no intentions of easing her into it.

McKayla squealed when the horse launched forward. Never was there a more profound feeling than that of flying across the wide meadow with a highland castle off to her left and jagged, majestic mountains rising into the incoming storm to her right. The speed and wind brought tears to her eyes and joy to her heart.

Even when the tree line loomed, they barely slowed.

A whole new rush blew through her when the horse entered the forest, navigating the trees with unbelievable precision. Eventually they slowed to a trot until Colin stopped in front of a raging river. The sensation of flying remained and she laughed. "That was incredible."

"I used to dream about doing this with you," he said and tilted her head so he could kiss her. This time his lips didn't linger but his eyes did, roaming her face. "We will make many more memories like this."

God, she hoped so.

"Aren't we supposed to stay close to the castle? Won't we be in danger here?"

"Nay." He pointed across the river into the woods then spanned his arms in both directions. "We've already got thousands of warriors on our borders and allied clans further out. He's not here yet, lass."

Though he might say all was well, McKayla sensed they took a risk. While she knew it didn't need to be said she wanted everything out in the open. "I never knew Seth had such strong feelings for me."

Colin eased her down from the horse then followed. "'Tis not something that needs further scrutiny. All is as it should be."

When she looked at him, McKayla realized he meant every word. Any jealousy that might have been was gone. She was more than content to let the matter rest. "Shouldn't you still be training him?"

"Bradon and Malcolm will take it from here. They are just as knowledgeable."

McKayla nodded, trusting in his decision.

"This is where my Ma and Da were married." He nodded at the river. "It was but a stream then."

"It's a pretty spot." She gazed up at the tall pines towering overhead. "They share a great love."

"As do we," he murmured. They walked hand and hand back through the woods, his steed trailing along behind them. The ring, as it did whenever he was close, heated. She twisted it, wishing Seth would remove it. Did he even remember he'd put it there?

"So we aren't staying out here long after all," she remarked.

"Nay, just long enough to have some time alone. There's been so little of it."

Her heart fluttered when a harsh realization settled over her. "You're afraid we won't have much more."

"'Tis logical to feel such before any battle, lass." He pulled her hand closer, eyes steady on the ever darkening forest. "Though I dinnae intend to die, if I do 'twill not be with the wish I'd but stolen a few more moments alone with you."

Thickness swelled in her throat but McKayla fought the emotion. The last thing he needed right now was for her to get sappy. "Then let's make these moments count."

"My verra thought exactly." With a devious grin, his near somber mood lightened and he said, "Perhaps a little light to lead the way?"

"It's not nearly that dark yet," she began but trailed off when a little box with spidery legs crawled out from behind a tree. The flashlight! Now she did tear up. Unable to stop herself, she went over and picked it up.

When McKayla turned back, she froze. Hand over her mouth, she shook her head.

Trevor.

"McKayla," he said quietly.

As handsome as ever he stood there looking at her...an old friend, lover and as it turned out, so much more. Words didn't need to be exchanged. She understood why he'd shifted. His door to the life they'd shared was closing and with it, who he'd been.

But who he had been was not who he was supposed to be.

She knew it was time to let Trevor go.

Crossing to him she set aside the flashlight, cupped her best friend's familiar face and whispered, "I love you."

"And I love you, sweetheart, more than anyone, anywhere at any time," he murmured.

"You know you're making me find my calm center, right?"

His brow arched. "Am I?"

"Aye," she said softly and leaned her head against his chest. "I want *you* back. Not the man you always pretended to be."

His arms came around her and he kissed the top of her head. "When it came to you I never once pretended."

But for the first time and what she knew to be the last, McKayla felt him change beneath her very fingertips. She breathed in the unmistakable and delicious scent of Colin MacLomain. This time when she pulled back, he cupped her cheeks and stared into her eyes. Unmistakable desire didn't just flicker but consumed his concentrated gaze.

Recognizing his intent she mouthed, "Here? Now? Should we?"

He offered no response but lifted her and walked forward.

Suddenly not concerned in the least if the timing was appropriate, she wrapped her legs around him. The next thing she knew he lowered her onto a patch of grass by a small stream that stemmed from the nearby river. She gasped when he cupped a large handful of water and trickled it up her exposed leg. Each drop explored her steaming hot skin.

He moved down and slowly, thoroughly, searched out each adventurous drop. Unable to do anything else, McKayla hid beneath her lashes and buried her hands in his hair. Uninhibited, she all but steered him where she wanted him. Pushing her skirts up around her waist, he willingly complied. His tongue flicked and teased until his mouth found her pulsing center. In near agony beneath his talented appetite she arched against him, again and again as she chased the pinnacle he kept out reach.

Close, almost there, she groaned and grasped at the grass.

Determined to keep her perched at the edge of release, he nibbled, stopped, then nipped again. Bordering on the precipice of what felt like insanity she shook her head. In an instant he moved up, taking her legs with him. Pressed wide and tight, he moved into her swiftly, his wicked eyes watching her every reaction.

Body blown into a mad mixture of chaos and sharp, spearing release, she stared wide-eyed through the canopy of pines. Tears ran down her cheeks as an orgasm ripped through her with such speed that she couldn't escape it. As she rode the waves of her pleasured prison, he found a rhythm that almost drove her mad.

He moved in and out. Faster. Harder. A mind blowing pace that she didn't think she could take for much longer. Before she could voice her concern, bright lights shattered before her eyes. She cried out, her body vibrating and trembling uncontrollably against his.

Now he had to work against her muscles as they clenched and locked tight around him. Sweat glistened as he breathed heavily. He slowed just enough to allow her body a scant moment to untwist and float back down from wherever it'd been.

Every last nerve was mouth-wateringly heightened when he thrust then slowed. Thrust then slowed. Again and again he did this, creating an energized rhythm that didn't for a second let her cherish any of the previous euphoric orgasms. No, he drove her toward something even higher.

Better.

Much more thorough. If that was even possible.

She never dreamed it could be like this.

Colors already swam in her vision. But now they ignited and exploded all around. Gripping the ground above her head, Colin's jaw clenched and his eyes closed. His muscles locked up so tight that when his release came, his body jerked and thrust against hers. She twisted and drifted in such pleasure and sweetness, floating, as if she were in another world.

A world made of man and warrior, of love and flawlessness.

Pressed into the warm summer ground, she breathed in the scent of grass mixed with the blistering sensual scent of their entwined, fulfilled bodies. When his cheek came against hers, he seemed as eager to inhale her as she was him.

"I think I must've loved you before I was born," he whispered against her skin.

It was hard to imagine it any other way.

When he finally pulled back, she flinched. Her body had been well used. Before she had a chance to acclimate, he lifted her, smoothed her skirts and then swung her into his arms. McKayla wrapped her arms around him, exhausted and grateful. Truth be told, she highly doubted she could stand on her own.

It was only once she was again cuddled and content high astride his horse that she said, "Wait, where's our flashlight?"

Colin chuckled, steering his steed back through the wind-whipped, darkening forest. "No worries, lass. 'Twill find its way home."

She smiled. "Good, it's a handy little thing."

When they departed the woods and entered the field a large fire struggled, its sparks and smoke rebelling against the mist and highland winds. The ocean, with white-tipped waves, crashed against the distant shore.

"It would seem that plume of smoke is a beacon," she mentioned.

"'Twould, wouldn't it?"

McKayla glanced over her shoulder at him then once more at the fire. "So I suppose that's exactly what it is."

Colin gave no response but eased the horse back into a trot. This time they didn't fly across the field but enjoyed an easy pace that soothed her heated cheeks and allowed her time to regain strength in her legs.

When they made their way back to her family it was to find Seth now kilted and sparring with Bradon. McKayla burst out laughing. Leslie and Sheila stood nearby, goblets in hand, and grins on their faces.

Sheila looked up, a mischievous sparkle in her eyes as she looked from Colin to McKayla. "Did you have a nice ride?"

McKayla didn't miss the innuendo and rolled her eyes as Colin helped her dismount. But she was feeling more alive and far more spunky than usual.

"Faster and more intense than I ever would've expected."

Her cousin giggled and Leslie cast them a bemused sidelong glance.

"Wow, look at Seth," Mckayla exclaimed. "He looks every inch the Scotsman."

"You should see him fight. He's got skills," Leslie said. "And he's almost giving Bradon a run for his money. Looks to me like he's having one hell of a good time."

"His magic will help him learn much faster than most," Colin agreed, as he watched the two men fighting.

McKayla shivered when Malcolm raised a sword in Colin's direction. Her husband nodded his agreement and caught the blade with ease when it was tossed his way. He'd not even started fighting and already McKayla swallowed hard. She wasn't so sure sparring with Malcolm was the smartest idea. Colin tied back his hair with a swath of plaid and tested the weight of the blade as he walked forward.

Sensing a good battle, everyone stepped back.

Colin and Malcolm circled around one another. Stalking. Assessing. Staring. You could hear a pin drop. McKayla held her breath.

Suddenly, both lunged forward.

They attacked with ferocious precision. Swords crashed together. The ground shook, and what sounded like thunder vibrated loud and strong.

She could barely breathe.

Malcolm was out for blood.

Each strike bounced off Colin's sword with vicious accuracy. Sweat dripped off their bodies, but still they battled, neither one willing to give up.

"Jesus," Sheila whispered and took a long swig of whiskey.

McKayla watched them go after each other with rapid, expert movements. She'd never seen anything so dangerously beautiful as Colin and Malcolm crossing swords. Supple, finely honed, muscles rippled and flexed each time they thrust. One second Colin pushed forward and Malcolm fell back, the next it was Colin who jumped, moved and evaded.

No dance had ever been more mesmerizing.

Sweat glistened and sinew slid over flexible frames as each anticipated the other. All the while, their faces remained impregnable masks of concentration. Neither let emotion cloud his judgment. They used the mud to shift and slide just out of the other's reach.

"Bloody hell, look at them go. Just like when they were bairns," Bradon murmured.

As if their deities cheered them on, lightening flashed across the sky and an earth-shaking clap of thunder crashed. If nothing else, the very storm brewing around them seemed to feed their energy. With deadly focus, Colin drove forward, moving his blade back and forth so quickly that for the first time, Malcolm slid out of control.

The crowd gasped.

But her husband's near victory didn't last long.

Taking advantage of his unruly slip, Malcolm twirled down and around then sliced back fast. Colin protected himself but not nearly soon enough. The slick ground pulled him down.

"Och," some murmured.

"He's got him now," others said.

As if he tasted victory, Malcolm made the mistake of thrusting when he probably should have waited. When he did, Colin dug his hand into the ground and used the wet mud to his advantage. He swiped his leg beneath his cousin and Malcolm hit the ground. In a move she knew all too well, Colin arched his back and jumped up, lodging his blade tight against Malcolm's neck before the Scotsman had a chance to move.

They stared at one another.

McKayla bit her lip praying Colin wouldn't do anything he'd regret. He loved his cousin, but what if Malcolm refused to lose? What if Colin didn't have any other choice but to defend himself? Would Malcolm cross that line? Did his hatred run that deep?

Water dripped off Colin and his body shook. Oh God. Battle lust. It was apparent in his dark, pinning gaze. McKayla had done enough research to know that even civilized men did horrible things when their mind was overrun by such rage.

Malcolm and Colin breathed heavily as the tense moments stretched. Thank the heavens it wasn't long before the crowd broke their silence and cries rose up. Warriors banged on their shields and clanged their blades. Colin held his sword against Malcolm's neck before hanging his head and rising. He took a deep breath, and then held down his hand. "Well fought, cousin."

A war raged in Malcolm's eyes. Almost impossible to miss, he fingered the hilt of his sword as if he envisioned running the blade through his cousin's gut. If any saw, none commented. But McKayla noticed.

At last, Malcolm made a show of amiable sportsmanship and took Colin's hand.

"Good," Bradon said under his breath and nodded with relief. "Verra good."

Though Malcolm didn't return Colin's slap on the shoulder, he nodded and exclaimed, "Defeated but only until next time, my friends."

"I believe he means that," Sheila said, eyes locked on Malcolm as he accepted a mug. In fact, she kept on staring as he took a long, thorough swig.

McKayla waved a hand in front of her cousin's face and shook her head. "Remember, he's married to the devil."

"It doesn't matter what his wife's *like*." Leslie looked skyward. "I'd think the focus would be first and foremost on the very fact he's married at all."

"Och, 'tis not always considered when dealing with us highlanders," Bradon offered.

Having clearly forgotten he stood there, Leslie frowned. "Well, it should be."

"Speak of the devil," Bradon said, smirking. "Watch out."

McKayla almost groaned when Loch Nessa sauntered their way. Stunning as ever in a dark blue, cleavage revealing dress, she stopped in front of Malcolm and Colin. Call it newly found wifely instincts or just a good old fashioned gut feeling, but when the devil talked to Malcolm she knew the words were meant for Colin. "If ever I saw a more striking sight. Never was there a more vicious warrior."

Sheila and Leslie's eyes were glued to Nessa, seemingly in awe.

Malcolm wrapped his arm around his wife's back and pulled her close, his lips crashing over hers almost as intensely as his blade had met Colin's minutes before.

Though Leslie looked away, Sheila couldn't. Or wouldn't. McKayla wasn't sure. *Great.* It seemed her cousin had a thing for Malcolm. She'd have to do her best to dissuade her of that notion, but it would have to wait until later.

Bradon leaned in close to Leslie and pointed at Malcolm and Nessa who were still engaged in a lip lock. "See, the battle lust is running rampant. And 'tis only bound to get worse."

"Then why aren't you off making the best of it," Leslie snapped.

With a snicker and a wink he said, "Mayhap I am."

McKayla sipped from her drink and tried to make sense of her cousins. But when Colin's arm wrapped around her midsection and his front came against her back, Sheila and Leslie faded away. He murmured against her neck. "What think you now of highland swordplay. Is it everything you imagined when you wrote about it?"

Every time this man touched her, the muscles in her legs all but liquefied. Leaning back, utilizing his solid wall of support, she reveled in the feel of his damp skin and hard chest. "More," she whispered hoarsely. "Everything about you is much *more*."

Colin spun her and cupped her neck, lips centimeters from hers. "Even when I fight I think about being back inside you." His lips curled a fraction. "'Tis most distracting."

"I would think," Leslie muttered from their left.

"'Tis good to know you think about it at all," Bradon said from their right.

Set to ignore them altogether, she stood on tip toes and met her husband's lips with her own. His arms wrapped around her and their kiss turned feverish. Even through the ever increasing gusts of wind and rain, they kissed. Only Ilisa's words broke a small hole in their self-created conclave.

"The pipers go to the castle wall walks. Let us go where we might enjoy both what the heavens offer and a wee bit o' protection for those soft of skin!"

McKayla pulled back, laughing as Ilisa swung onto a horse and hooted all the way back to the castle. "She really is insane, eh?"

"More than you know," he guaranteed and took her hand.

His steed had been brought back so they trotted alongside the crowd. If she didn't know any better she'd think the clan celebrated, not prepared for war. But even as they went she saw many horsemen pass, weapons scattered along their bodies. Even more strolled along the castle's numerous wall walks.

By the time they reached the largest wall walk, night had fallen and more torches than usual burned. Bagpipes fired up, their trill echoing off the castle walls and catching on the wind. Like her, Sheila and Leslie were enchanted, caught in a time and place they never could have imagined.

"I love you honey but even your book didn't bring it like this," Sheila said, her eyes covering everything at once.

"Nothing recorded portrays it like this," Leslie said.

"Like a fairytale but not," McKayla said.

Leslie's expression soured. "Right, so says that dreadful latrine in the back of the castle. I think I'd rather go behind a tree."

"Or in the ocean," Sheila said.

McKayla sighed but couldn't help agree. "Way to kill the romanticism."

"Oh, it shouldn't," Sheila said. "It's clean here. Much cleaner than I would've thought. Even the men don't reek of body odor." Her gaze landed on Malcolm and Loch Nessa. "Even the ones who recently fought." She crinkled her nose. "But maybe after days of it."

"I assume we won't be around long enough to experience days of it," Leslie said.

"Right." Sheila sipped from her drink.

Seth came out of nowhere and managed to wrap his arms around all three, one around her cousins, the other around her. He was a muddy mess but happy as could be. "This place seriously kicks ass. Forget all the haunted houses back home, I bet this castle is teeming with paranormal activity. Seriously, the energy around here almost pulses." He looked at each of them, excited. "Can you feel it?"

Colin had just returned with a fresh mug of ale for her. Bradon trailed after him, carrying mugs for the girls. It seemed his brother was their newfound shadow. She suspected it had more to do with Leslie than anyone else.

"What happened to your *servants*?" Sheila asked, not all that pleased.

"They're about," Colin said. "And they're paid so servant isnae the word you're looking for."

"Are they?" Leslie asked, surprised. "I didn't think that sort of thing happened in these days."

"Normally they dinnae," Bradon responded. "But we MacLomains have never made slaves of men."

Sheila grinned. "I'm impressed."

But it wasn't her approval he was looking for. Leslie, eyes anywhere but on Bradon, said wryly, "Who would've thought?" She looked at McKayla. "We'll have to add that into your book. It's a nugget of information readers would appreciate."

"But might not think realistic," she responded and smiled at Colin. "I tend to think the MacLomains are rare."

"Oh, they're rare all right," Leslie muttered when a girl with big brown eyes and a come-hither smile winked at Bradon. He took her hand when she offered it, and vanished into the crowd to dance.

Colin, clearly aware of the attraction between Bradon and Leslie, said, "'Twould have been rude had he not danced."

Leslie's brows shot together twice before her expression smoothed over. "What do I care who he dances with?"

"No doubt," Sheila said, the whiskey warming her already rambunctious tongue. "There are always other men to be had, cousin." She winked. "Men without such *God awful* hair."

Leslie glowered. "Why don't you go try to break up a good marriage then, eh? You couldn't be any more obvious. Better watch yourself or all those biblical characters you love so much might get around to judging after all."

Colin chuckled but ceased when McKayla frowned.

"You're such a bitch," Sheila muttered.

"And you're a…"

Ilisa climbed onto the wall and raised her arms in the air, stopping Leslie from spitting out a stinging retort. "I've something to say, my brethren!"

McKayla edged her way through the crowd and stood by Ilisa's side. The girl was crazy. Stone cold. And she knew it. Used it. McKayla stood with her heart in her throat. One wrong step and… She didn't even want to think about it. There was nothing but a long drop onto the hard ground below. But the highland lass didn't seem fazed. Not drunk in the least but acting it, she peered down at McKayla.

"Oh good, you're here!" she said, and then grabbed the protective hand McKayla had snaked toward her foot. With one mighty swing she pulled her up. Wide-eyed, McKayla flailed before Ilisa steadied her with an arm around her back.

Anxious, trying not to appear frightened, she looked out over the crowd.

Colin stood, arms crossed over his chest. Though clearly alarmed he hadn't moved.

When she looked down she realized why he wasn't worried. Of all people, Malcolm had appeared out of nowhere and stood by her side. Or should she say below and by her side. With an arm draped casually on the wall behind her feet, he said nothing.

Ilisa, still grinning, said, "I've been giving my new laird's wife a lot of thought since she chopped off all my hair." With a whip of her head, that very hair flew about as much as it possibly could.

"Bloody bonnie!" a man yelled.

"Makes ye look fine indeed!" another cried.

The crowd laughed, agreeing wholeheartedly.

"Aye," Ilisa cried and pulled McKayla closer. "And I've my new sister to thank for it!"

Not just anyone gained Ilisa's favor. It was a gift indeed. And all in the clan knew it. McKayla eyed Ilisa, amazed. *Sister?*

"That's right," Ilisa said more sternly, her hand squeezing McKayla's. "I've been needing one." She looked at McKayla. "How about you, are you needing a sister?"

Um, no. But…okay. Maybe. What was all of this about?

When she looked for Colin he was gone.

Sheila and Leslie stared back, eyes the widest she'd ever seen them.

"Well, are ye then?"

McKayla blinked. Silence reigned. Everyone was waiting for her to answer. Much like the sacrifice with her hair, Ilisa was now offering her something she would not be able to attain on her own. She only wished she knew what it was. One thing she knew for sure was having Ilisa in her corner was a good thing. It never hurt to have someone like her on your side.

Ilisa squeezed her hand again and though McKayla saw the craziness in her eyes, there existed something else altogether. Determination, persuasion, assurance. Lulled, wanting to please, needing to, she nodded.

"Verra good," Ilisa whispered.

Raising their hands in the air, she yelled, "It seems she'll have me then!"

The crowd roared. Torches flickered. And, though it must've been her imagination, a tiny bolt of electricity passed between their joined hands.

Before Ilisa could further her unexpected display of kinship, Malcolm grasped Mckayla's hand and pulled her down. He said nothing, only led her through the over-joyed clan folk, many of whom patted her on the shoulder and smiled, murmuring words of pleasure. After he deposited her with Leslie and Sheila, Malcolm vanished into the crowd as quickly as he'd come.

"What the heck just happened?" Sheila said.

"Damned if I know," she said softly.

"I'll research this when I get home," Leslie said, her eyes still on Ilisa as the Scotswoman hopped down from the wall into the waiting arms of several suitors. "It's got to be a custom we missed."

"What did Colin say about it?" McKayla asked.

"Nothing," Sheila said. "He watched until he knew you were safe then took off."

McKayla looked around. "And where's Bradon?"

"Gone too," Leslie said. "He went with Colin."

"Should we go after them?" Sheila asked.

"And say what?" Leslie said sardonically. "Why did you leave our side for even a second?" She rolled her eyes. "Please."

Yet McKayla knew and her cousins clearly suspected that something wasn't right about any of this. Fleeing the scene however was not an option. The crowd soon turned their attention toward the girls. And they were far too interested. Men had been flocking around her cousins all night. Now, with their laird and his brother gone, the fresh-faced foreigners seemed far more accessible. Even Seth had vanished, no doubt off exploring the castle.

"I never thought I'd say this but I wish Colin had stayed with us," Leslie said.

"Ya think?" Sheila said, smiling but shaking her head when yet another Scotsman tried to take her hand and pull her into a dance.

McKayla suddenly found herself in a very unusual situation. One wrong move and the rapport Ilisa helped her build with the clan could be gone. Wiped out. She was the laird's wife. And so she walked a fine line. She had no desire to be rude. But she wanted to haul her cousins away from the celebration. Was she not in a position to do exactly as she wished? Right now she needed a savior.

As if reading her thoughts, Ilisa appeared. With a quick peck on either cheek she pulled back and said, "Me thinks my kin might need you below, aye?"

"Maybe there is a god after all," Leslie mumbled when McKayla nodded and Ilisa led them off the wall walk.

Ilisa leaned close so that only McKayla could hear. "I needed to create a distraction." She nodded. "But 'tis good we're bonded now. 'Tis verra good indeed."

A distraction? Whatever for?

But it appeared she wouldn't be finding out. Her new sister waved and cried out in pleasure as she was swung away in another highland jig. Not sure where she should be going, McKayla headed for the great hall. Thankfully, Bradon appeared when they reached the second landing and urged them to follow. "Come be where 'tis quieter."

They traveled down the hall and up another set of stairs to a smaller landing that while well lit, appeared far more hidden than the others. The castle jutted up sharply on one side and left only a swath of churning loch below.

A semi-round, stone table wrapped out from the side. With plenty to eat and drink, this corner of the castle was set aside for immediate family. A piper played a soft song as Arianna and Iain danced. Malcolm and Loch Nessa sat in a corner, heads bent close.

Ferchar stood with William, sharing a cup of ale. Colin greeted them when they arrived, pulling her close. "Sorry to have left you like that. 'Twas a moment for Ilisa alone."

Arianna broke off her dance and joined them. Though she took McKayla's hands her warm gaze covered all three girls. "Welcome, lasses. I do so hope you've enjoyed your eve so far."

Sheila nodded, captivated by the older woman and her gracious nature.

Leslie worked at a smile and nodded.

"I know you met everyone earlier but let me again introduce you to those you've seen the least." She turned to the older men. "My husband, Iain and of course, William." Her eyes flickered over Sheila with interest. "Malcolm's father."

As if she sensed rather than saw the brief look Arianna had given, Sheila's eyes shot from her hostess to William. "Hello. Nice to see you again."

"And you as well, lassie." McKayla noticed the speculative way the former chieftain looked at her cousin. What did he see when he looked at Sheila? It was impossible not to wonder. Because anything he saw in her surely had to be better than what he saw in his current daughter-in-law.

Sitting on one of the walls with a hundred foot drop to the ocean below, Bradon grinned. "More family is always welcome, indeed."

Leslie's gaze flickered to the water then to him but she said nothing.

Colin guided McKayla to the table, content to let his family care for her cousins. As if sharing a small secret over a country picnic he said, "There is movement to the north and by sea. They will soon be here."

Distressed, she started to speak but he put a finger to her lips. "Nay, dinnae alarm your family. Everything thus far has gone according to plan." Almost too calm his eyes locked with hers. "When you leave here, take your cousins and head to our chambers. Open the trunk at the foot of our bed. In it you will find what you need to get home."

Petrified, she shook her head. She didn't want to go home. Not yet. Not now. How could he expect her to just walk away? After all they'd shared. Was it that easy for him? Because it sure as heck wasn't for her.

"My love," he said and cradled her face in his hands. "We will distract and destroy Keir Hamilton while you and the others return to the future." His hands clenched tighter. "Trust me in this. If you dinnae listen it will be at the cost of not only your kin but mine."

"Why does everything have to be a secret?" she asked through clenched teeth, refusing to tear up. "Don't you trust me?"

"Of course I trust you, McKayla, I trust no other more."

He tried to pull her in closer but she jerked away. "Then why can't you tell me what the hell's going on?"

"Because the less you know the better," he tried to reason with her.

"And what about Seth?" she argued.

"Seth will join you eventually. Until then," he pleaded, "Please do what I ask of you."

He again tried to pull her closer but she wriggled out of his grip. "Don't think for one minute that a little embrace is going to make this all right."

"Aye, I know." Colin dropped his hands to his side. "I cannae stand the friction between us. You have my heart. You must know that McKayla. But I have a duty. Not only to you, but to my clan. They depend on me. And as it stands you are a threat to their security. So what would you have me do? Ignore the fact that there is a solution. A way to ensure your safety as well as theirs? As much as I want too, I cannae do that. 'Twould be selfish for my needs to come before those of my clan. I took an oath. A pledge to stay and fight. And that is what I must do. If anything happened to you I would never forgive myself."

He sighed and pleaded with his eyes before he continued. "I wish you could understand that. I will keep you safe at all costs … even if that means sending you home. This was not a decision that I came to lightly." His voice trailed off as he studied every inch of her face. "Do you not think this is killing me?"

McKayla frowned. "I know you love me. And I do understand. I know you have a duty to your clan. I get that. I do. That's not the problem. You're not up front with me. You hide things, deceive me, and then tell me it's for my own good. But it's not. That's not how marriages work."

She stood up a little straighter. Whining wasn't her style so she kept her voice level. "You don't have the right to determine my future without talking to me about it first. I know we're not in the twenty-first century right now and women tend to have little say in your world, but this is me, Kay, the woman you love. All I want is for us to talk about it. For you to give me a choice."

"Lass, there is no other choice."

"See that's exactly what I mean. You're deciding for me. And you expect me to obey you without even knowing why."

"All right," he said, his hands once more cupping her cheeks. "I cannae tell you much but I can offer you some truth. But first I need you to do something for me."

"What?" Mckayla whispered.

"Tell me more about Iosbail from your book."

"Please," she pleaded. "Don't try to change the subject."

"That's not what I'm doing. I promise. Tell me about your character."

"I don't know what difference it will make but fine." McKayla sighed. "Iosbail's voice always told the heroine to follow her heart. To rely on her instincts, no matter the consequences." It was impossible not to narrow her eyes. "Did you know a woman by the name of Iosbail MacLomain actually existed?"

He kissed her then leaned his forehead against hers. "I've always known of Iosbail, lass. I wouldnae be here without her. Nor would you. She was Adlin MacLomain's sister. My guess is that she was one of your muses."

Daunting thought! Yet it wasn't all that surprising considering everything else she'd learned thus far. "But what does Iosbail have to do with what's happening now?"

"I think if anything should go wrong this eve you should draw on Iosbail's voice, her advice. Think how you imagine she would have. You cannae go wrong if you do."

217

"You make it sound as if she's truly about," McKayla whispered.

"Do you think Seth is wrong for believing in ghosts?" His eyes glinted with mystery. "I wouldnae put it past Iosbail to whisper in your ear on occasion."

She was about to respond but he spoke instead. "We will talk more about this later. And there *will* be a *later*, McKayla. But for now, you must focus on staying strong." He brought her hand to his chest. "Remember, I'm but a heartbeat away."

McKayla closed her eyes. "Then why do I have the terrible feeling that I'm getting ready to lose you?"

His lips brushed over hers. "You willnae ever lose me, lass. Not there or here. *Never.*"

She didn't believe him in the least. And it scared her to death. But Colin was determined to remain vague. She'd not get more out of him.

"Think of your cousins," he implored.

Their safety was the only thing that kept her from screaming. If they weren't all part of this she'd throw his words to the incoming storm and be done with it. She'd never leave.

But it wasn't all about her.

"I hate all of this," she murmured, eyes still closed.

Gentle, brief, his lips pressed against her closed lids. Then those same lips covered hers, slow and easy, forgiving. She stifled a whimper and kissed him back. Fierce, wholesome, she kissed him. When she pulled away his gaze was emotional though quickly tempered.

"Go now," he urged.

As if acting out a part she was never meant to play, McKayla put her hand on her stomach and smoothed her skirts. "I'm not feeling all that well," she said, swaying as she looked at her cousins. "Would you mind helping me back to my chamber?"

Both shot her an odd look and rushed to her side. She felt clammy. Warm. Dizzy. Nauseous. Though he didn't really tell her what was about to happen, she wouldn't go against Colin's wishes. As much as she hated to admit it, he had her best interests at heart.

Leslie held McKayla's elbow and steered her toward the door. Once they reached the threshold, McKayla looked back one last time.

Colin nodded and offered her a small, encouraging smile.

She had to trust him.

Still, as she walked down the long hall she had the sinking feeling that this was wrong. All wrong. That she should have remained impassive, stubborn. That her destiny somehow wasn't what Colin believed it to be. But it was too late now. The plan was in motion. And when a loud roar rumbled all around the castle, proof that trouble came, McKayla knew…

She never should have walked away.

****

In the end Colin found a way to ensure McKayla and her cousin's safety while remaining close to his sister. Yes, he'd done what he'd planned all along. He'd put the strongest members of the next generation and their token warlock as close to Torra as possible.

It'd been important not to reveal his plans to his family until the very end.

But his father, William and Ferchar were pleased.

Arianna, terrified, but willing to follow his instructions.

Malcolm, Bradon, Ilisa and Seth would protect Torra. The others would protect McKayla and her cousins. After all, if what Bradon divulged was the truth, his sister had always been the intended target.

"I will go see her soon," he said softly.

Heart in his words, his brother said, "She has only seen Ilisa and me. You might not…"

His brother trailed off, unwilling to look him in his eyes.

Yes, he now knew the truth. When he'd left, Torra had not closed herself off entirely. Over time she saw first Bradon then Ilisa. Now, as they had every right to, they protected her from anyone or anything that would do her harm.

Even her own brother.

"I owe her an explanation," he whispered.

"You owe her an apology," Bradon said. "While we have worked through our hurt, she's had no such benefit."

"Ma told me not to go near her, that she received no one. Does she speak now?"

"Nay," Ilisa said. "Still just the sixteen words a year."

"I will go in first." Colin stood. "You all know what to do." He met each gaze. "May this go well."

They nodded but said nothing.

Claymore strapped to his back and more than four daggers hidden on his person, he walked down the narrow, arched hallway to a barred chamber. Magically enhanced, the iron around Torra was meant not to imprison but to protect.

His sister sat very still, shoulders slumped with her head bent.

He watched for several moments before he knelt in front of her, and whispered, "I have never cherished another as I do you. Can you ever forgive me, lass?"

She made no movement.

"A man's soul can get twisted, misplaced, confused," he continued. "Though once lost I am no more."

Boom. Crash. The sound of warfare echoed in the distance, shaking the castle. Yet Torra remained rigid as stone. Colin hung his head. She was as withdrawn as ever. Would he be able to get through to her at all? Did she even remember him? It was no use. She was unreachable. Colin went to stand. Just as he did, Torra's hand shot out and grabbed his arm. Surprised, he remained kneeling.

Inch by inch her head rose and Colin's heart stilled when her eyes met his. No longer were they sage green but white gold.

"*Nathair sgiathach,*" he whispered and instantly bowed his head, respectful and awed.

This is why Bradon's hair had turned white, why McKayla's had streaked. They had seen Torra as her true self. They'd suffered the magical repercussions of her immense power. Yet McKayla's white streak was already returning to its normal color so he suspected his brother's would as well.

Clenching away the tremble in his hands, he cupped Torra's cheek. "I will protect you always, my sister. Please know that I will never again abandon you." He put a hand over his heart. "You have my solemn promise."

"And mine," Bradon said as he entered the chamber.

"Aye, and mine as well, luv," Ilisa said softly, not far behind.

Torra, silent as ever, looked up.

As if wind whistled through unseen cracks she started to release a long, low keen.

Colin met Bradon's eyes. His brother nodded. Ready.

Calm, Seth and Ilisa stood next to one another, waiting, prepared.

They might very well be getting ready to live their last moments but none showed an ounce of fear. A new MacLomain era unfolded this eve.

Hands folded over his sisters, he said one last prayer to the gods.

For the time had finally come.

Chapter Fourteen

McKayla sat on the bed and debated her next move.

Leslie put the back of her hand against her forehead. "See, this is the thing about the medieval period. The food. No FDA to screen whether or not it's healthy. What did you eat tonight? List everything."

"No, I'm fine." McKayla stood and walked over to the window. Sure as heck, a line of bobbing lights glimmered on the distant shoreline. "I think."

Sheila joined her and frowned as she stared out. "Are those what I think they are?"

Leslie peered out as well. "They look like ships."

"Enemy ships I'd guess." McKayla swallowed and leaned against the eave. "A lot of them."

"Do the MacLomains not have ships?" Leslie asked.

"I have no idea." Worry brought her brows together and a nervous bit of humorless laughter escaped. "Can you believe I never thought to ask? And here I call myself a historical writer."

"You've got a lot on your mind, sweetie. Don't beat yourself up," Sheila said.

"Listen to the wind and see the waves. They're immense," Leslie pointed out. "The enemy is foolish to come in by sea. If the MacLomain's have ships and they're not using them, then they're the smart ones."

Now that's the way she should be thinking right now. Logically. Not with her emotions. Because right now she was letting a heart near paralyzed with worry jumble her mind. What sort of chieftain's wife would she truly make if she allowed such to continue to happen? "I never even asked how to use my magic or how to fight with a bloody weapon. I assumed all along he'd protect me." McKayla frowned. "Ugh, I've been such a girl! In a frilly, damsel in distress sort of way."

Leslie put a firm hand on her shoulder, voice stern. "Don't you for a second blame yourself for not being better prepared. You've only been here for a few days." Though she hesitated momentarily, her cousin decided to continue. "Colin has known long enough that a day like this would most assuredly come along. And it did. So this falls on him entirely. *Not* you. Once we get through this you'll learn everything you need to know. We will too."

Sheila nodded. "For once, I completely agree with Leslie. Colin knew. And though I remain in his corner, I'm not good with you taking any blame or responsibility for his lack of action when it comes to your knowledge of magic or weaponry."

They weren't just cousins but good friends, which brought her back to another concern…their inevitable involvement. An involvement that no matter the circumstances, she *did* take responsibility for. As such, it was time to stop whining and start showing a bit more gumption. Though she dreaded every step, Colin had told her how she could get them home and it was past time she do so.

Determined, she crossed to the trunk at the end of the bed and crouched. Large but not ornate it'd been here all along. An unassuming piece of furniture. What better place to hide a treasure?

"What are you doing?" Sheila asked and joined her.

"I was never sick at all. Colin told me the enemy had arrived. He urged me to come back here and open this trunk. In it I'd find an object that would get us home."

Leslie came over as well, crouched beside her and put a hand over the trunk. When her eyes met McKayla's she was surprised to see her cousin's eyes glistening. "If you were the heroine in your book and the voice in your head, also known as Iosbail, said not to…what would you do?"

Gone was her steadfast agent, in her place was someone who truly cared. In truth, Iosbail always tended to sway her heroine to do the opposite of what she should. Mostly because there was always a greater outcome to be had when following the path less traveled. And what if Colin's implication was true? What if Iosbail was an ancestral muse who inspired her through magic or as a ghost?

McKayla understood what Leslie implied. She glanced at Sheila. "Are you of the same mind?"

Sheila, who had crouched on the other side, met her eye. "What, that we don't flee home but stay and help out our new friends? You bet your ass I'm of the same mind."

Screeech. Thwap. Crash.

The castle rumbled and the floor trembled. Sheila fell back. McKayla pulled her to her feet and the girls leaned against the wall as another crash resounded overhead.

"What the hell?" Sheila said.

"Hell itself so it seems," Malcolm said, walking into the room. With sure strides he walked over to the trunk and shook his head, casting them a frustrated glance. "McKayla, you *must* open this trunk now."

Again, about the last person she expected to join them was Colin's moody cousin. But moody might be putting it delicately right now. No, he was seething mad. Turbulent pale brown eyes met hers. *"Now."*

"Dinnae do it!" Loch Nessa said from the doorway, eyes upset as she wrung her hands. "If you do, Colin will be lost."

A heavy, disappointed frown ruined Malcolm's face as his tortured gaze met his wife's. "Go back to our chamber where 'tis safe."

"'Tis safe *nowhere*," she said vehemently. "And we both know it."

"I know verra little," Malcolm ground out and turned his gaze back to McKayla. "Do as your husband asked. I beg of you."

Who to believe? Malcolm who clearly hated Colin...or his wife, who clearly loved the laird? It was impossible to know. Wind screamed. The window skins ripped away. Torch flame bent and spit, struggling to survive.

Her cousins gasped when black fog started to seep over the eaves.

"Now!" Malcolm yelled. Not willing to wait a moment longer he reached out to grab her while simultaneously opening the trunk. But when he did Sheila blocked her and instead was yanked forward.

224

"McKayla, Leslie, touch Sheila's arm now," screamed Seth as he rushed in from a hidden entrance with a girl in his arms.

Not hesitating, trusting him as one of their own, they did.

Both chill and warmth ran over her, and then a sharp bolt of what felt like static electricity. Not only hers but her cousin's legs buckled and they fell. Frozen in place, she watched Malcolm tuck a small chunk of stone into her palm. It seemed movement was impossible. Malcolm, aware that this would happen, pulled free his blade and stood in front of them.

Swords began to clash just outside the door.

A fire roared to life on the hearth.

Terrified, McKayla met the eyes of the girl who hung limp in Seth's arms. Torra. She wouldn't allow her to get hurt. As hot as the fire, a burning started deep down inside, rising up through her core until bit by bit she was able to move.

Bradon and Ilisa were right behind Seth, weapons drawn as the black, oily fog started to ooze around the chamber. It smelled as though a corpse rotted. As if she were a child being punished, Loch Nessa fell to her knees and crawled across the room, sobbing. "I tried to stop the chest from opening. I didnae know about it soon enough or it would have been destroyed somehow, master," she whimpered. "I swear it."

Who was she talking to?

Horrified, Malcolm ran to her.

This left them exposed. As if sensing weakness, the blackness ebbed and flowed their way. Not sure what else to do, she leaned in front of them and flung her arms back. There was no way it was getting them.

"Oh, I think the hell not," Seth muttered.

Not losing his grip on Torra, he ran and swung fast, somehow managing to crouch with his back to the blackness, defending all four women. This put Colin's sister eye to eye with McKayla. Caught in the glowing white gold orbs she heard a voice, *Torra's voice*, enter her mind.

Tell Colin he never needed forgiving. He but fulfilled his destiny.

McKayla nodded before her attention was snagged away by the horror show unfolding. Pure havoc broke loose and war erupted in her chamber. Men formed of the greasy, enemy darkness. Inky warriors with jerk-like movements came with sword and ax and magic.

With a wild, berserker cry, Ilisa jumped up on the large bed and used one of the end posts to swing and kick. All the while she released three blades, each aimed true. Blood gushed. Nearby, Bradon sparred with one warrior while he threw a dagger that efficiently sunk into the forehead of another.

Meanwhile, William, Iain and Ferchar rushed in, all armed, all deadly.

While McKayla might have thought the chamber large upon first sight, now it seemed far too small. And as she learned fast enough, no battle should be had in closed quarters. Then again, it'd be gruesome anywhere. Warfare was a thousand times more petrifying when not on TV or in a book but executed in real life. Even despite the fact that this battle was a *little* different. Though blood sprayed, none fell. Made of black magic and supernatural limbs, the enemy warriors vanished as quickly as they'd appeared.

Bradon, furious, seemed to cut down even more than most, working his way to stand in front of Seth and the women. Malcolm now fought over his wife, a whining useless woman who pleaded to some unknown face.

Until, bit by bit that face formed.

Even Seth shuttered and grew more determined as warriors started to fade and one, all-consuming presence became more and more obvious.

Kilted, tall, with a long black cloak and hood, a man appeared.

Sound ceased.

The air smelled of burnt plastic and sulfur.

Black, throbbing fog wrapped around his legs and pulsed around his body as blacker than night eyes swept over the room. Any remaining enemy warriors bowed then faded away. Booted feet smoking on the now chilled stone floor, he took one step. In reaction, the dark fog sunk against the walls like saran wrap.

As if he had the power to control time, all started to move slowly.

Ilisa, still standing on the bed, slowly lifted her blade in his direction, blackened blood dripping from it. Bradon pulled free his ax, caught halfway in the otherworldly sluggishness. Iain, William, even Ferchar, struggled with various weapons, faces enraged.

Malcolm, determined, tried to cover his wife.

Where the hell was Colin?

"*Shhh.*" McKayla heard Torra from deep inside, her voice though distant was reassuring. "*Time to find your calm center.*"

Seth, face straining, looked back through jet black eyes. As slick and evil as the warlord standing in the center of the room save one difference...he still protected. Despite the darkness in him, Seth was good...or at least used his magic for such.

"Keir."

Her eyes shot to the corner of the room when she heard the strange voice.

As if part of the wind raging in through the window, a man formed then dissipated then reformed. As tall as their dark enemy, the Scotsman shifted and fluctuated. His...*its* voice when it came was wispy, hoarse. "Da."

Expression partly hidden behind the hood, Keir stared back. When he spoke it sounded like a blade being dragged over gravel. "Son?"

"Caught," the form responded. Half of it flipped and caught in a burst of wind. Half of it was sunken in by blown rain. "In between."

A ripple of fury made Keir's cloak twist around his legs. "This cannae be."

If all of this wasn't horrific enough the same face that'd formed in the fire from her dream once more appeared.

Colin MacLeod.

Disgusted, his fiery voice whiplashed at his sister, Nessa. "All I needed was the MacLomain's lass. Her capture would have led the laird straight to me and his sister would have pursued! All you had to do was keep the MacLomains away long enough so that I could lull her to me. 'Twas simple really. I'd already entered her

227

subconscious so she knew my name. But you turned and ran from Torra's chamber when faced with a challenge."

Loch Nessa had been there in her dream?

But as it turned out it had been no dream at all.

And now McKayla knew where she'd got the inspiration for her hero's name. Colin MacLeod himself had somehow planted it there!

Nessa, shaking violently, looked from Colin MacLeod to her seething master.

"My laird, please forgive me. Give me another chance," she cried as she looked up at Keir. Her words were long and stretched in the strange otherworldly place they all existed. After Nessa shook her head at the ghostly visage of Keir's son her wild eyes turned to the fire. "Brother, I tried to help you but their magic was too strong!"

As if discovering an ant beneath his foot, Keir said, "You never gave anything you promised, lass." As if two aircraft carriers crashed together, he lashed out and sent a bolt of pure blinding death from his hand. Malcolm tried to defend but it was too late. The dark laird's wrath hit the floor, wrapped around Nessa and strangled her to death in a split second.

"Noooo!"

McKayla was surprised the sound came from behind. Sheila?

But as soon as she heard her cousin's cry, all sound snapped shut again.

Then, *boom*. A terrible moment made of screams and death and vengeance raged around the chamber. Echoing, horrific, she watched, terrified, as he who had called himself Keir's son rushed at the powerful warlock.

With a wide thrash, Keir shot out his hand and black lightening erupted.

As if materializing from thin air, the mysterious stranger formed into Colin. He flung his arms up in the air and started to chant.

"Ecce terra mea, et in arcem ex me tibi iniqua interdicunt. Nunc et usque in sæculum."

Seth, teeth gritted, started to repeat the same words.

228

A voice, maybe Torra's, entered her mind and said the words so that she would understand.

Here on my land, in my castle, I ban you from this ground. Now and forever.

Over and over, Colin and Seth chanted.

Then, through all the chaos, the ghostly form of a robed man with long white hair appeared. Just like in her dream! He said nothing but lashed out against the fiery form of Colin MacLeod. Soon caught in their own private war, the two struggled within twisting tunnels of fire and wind.

Meanwhile, her husband and Seth shot bullets of black and white lightening at Keir. Caught between a warlock and the magic his own son had taught another, the dark enemy began to struggle. But he was by no means ready to give up. Infuriated, he lashed out at Seth first.

When her friend took a direct hit, pain sliced across his face. His shield over them weakened and she felt a portion of what he'd felt when her muscles suddenly tightened. She could only compare the feeling to one big body-ridden Charlie horse. Inhaling sharply through her teeth, McKayla looked at her cousins as best she could. Blatant pain was apparent on their faces as well.

Though her eyes shone brighter and brighter, Torra seemed at peace.

Worried about Seth and her cousins, it took several long seconds to realize that Keir had swiftly turned his attack back to Colin. His fellow MacLomains, still caught in a time vortex, could do nothing but watch. Terribly enough, their laird was somehow trapped, ensnared and imprisoned magically by their adversary's rage. With a crazed roar, Keir unleashed an even stronger bolt of energy at Colin.

McKayla watched in horror as a tornado of darkness wrapped around Colin, whipping him up the wall so fast that it appeared his head snapped against the ceiling. Like a ragdoll he fell to the floor.

"Ecce terra mea, et in arcem ex me tibi iniqua interdicunt. Nunc et usque in sæculum," Seth croaked over and over.

Like a cool wind over sunburned skin, another soft voice joined him. *"Ecce terra mea, et in arcem ex me tibi iniqua interdicunt. Nunc et usque in sæculum."*

Keir Hamilton's aura bubbled with sparks and what almost appeared to be the misconstrued pixels on a fuzzy television screen. Staggering backwards, he swung his gaze her way.

But it wasn't actually directed her way at all.

No, he looked at Torra MacLomain.

"I'll find you no matter where you go *Nathair sgiathac.* You belong to *me,*" he promised, his tongue sluggish. Now he was caught in the same anti-gravity he'd inflicted on everyone else.

The energy that Seth had maintained fizzled away as he fell back and Torra stood. Fine boned and stunningly beautiful, her gaze fell on all in the room. There was compassion and trust in her surreal gaze.

Her eyes, shining with a ferociousness meant only for him, once more connected with Keir's and she repeated, *"Ecce terra mea, et in arcem ex me tibi iniqua interdicunt. Nunc et usque in sæculum."*

Then, fleet of foot, she dashed across the room and leapt onto the window's eave.

For what felt like several long excruciating moments, she hovered there.

What was she doing? Oh God, no. Don't do it.

After a long inhale, Torra's body rippled and she jumped.

With a mad cry of outrage, Keir was sucked unwillingly into the fire. Before he faded away, the ghostly man with long white robes shot one last ravenous bolt at the vanishing form of Colin MacLeod. In an instant the fire sizzled down then puffed out, taking the evil creatures with it.

As soon as Keir and Colin MacLeod warped away, the blackness on the walls turned to water and trickled down. All were released from whatever spell they'd been under. Blades still swinging, they were met with an empty room.

Horrified, McKayla ran to Colin. "Please don't be dead," she said over and over and over. "Don't you dare be dead."

All stumbled to them, their attention torn between their laird and their kinswoman, Torra.

As McKayla ran her hands over Colin, she murmured that his gods bring him back from wherever he was. "Please, my love," she prayed.

"Holy hell, look," Sheila whispered, one concerned hand on McKayla, the other on the window sill.

Stone still clenched in her hand, she barely glanced but that was enough. Hands on her husband, her jaw dropped as she stared.

As if whipped away by the events, or perhaps created by the events themselves, the hurricane was veering off to sea unveiling a large round moon. But that's not what Sheila referred to.

Not at all.

No, her steadfast gaze was on Torra as she sailed away with wings spread wide and her strong body fluid in the air.

Not a woman at all...

But what could only be a dragon.

Chapter Fifteen

"Ouch!" McKayla ripped away her riveted gaze and tossed aside the stone. *Hot!*

But there was little time to wonder why.

Suddenly, a horrible sucking sensation pulled at her. The smell of burning sugar stung her nostrils. Mortified, she looked down at Colin only to find that he'd vanished. Crippled beneath what she knew were the side effects of time-travel, she wrapped her arms around her mid-section and put her head to the ground.

"No, no, no," she whispered.

As fast as it'd happened the terrible jarring sensation soon passed.

"McKayla," Sheila groaned.

"It's okay. We're home," Leslie reported, her voice shaky.

Careful, still trying to adjust to her surroundings, McKayla sat up. They were on the front lawn of the old colonial. Head in hands, she said, "Please tell me I didn't imagine all that."

"You didn't. We were there," Leslie assured, holding her head as well.

Sheila grabbed the bench to steady herself. "But how? The last thing I knew Colin and Seth had sort of defeated a real nasty guy, the next we were looking at a…"

"Dragon," McKayla whispered.

"Still undecided on that," Leslie said, blinking to adjust to her surroundings.

"Really?" Sheila rolled her eyes. "You saw the big winged creature with scales and claws yet you're not sure?"

Leslie frowned. "We witnessed things in that chamber far beyond our wildest imagination. While I concede things were crazy I certainly won't agree to having seen a *dragon*. That's a bit of stretch."

"Seriously, you're going to play Agent Scully after all of that? Good thing there's no Mulder to say, "Uh what?" because he would. God, again, *really* Leslie? Time froze, people were speaking Latin, and oily black stuff was everywhere."

"And I concede to all that," Leslie granted, pulling up until she sat on the swing. "What I'm saying is that there's no proof what we saw was a dragon."

"Alrighty, Scully." Sheila rose to her feet, hand braced against the tree.

"Enough!" McKayla said.

Both looked at her and quieted.

"Enough," she repeated softer. "And I won't apologize for being sharp this time." It was hard not to panic. "Last I knew Colin was very ill. I have no idea if I healed him or not. He could be dead."

"You can heal people?" Sheila said.

"I don't think he's dead," Leslie added.

"Yeah, I guess it's my gift," McKayla said, coming to her feet. When the world swayed she braced herself against the bench. "Or at least I thought it was. But then Colin was hurt and I'm pretty sure I wasn't able to help him."

"Pretty sure you did," Leslie said.

"I appreciate your optimism but if I had wouldn't I still be there?"

"Not sure it's necessary." Sheila nodded toward the house.

Her eyes flew back to the colonial. Heart skittering like a mad animal in her chest, she stared at the man standing in the doorway. Colin, kilted and well enough considering.

Afraid that if she blinked he'd vanish, she ran.

Still weak, she stumbled a few steps but it didn't matter. He met her halfway and swung her around. The minute her feet hit the ground his lips were on hers. Warm, alive, he was right here. Not dead at all. Pulling back, she cupped his cheeks and asked, "How are you here? Are you okay? I don't understand."

"There's plenty of time to understand."

She studied his eyes, the trauma of what they'd just witnessed still rippling through both her body and emotions. So much had happened. Terrible things. Why *was* he here alone? Almost afraid to ask she whispered, "Where's Seth?"

"Seriously? You have to ask?" With a wide, devilish smile, Seth appeared in the doorway. "I would've been out here to greet you but Colin says I need to rest."

Overjoyed that they'd all made it home safe she gave him a long, heartfelt hug too. When she pulled back the strain in his face was clear. What he'd done back there had taken a lot out of him. "Are you all right?" she asked, worried.

"If I'm alive, I'm okay," he said. "Trust me on that one."

Seth looked over her shoulder at Colin. "Your man, however, not so much."

"I'm fine," Colin muttered.

But he wasn't. She was so happy that he was alive that she hadn't seen he was hurting. Yet this hurt had nothing to do with Keir.

"You healed me," Colin assured and sat down on the bench.

Still off-kilter, Leslie said, "Hang on. I'll get something for him to drink."

McKayla sat down next to Colin and frowned. "Oh no. The mark on your side. You were never supposed to travel to the future again!" Frightened, she studied the circle. Angry and red, it appeared almost closed. "What the hell are you doing here?"

"He's stubborn," Seth muttered when Leslie brought out both water and whiskey.

"I had to know you and your cousins arrived safely," Colin said, taking the water.

She looked around and frowned. "Where is Ferchar?"

"Home already, glad to be reunited with his family."

"And what of Keir Hamilton? Was he destroyed?" Sheila asked. "And is your sister *really* what I think she is?"

"Enough with all the questions," Seth said. "Can't you see the man's in pain?"

"Nay, 'tis fine," Colin said and downed his water. "Though we've banned him from the castle 'twill not be the last we hear from Keir Hamilton. And now we know that Nessa MacLeod was his minion and Colin MacLeod his ally. No doubt he will strengthen his army and pursue Torra. While I'm sure he'll not give up on his blood oath to destroy me, his main focus as it has always been will be my sister."

"So there truly is a Colin MacLeod," McKayla murmured.

"Without doubt," Colin reported. "A wizard who can manipulate fire like Ferchar but possesses a darker heart. Keir has partnered himself with a formable power indeed."

"Colin MacLeod said he'd planted his name in my mind." She shivered and touched her fingertips to her temple. "How do I know he's still not in my head?"

"He's not," Colin assured. "He but used the power of suggestion via magic. A timeless trick that inspired you to write his name. 'Tis a simple bit of magi that is untraceable."

"Are you sure?"

"Never more so."

Then she would have to take his word for it. Nothing good could come from dwelling on the idea that a monster had influenced her thoughts

Puzzled, McKayla said, "And the old man from my dream was there. It seems he's defended me twice now. Or should I say us."

Colin nodded. "Aye. 'Twas the ghost of Adlin MacLomain. I suspect our paths will cross again." He and Seth exchanged a bemused look. "As we learned briefly before, it seems my kin has already visited with your warlock several times."

That's right! Interested, she looked at Seth.

"During the unraveling of Calum's curse when I discovered what I'd become," he reminded. "But those stories are better left for another day."

"Stories we'd be interested in hearing for sure," Sheila said, eyes round.

Seth winked but said nothing more about it.

McKayla, though still processing everything, found her mind wandering back to his sister. Awed, she looked at Colin. "Torra is a dragon, isn't she?"

For a moment, his gaze seemed far away. "Aye, at least partly. 'Tis why she became a recluse. The beastie inside of her struggled for freedom. But Torra didn't want to leave her clan, her brethren, so she fought to repress it all these years."

The girls, even Seth, stared, expressions equally slack with disbelief.

"She must be incredibly strong," Leslie said with admiration.

"More than we ever knew," Colin acknowledged, emotion in his voice.

Sheila nodded. "She'll be okay. I don't doubt it for a second."

Colin worked at a weak smile.

"So I assume Keir's anti-time-travel gate is destroyed?" McKayla said.

"Aye, and much to William's relief, Coira made it back to the castle safely."

Glad to hear it, McKayla rested her hand on his shoulder and squinted. A small mark was forming just above his collar bone. Her eyes widened. "This…this looks like the tattoo that was on my book's cover model. And it's in the exact same spot!"

Leslie and Sheila leaned closer, slack-jawed.

"*Exactly* like it," Leslie said.

"Your story has always interwoven with all that has happened," Colin said. "I believe 'twas the magic in you, lass. A magic determined to bring you closer to me and Scotland."

"The mark seems to darken even as we speak," she murmured, running her finger over it.

"Bradon and Malcolm developed the same mark but in different areas. They began to form when Torra left so we're guessing they have to do with her. Though we cannae be sure yet her reasoning."

"Interesting," Seth said.

"Verra," Colin said.

"And what does that circular tattoo mean?" Leslie asked.

McKayla took a deep breath and swigged down some whiskey. "That he never should have come. It has the ability to trap him here."

"And as it turns out 'tis not of Keir's device," Colin said. "'Twas of the MacLomains. My ancestors. Mayhap even Adlin. A punishment of sorts for manipulating time travel as I did when I killed my mentor and brought McKayla back with the Lucid Dream mask."

"That's terrible." McKayla shook her head. "Why would they do such a thing to one of their own?"

Colin didn't seem overly troubled by it. If anything, his response was somewhat reverent. "To reiterate that traveling through time is to be respected. Doing such has the ability to change the course of history. We must always be verra careful. This mark reminds not only me but my brethren and future generations that such negligence willnae be tolerated."

"So you're not upset?"

"Nay, I have no right to be. I've learned my lesson," he said. A flicker of pain crossed his face and he held his side.

"You need to get home now, friend," Seth said.

McKayla looked from Seth to Colin. "He's right, isn't he? The door is almost closed."

"Almost," Colin said, expression stern as he looked at Seth. "I need to know they'll be safe."

"Really?" Seth asked. "If you hadn't noticed, I'll protect them with my life."

"Right," her husband said. "But I expect more than that."

"I know a few more warlocks. Trust me, they'll protect all in this time period just as readily," Seth pledged.

McKayla looked between the men. It seemed they were no longer enemies but allies.

A strange look passed over her face when Sheila asked, "How did Malcolm fare? I know his wife wasn't well liked but still…"

"He's in a dark place right now, lass," Colin said. "I was only home a day after but 'twill take much time for him to recover."

McKayla was shocked to see her cousin's eyes glass over. "Of course, I can't imagine the heartache."

"May none of us come to such an end," he murmured a prayer to the gods.

"So true." Leslie cleared her throat, uncomfortable. "And what of your brother? He put up a good fight. Is he well?"

Colin's eyes met McKayla's, amused before his attention turned to Leslie. "He's well enough. Much thanks for asking." But then her husband's eyes grew troubled. "It seems he's made a vow to find, protect and bring home our sister."

Leslie thought it over briefly. "That's a good thing, right?"

"The vow of a highlander is always a good thing. But 'tis a quest he wishes to make on his own. As his brother, that worries me."

"Right," Leslie agreed. "It certainly sounds like a strong promise."

Once more, the ring on her finger burned so McKayla held up her hand and twisted it. "Seth, don't you think it's time to remove this?"

Sheila and Leslie looked at her, twirling similar rings and almost at the same moment held up their hands.

"Why have I got one?" Sheila asked.

"I don't do Claddagh rings. Please remove mine immediately," Leslie said.

"No can do," Seth said, a speculative look on his face. "While I put the first one on McKayla's finger, it seems hers and yours have since taken on a new purpose."

"What?" Leslie and Sheila said at once.

Sheila was thrilled.

Leslie was upset.

"I told you this might not go well," Colin volunteered.

Seth shrugged. "Again, it's not all me." He looked at Colin. "And you did have a small part in it. That rock says it all."

"What rock?" McKayla asked, then trailed off.

The rock from the trunk.

The very stone she'd been holding before they'd traveled back to the future.

"Aye," Colin admitted. "Mayhap I had a wee bit to do with it." He looked at Seth. "But so did you and Torra to be sure."

McKayla frowned, remembering. "The rock in the trunk that Malcolm was so determined that *I* open."

"Oh, sure," Colin conceded. "He didnae want to be enveloped in its magic." His eyes grazed over Sheila. "You all now wear the Claddagh ring that ties together the MacLomains and Brouns. The white stone at the heart of your ring was broken off the original Highland Defiance, giving you the power to travel through time. 'Twas Torra who somehow had a hand in that. Thanks to Seth, the ring itself will only warm and shine when you're near your true love." He winked. "'Tis his way of ensuring you know without doubt you're always with he who truly loves you, not a possible shape-shifter with questionable intentions."

Colin cast an amused glance at Seth. "Despite the evil, who knew the lad had such a romantic heart."

McKayla looked at Seth as well. "You are outstanding, my friend."

Seth shrugged in resignation. "I am, aren't I?"

Colin doubled over, holding his side tighter.

Uneasy, she put her hand against the mark.

Nothing.

Her touch would not heal this time.

"He needs to get home," Seth said, worried but hopeful. "Or stay here and learn more about us warlocks."

Looking more and more ill, Colin stood.

"Come on, brother." Seth was at his side in an instant, arm around his back. "Let's get you to bed."

"Aye," Colin mumbled.

"Nay," McKayla whispered. She stood and twirled the ring on her finger. Looking at Seth she said, "We need to get him home. *Now.*"

"I can be trapped in one time or the other, lass," Colin said. "It doesnae need to be there."

But she knew he said that to comfort her. He would go back to his clan.

And he wouldn't be going alone.

Her eyes met Sheila's and Leslie's. Did they know? She looked at Seth. He knew.

Heart in his eyes, he nodded. "I think she has the right of it. You need to go back to your clan." Seth ground his jaw but said exactly what she needed him to. "You made them a promise, eh?"

Colin said nothing as Seth walked him away from the house.

"McKayla," Sheila whispered. Emotion seemed to clog her throat. "What are you doing?"

"I have always loved him," she said absently, unable to look her cousins in the eyes. "So very much."

Leslie grabbed her hand and wiggled it, forcing her to meet her eyes. "I know you love him. And I'm good with that now. Really I am." She looked at the colonial and straightened her back, fighting emotion while she tried to gather her thoughts. "I'm not sure I ever told you how proud of you I am. What you accomplished here was remarkable. I think this house made it possible for you to write a bestseller. You couldn't do it alone. Sometimes we just need to be shoved in the right direction."

"As in she couldn't do it without *you*?" Sheila said.

Leslie teared up as she looked at McKayla. "No, she couldn't do it without *herself*. And she found herself here."

"Oh, well then." Sheila nodded. "That I agree with."

"Get it published. I'll write more," McKayla promised.

"You better," Leslie said.

Her cousins understood what she was doing when they pulled her in for a hug. Squeezing, she held on tight. If what they'd been told was true, their Seth/Torra magically enhanced rings ensured they wouldn't lose touch but what if...

When at last she pulled away, they all had tears in their eyes.

Sheila wiped away hers. "We're going to have to toughen up if we're going to be MacLomains."

Leslie released an unladylike snort. "I have no intention of becoming a MacLomain."

McKayla turned away from their chatter to find Seth standing behind her. Colin slumped against the barn door.

"Are you going to be all right, hon?" Seth asked, seemingly laid-back. But she didn't miss the pain he tried to hide.

"What do you think?" she asked, determined to give him the response he expected.

Arms akimbo, a challenge in his eyes, he said, "I think you better love him half as much as I love Alana or this shit isn't going down."

"As Ilisa would say, like horse and cow manure?"

"Exactly," he mumbled. But their eyes held. He'd never been more serious.

"Thank you so much for all you've done, Seth. I hope Colin said as much."

"He did. We're good." Seth scuffed his foot. "I even like him now. As much as any warlock can really like a wizard that is."

She chuckled. "Don't let him hear that."

"No doubt he already did. The man's extremely tuned in when it comes to you...*lassie*."

Colin continued to lean against the barn door with his head down.

"I have to go to him."

"And you always will." Seth pulled her in for a tight hug. "May your life be half as interesting as mine."

"No doubt it will be," she managed, fighting a rush of emotions as they pulled apart. "I love you wicked, my friend."

He squeezed her hand. "Back at ya."

She smiled. "Time for you to go home to Alana."

"I can't wait. You've no idea."

"Yeah I do."

They walked backwards away from one another. "This isn't goodbye."

"Never is," he said.

"Hey Leslie," she said, looking over his shoulder.

Her cousin, who had never turned away said, "What?"

"I'm sick of being told what's what. Let our publisher know that the new title is..." She paused. "*Mark of the Highlander*. And have a ghost writer rework it a little. Instead of Iosbail being the heroine's subconscious voice let's make her a woman that she travels back further in time to consult with."

When Leslie seemed undecided, McKayla said, "Love you cuz, but this one's not up to you. If the book's to be published introduce a wee bit o' time travel." She grinned and couldn't help herself. "And if you're so inclined maybe a bit of magic?"

Even as she turned away she heard Sheila say, "Ha! Look at her go."

"A little too assertive if you want my opinion," Leslie said.

Their voices, however, faded fast when she again focused on Colin. Though he remained standing, it was but barely. Next to him once more she said, "Sorry. They talk a lot."

He grasped her hand. "McKayla, you dinnae need to do this."

"Do what?" she said and entwined their hands.

Sweat glistened on his brow. "I want you to be happy."

Twirling the ring on her finger she said, "Me too. So let's make that happen."

Power started to slip and slide around them.

They leaned against the old barn as the world shifted. The sugary smell came and went. The barn was there and it wasn't. Then it reappeared. This travel through time was different. Precarious almost.

Would they make it?

Then, as if it'd never been there, the barn totally vanished and they fell back. Luckily, his horse was ready to support them. They were back in medieval Scotland. Arms now wrapped around her, Colin whispered. "Why did you return?"

"Because I needed to make sure you were safe."

"Simple answer."

She pulled back and looked up at him. "The same answer you gave me."

"Was it? I dinnae recall," he murmured, smelling her hair, running his hands over her arms. "I dinnae expect you to stay, lass."

With a disappointed tone she said, "Well then I'll see you home safely and be on my way."

"Aye, if you wish." But there was a defiant glint in his eyes. His energy and vitality had all but returned.

Her gaze drifted to his abdomen.

Colin understood. "'Tis a closed circle now. As far as I know, I cannae travel through time anymore."

"I'm so sorry," she whispered. It was impossible to comprehend how that must make him feel.

"Dinnae be," he said, pulling her close. "I am where I need to be. And now you are free to be where you need to be as well." Colin brought her ringed finger against his heart. "'Tis a fine gift Seth gave you. He's a good man."

McKayla titled back her head and felt the warm highland wind caress her face. Never had she felt as alive as she did now, standing with him in a time only recorded in history books.

"You're right. I am finally free to be where I *need* to be. I moved from the Cape because I was lost. At the colonial I found myself but only through a book I'd written." Her eyes met his, reflective. "Then there was you, always you."

When he started to talk she put a finger to his lips and shook her head. "*You* will always be on the next page in my book. In the life I want to live. Sure I'll miss the twenty-first century but what's the point of all that if you're not there?"

"So again you sacrifice for me."

"Is that what this is," she said, coy eyes on her highlander. "Then I guess I'm more than content offering myself up."

Colin, her best friend, the love of her life, shook his head. "I am so verra blessed."

"*We* are so verra blessed," she whispered.

When his lips closed over hers, everything seemed to fade away. Beneath his touch, beneath his love, she cherished the journey ahead. In the midst of their never-ending kiss she smiled against his lips, sure she heard the sound of bagpipes. When at last they pulled apart her suspicions were confirmed.

Kilted, little legs crawling along, a flashlight bobbed away to a merry highland jig.

Colin grinned and winked.

McKayla laughed and released a little yelp when he scooped her up and planted her on his horse. Swinging up behind, his husky words came close to her ear. "Do you recall me speaking of the lusting that follows a battle?"

"Aye," she said softly.

"Well, I've had the battle but still I lust."

"Then we better hurry home, my laird."

"Aye, we better."

McKayla held on tight as the horse took off, once more flying around the trees. When it broke free and sailed across the meadow she knew they raced not only toward a magnificent castle but an extraordinary future.

Memories would be created.

Love would flourish.

But best of all, though many chapters in...their story had only just begun.

The End

Continue the series with *Vow of the Highlander.* (Bradon's story).

Follow the MacLomains from the beginning in The MacLomain Series- Early Years and then in the original MacLomain Series.

Read Seth's story in The Tudor Revival. Also available in the Calum's Curse Series Boxed Set.

PREVIOUS RELEASES

~The MacLomain Series- Early Years~

Highland Defiance- Book One
Highland Persuasion- Book Two
Highland Mystic- Book Three

~The MacLomain Series~

The King's Druidess- Prelude
Fate's Monolith- Book One
Destiny's Denial- Book Two
Sylvan Mist- Book Three

The MacLomain Series Boxed Set is also available.

~The MacLomain Series- Next Generation~

Mark of the Highlander
Vow of the Highlander
Wrath of the Highlander
Faith of the Highlander
Plight of the Highlander

~Calum's Curse Series~

The Victorian Lure- Book One
The Georgian Embrace- Book Two
The Tudor Revival- Book Three

The Calum's Curse Boxed Set is also available.

~Forsaken Brethren Series~

Darkest Memory- Book One

Heart of Vesuvius- Book Two
Soul of the Viking- Book Three- Coming Soon

~Song of the Muses Series~

Highland Muse

About the Author

Sky Purington is the best-selling author of nine novels and several novellas. A New Englander born and bred, Sky was raised hearing stories of folklore, myth and legend. When combined with a love for nature, romance and time-travel, elements from the stories of her youth found release in her books.

Purington loves to hear from readers and can be contacted at Sky@SkyPurington.com. Interested in keeping up with Sky's latest news and releases? Visit Sky's website, www.skypurington.com to download her free App on iTunes and Android or sign up for her quarterly newsletter. Love social networking? Find Sky on Facebook and Twitter.

14012147R00141

Made in the USA
San Bernardino, CA
12 August 2014